DEAD
AIM

DEAD AIM

A CHRIS KLICK MYSTERY

Wendell McCall

St. Martin's Press • New York

Design by Joan Jacobus

Library of Congress Cataloging-in-Publication Data

McCall, Wendell.
    Dead aim / Wendell McCall.
        p.   cm.
    ISBN 0-312-02184-4
    I. Title.
    PS3563.C3343D44 1988
    813'.54—dc 19   88-14755

10   9   8   7   6   5   4   3   2

For Ollie Cosman
and Chandler Lyell

DEAD
AIM

The condition of the sky sets the tone for the day, more so than temperature or wind. Even on the coldest of days, with a brittle northerly blowing hoarfrost along the hardened surface of snow crust, a bright, crystal sky elevates my mood. Such a sky is intoxicating.

On that day in early September, the sky was a flawless expanse of mountain-air blue. It said, "Smile." It said, "Enjoy." I was doing both. My binoculars were trained on a pair of mergansers, members of the diving-duck family, the male richly colored, the female less so. The deck off the east side of the log cabin I regularly house-sit allows me a slightly elevated view of the slough that snakes along the border of the property's five acres. The slough is a slow-moving, spring-fed creek that doubles as a source of irrigation water for the local farmers fortunate enough to own water rights. It is also haven to waterfowl, brook trout, songbirds, and a variety of bushy vegetation that grips its banks stubbornly. Arctic willow hugs its edges in dense clumps that stretch fifteen feet high, obscuring both sight of the creek and a neighbor's nearby horse corral. The slough is the lifeblood of all flora and fauna along its edges, for the five acres are considered high desert, and if left to nature, little grows other than knee-high sage and an assortment of hearty wildflowers and weeds.

The mergansers motored silently from right to left—upstream—seemingly effortlessly, narrow silver wakes trailing behind, breaking the slough's mirrored surface. How beautiful they were in their motionless swimming, paired, black agate eyes peering back into my non-glare lenses. The binoculars were strong enough to allow me to spot a flotilla of water bugs navigating the oscillating motion of the wake as they randomly scooted about, their tiny legs miniature pontoons on the hard glass-like surface of the slough's dark water. They looked like pleasure craft avoiding the much larger ferry as they darted in behind the passing ducks.

I heaved a sigh of contentment. Birding was something new to me. Previously I had considered it a decidedly effeminate hobby meant for bald-headed, red-lipped bibliophiles. But a few months earlier, on another of my visits, curiosity and admiration had won out. The great blue heron was to blame. It, like well-postured women and vintage champagne, I found irresistible.

I was thankful that I had the good fortune to relax in a deck chair while watching mergansers feed. Tough life, this. But I also felt the torment of the child who has built a multi-towered sand castle and now must face the change in tides and the inexorable advance of the threatening waves. I had earned this time off—I had a sore shoulder and insurance claims to prove it—and it was passing much too quickly. Soon I would face a jetway again, and the short flight back to Horrorwood. Ugh.

That's one reason I was annoyed when the mergansers took to wing, although I confess that ducks landing and ducks taking to flight are wonderful sights to behold. Had it been a natural response to a predator, or simply a desire to change diet for a few hours, their departure might not have bothered me. But it was because of the Jeep Wagoneer that pulled into my gravel driveway and the subsequent sounding of its horn that they flew, and I knew they would not return today. Probably not ever. My enjoyment of these particular two mergansers was over. In all, we had shared some twenty-five minutes together, and I could only reflect on what the rest of their lives might be like. It was duck-hunting season, my slough a sanctified retreat preserved from the scattering steel shot of anxious hunters. This Wagoneer had startled my comrades back into the sky, back into the game, and whether they would even survive the evening was now a matter of conjecture. By leaving here they had thrown themselves back into it, and I was anything but pleased.

●

I was wearing tennis shorts and a layer of number 4 block (I figured the September sun couldn't do anything but enhance my summer bronze). I made no attempt to slip on the T-shirt that lay next to the St. Pauli Girl. This was my house, my time off, and this Wagoneer was uninvited. If the driver didn't like looking at a bare chest and abdomen, then that couldn't be helped. They weren't bad, as far as male chests and abdomens go, and I wasn't feeling modest. I was feeling intruded upon.

"Hello," I offered in my best neighborly voice.

She waved with three fingers as she struggled to fix a scarf about her hair, securing it against the light breeze that had intruded as quickly as she had. I shielded my eyes against the harsh afternoon sun and fished blindly for my sunglasses, which lay somewhere near the T-shirt and beer bottle. My fingers struck plastic and I raised them toward my eyes.

"Mr. Klick?"

"Chris or Christopher," I corrected.

"I'm sorry to barge in on you like this, unannounced and all. I tried to find a phone number—"

"It's not under my name. I'm house-sitting."

Her shadow stretched to my thighs. I could only see a silhouette, yellow fuzz burning its edges. "I asked Nola where you lived," she explained, referring to our small town's beloved postmistress. "I told her it was an emergency."

"Is it?"

"I think so."

"With emergencies they either are or they aren't. They're quite dependable that way—you know when you've got one."

"You're angry. I have violated your privacy. I can understand your anger. I have to admit right up front that I'm not much on popular music. Stopped listening to the radio ten years ago. Would I know any of your songs? I understand you're a producer."

I debated correcting her. I had been an unpublished songwriter once—maybe that counted. It struck me that she didn't care about any of it anyway, so why bother with it? She probably didn't know the difference between a back-up singer and a lead singer, a producer and an arranger, a gig and a session. Not many did. Upon hearing that I had found Brenda Catiglio and had bailed her out of some trouble, a local rag had decided that qualified me for celebrity status. I had refused the interview, but even so they had managed to dig up some dated misinformation, and had spread it across page 17—of 20. She was trying to build me up. We both knew it. I wondered why.

I climbed out of the deck chair and motioned to it. "Have a seat." She hesitated. "Sit down. I'll grab another chair. Beer?"

"No, thanks."

"Sure?" I asked over my shoulder.

"Oh, okay." She shrugged. It was a nice shrug. Genuine. Self-conscious and insecure. "If it's no trouble," she added.

"All I do is open 'em and pour 'em," I reminded. "Back in a jiffy."

When I returned a few minutes later, she was poised in the chair with her neck resting on its rim, eyes closed behind sunglasses, blouse unbuttoned and hanging at her sides revealing a skintight leotard made of purple Lycra. It pressed her breasts flat and smoothed her narrow waist. A chain of perspiration specks clung to tiny hairs on her breastbone. She had the skin of a sunworshiper. I placed her in her late twenties, early thirties. I had a decade on her, stood a good foot taller, and probably weighed in eighty pounds heavier. She was a little too perfect for my tastes. She had a very feminine jawline and a very delicate neck. I wondered what that body looked like when it wasn't being flattened by Lycra. How far did that tan run? I dragged my chair with my foot so it would make a racket, and I sat down facing her, but with one eye still on the slough. Still hoping for a second curtain call by the mergansers. She made a sound like a vacuum cleaner coming to a stop—winding down—and sat up. "Got to take every advantage of that sun," she said. "Won't be with us much longer."

"Agreed." I handed her a glass of beer. She seemed perfectly comfortable in the leotard. To her it was obviously acceptable summer dress—just like my tennis shorts were to me. I was less comfortable. I found myself distracted. I'd been alone in my little cabin for a few too many weeks, I decided. The slow, steady movement of her as she breathed had me mesmerized.

"I read that you visit here often," she began.

"Off and on."

"When you're not out doing what it is you do."

"That's right."

She sipped the beer. I swigged. She said, "You like it here?"

"It's quiet. I like that. Open. That's nice. I spend a lot of time in the city. This is better for me."

"Then you like the city?"

"Some of them. Yes."

"I'm from southern California originally. Came up here to Idaho to ski. Fell in love with it. Me and a thousand others," she said, laughing gracefully. "Couldn't stand the hustle of Snow Lake. Moved down here to Ridland, away from it, but still close enough for the restaurants and the powder days. You like to ski?"

"Yes."

She looked over. "I'm bothering you."

"To what do I owe the pleasure of this visit?" She toyed with the idea of buttoning her blouse, but I must have willed her off. She nervously fooled with a button and let the fabric fall open again. I wondered if she caught my smirk. I have trouble hiding my smirks.

"We've only lived in Ridland about five months," she declared somewhat loudly. She wasn't ready yet, and she wouldn't be pushed into it. Her use of *we* did not go unnoticed. I noticed the ring then, the little band of gold that says "I do," or "I did," and almost never "I will." I had trouble masking my disappointment. I swigged again and tapped out a rhythm connecting the bottom of the Pauli Girl with the beige metal armrest. I looked back out at the slough, hoping to see my winged friends, wondering why this woman had come along to scare them off. "We met up at Snow Lake at the end of last season," she continued. Then she spun the ring to make sure I'd noticed it. "I read how you saved that woman's life—Brenda Catiglio—and you seemed like someone I should talk to."

"The press exaggerates. I found her is all. I was actually looking for someone else, someone owed some back royalties. It was a fluke. She was in some trouble. I was handy."

"And she's Carmine Catiglio's daughter?"

I nodded.

"I bet he was pleased."

I nodded again. I was still uneasy at having an Atlantic City casino owner claim he owed me a favor. Probably the same feeling as being a close friend to a politician.

"The article said you make a living at it. You track down former pop musicians who are owed royalty checks and then help them get what's rightfully theirs. Isn't that what it said? I mean, besides writing your own songs?"

"That's what it said. Yes."

"So you obviously *like* to help people."

"I like music. This happens to be the side of the business I've ended up in. I got here via a very circuitous route. And it's not all Robin Hood—although I admit I like that part of it. I do it for money, for a percentage, Mrs——"

"Oh. I'm sorry. How rude of me! Nicole Russell. Call me Nicky."

"Nicole suits you better."

She shrugged again. She had a patent on that shrug. Careless and indifferent. "My father always called me Nicole." She hesitated just long enough for me to feel her grief. The mergansers could have felt it had they still been swimming out there. It probably would have scared them off, it was so intense. "You can call me that if you like."

"I like." That made twice she had used language to tell me something. First the *we,* and now the past tense in conjunction with her father. So it would be a contest of subtle semantics and nuances. I hoped she wasn't going to make me pry everything out, a bit at a time. The green Pauli Girl bottle was half empty and my September sun was slanting quickly through the sky. I nearly ended our conversation with a blunt rudeness—I keep them handy for such moments—but Nicole had aroused my curiosity, at *least* my curiosity, and now I wanted her mystery as well. I feared I had taken the job before I even knew what it involved.

She moved in the chair and the Lycra flexed with the effort, softly shifting the flesh beneath. Again she sipped the beer. If she kept it up it would be flat by the time she was half finished. It made me uneasy. Beer—especially my green Girl—is to be appreciated.

"Fall's a beautiful time of year, isn't it?" she asked.

"I like the migrations. Fall and spring are special because of that. They're the seasons of change. Winter and summer, they're the seasons of stability."

"Birds or big game? The migrations, I mean. Are you a hunter?"

"Birds. And no to number two. I like to watch." I saw her blush and wondered why.

"I get so angry at his hunting," she spit. Her jaw muscles hardened and tensed. Again the Lycra flexed, and again my mind wandered. I'd been cooped up too long. "If he hadn't gone hunting, none of this would have happened." It was a private comment—her way of telling me a little bit more.

"It might save us some time if you'd just explain."

She cocked her head toward me.

"Don't move," I demanded sternly. Behind her soft-green lenses her brows cinched down tightly and her forehead wrinkled.

By the time I saw them, their wings were set. Two mallards just at the tips of the willows. Nicole obeyed and remained still. I had heard the whistling of their wings that is unique to ducks. I wondered if she had. They dropped steeply and skidded into the slough, webbed feet dragging behind them and frothing the surface. They ruffled their wings in unison, shaking off the water they had gathered on landing. "Okay," I said, "if you move real slowly." She brought her head around to look and I saw her smile.

"I love that color green," she said. "I think that's my favorite color green."

"Iridescent."

She nodded slowly. "A couple," she whispered.

"It's Mr. Russell, is that it?"

She nodded again, still watching the mallards.

"He didn't show up last night," I suggested.

She agreed with that, in her own way. At least I took it for agreement. Then she added, "Two nights ago," and confirmed my suspicions.

"And you've spoken to the police?"

"I didn't want to at first." She wouldn't look at me. "Ridland's such a small town. So off on its own. Self-contained, really. Everyone knows everybody's business. You must get the same treatment as we do. They like us, but we're not really part of it here. They have their own group here and there seem to be some unspoken rules to the club."

"What did they say? The police, I mean."

"They? You mean *him*. He pointed out rather crudely that forty miles up the road is a world-famous resort with a lot of 'young things,' I think is how he put it. I challenged that notion. I told him I had already been up to Snow Lake and made the rounds and that none of his friends had seen him."

"And?"

"It's the truth. It's the first thing I did. I know all about failed relationships, *believe* me. But that's not the way it is."

"What'd he say to that? To your looking around, I mean."

"He pointed out that there are eighteen hundred condominiums for rent—especially this time of year—and another three thousand motel and hotel rooms. He suggested that finding anyone up there wouldn't be easy."

"He's right."

"You're missing the point. That's not where he is."

"Where is he?"

She took a deep breath and watched the mallards poke their necks into the water, biting off food from the bottom. Their white tails stuck straight up in the air. They looked fake, like capsized decoys. "You know they say there's a feeling, in here," she said, depressing the Lycra beneath her breasts, "that tells you when something bad has happened. I always thought that was some sort of romantic notion—fanciful, you know—bullshit," she said harshly, surprising me. She sniffled and I saw her swallow away another attack of tears.

"Anything's possible," I said tenderly, drawing on my beer.

"It's not him. It's not Paul," she said, confusing me.

"Meaning?"

"I don't know about Paul. Not in here, anyway. Not in my heart. We were convenient for each other at the time. It's pleasant enough—but no fireworks. No infatuation. Just convenient, that's all. With Paul I can't be sure. With Paul I can't feel anything in here. There's too much clogging it up. Too many impure emotions in the way. With Paul it's different."

"I don't think I follow you."

"It's Harper. It's Harper I feel in here. Something's happened to Harper."

"Harper?"

"My black Lab. Paul used him to hunt. He's a retriever. The best damn dog in the world." She sat forward and crossed her arms tightly. She buckled over and sobbed uncontrollably. "Harper's hurt . . . or dead," she blurted out after a while. "I just know he is."

It took me another fifteen minutes to get the whole story. Her husband had been missing for the better part of two days. Last night, going to bed, she'd been struck in her heart with a violent pain she attributed to her dog Harper. A dog! I saw my obituary fifty years from now: Finder of Missing Persons—and Pets. She had checked the kennel. Harper was missing, food still in the bowl. She couldn't remember seeing him. Had he been there the first night? Had Paul taken Harper with him? She couldn't remember.

"Goddammit, Mr. Klick, I'm scared!" she said, frightening the mallards who flew off in unison. "And no one seems to care."

"I care," I told her, my eyes staying with the mallards who circled, saw us, and rose quickly into the blue, darting over toward the river and an uncertain future. "Go home and stay by the phone. Your husband may call." I didn't tell her what I was envisioning: a twenty-year-old waitress with a middle-aged man.

"I can pay you. Money I have."

"I don't work for a fee," I explained. "Not exactly. It's kind of complicated. I don't handle things like this. This is for private investigators." I didn't have the heart to tell her I had no interest in a missing-dog investigation.

As she stood to leave I heard five quick dull pops from a shotgun far in the distance. *The river,* I thought gravely.

The mallards.

"Iridescent," I whispered.

Nicole Russell looked at me curiously.

By the next morning I had the first two verses of a song about a woman losing her dog—her companion. It was a sad, pleading ballad that begged to "see my friend again." I felt good about it, even after a quick review following a bowl of Shredded Wheat, which for me is the ultimate test. The lyrics stood alone well, worked well as a poem, and the first hint of a melody twisting through my head complemented the sentiment well.

The living room—the central room of the house—has a lofted ceiling with globe lights and a large Vermont Castings stove in lieu of a fireplace. The stove is faced by overstuffed chairs and a sturdy couch upholstered in a gray wool nap. Between the chairs and couch, in front of the black, four-legged stove, is a thick glass coffee table resting on milled house logs and covered with hurricane lamps and recent issues of *Forbes* and a week-old *New York Times* Sunday Magazine. Ridland is too far off the beaten track to receive the current *New York Times*. I was sitting on the couch, pencil in hand, conceiving a third verse, staring at a crayon-pastel four-by-four-foot Julie Scott painting called *The Man With Blue Hair,* which was thumb-tacked along the wall of the stairs to the second floor. It is pinks and turquoises, a single man, head tilted, standing passively on a beach, the sun setting directly behind his head. The expression on the man's face—in his eyes, really—is so marvelously whimsical that I felt tempted to go ahead and buy the thing. It was on a trial loan, and despite the fact that it was too big for this room, he and I had become friends, and parting with him now would be a great loss.

The Man With Blue Hair inspired the third verse, and I set about scribbling it down as quickly as the words and images flooded my brain. It dealt with loss and parting and that inexplicable pang in one's heart as certain realizations of self-grief come to light. Is it for the lost one we grieve? Or is it for ourselves?

Nicole Russell remained with me, like the Man With Blue Hair remained with me even when I wasn't in this room. I saw the genuine concern in her eyes, the frustration of helplessness, and that seemed good enough for me. I'm a sucker for people in distress, especially women. Especially kind, sensitive, attractive women.

●

The man arrived at my door uninvited, I thought. Had I not had the security system on, I might have greeted him in boxer shorts. As it was, I slipped into a pair of tennis shorts and greeted him before he had a chance to knock.

"How may I help you?" I asked.

"Chris Klick?" He was young, pale, and hosted a drawn face with a five-o'clock shadow. He carried a tape recorder and a notepad, and moved his sneaker-clad feet nervously, insole to insole. He spoke with a slight speech impediment. He sounded like Sylvester the Cat. "My name's Scott Shearson. I'm with KKSI. I called," he reminded.

I had forgotten all about the interview. Following a short piece in the *Snow Lake Express* on my efforts in Atlantic City, I had been asked by the local radio station for an interview. I'm not fond of publicity, but the young reporter had somehow won my sympathies and talked me into it.

"Coffee?" I asked, leading him inside and then, a few minutes later, out onto the deck overlooking the slough.

Scott had been doing this a long time, that much was clear. Despite his initial nervousness, he was now focused and poised, pencil in hand, tape recorder running. We had a couple of laughs about my friend Lyel—everyone knew and loved Lyel—and he had effectively broken the ice. I felt comfortable with him.

"So, listen," he said. "I don't want to appear ignorant or anything, but I read that article twice, and I still don't quite understand what it is you do for a living. I had a friend read it and try to explain it to me. He didn't get it either."

"I read it and I didn't get it either," I kidded. "After reading that, I'm not sure what it is I do."

"For the sake of our listeners," he said, smiling, "how about taking it from the top?"

"Sure. First of all, there's nothing real mysterious about what my partner and I do. The same thing is done by banks, oil companies, investment companies—you name it. I had a great-aunt," I said, digressing. "She received a knock on her door one day. A man in a suit—this is the middle of Kansas farm country, mind you—tells her that his company's records show she is a stockholder. If she can dig up the certificates, she's entitled to decades of past dividends. She found the certificates—true story—in a chest of drawers. She had used them as shelf paper, to line her stocking drawer. Anyway, she produced the securities, the man produced a check. My family's been making money off that stock ever since. It doesn't amount to a whole hell of a lot, but it's something.

"I do essentially the same thing as that man in the suit. My partner in Los Angeles, a lawyer named Bruce Warren, specializes in back royalty settlements. Let's say the Marvin Gaye estate hasn't seen any royalty payments for the past two years despite the fact that "What's Going On" is still played by a hundred radio stations a day. ASCAP or BMI keeps track of the air play, but getting the money out of some of these record companies and publishing companies can be real rough. So the estate hires Bruce. Bruce puts pressure on whoever is at fault and gets the estate its money. And he charges a fee for that, right?"

He glanced at the tape recorder and indicated for me to keep talking. I was enjoying this.

"What Bruce discovered along the way was that there were

other musicians out there who were owed small, and not so small, fortunes from back royalties. Guys you've never heard of, because they only had one hit, and that hit was a long, long time ago, even though it's still getting air play; or they wrote a song that someone came along ten years later and made a hit out of, and the record company claims to own the rights to the song. There are a million shades of gray in the music business. Several million, depending on who you talk to. People get ripped off right and left.

"Well, a lot of these guys don't ever see their royalties, and don't have it together enough to find Bruce Warren and hire his services, so we go about it the other way around. We find them."

"For a percentage?" he asked.

"Exactly. Bruce will stumble onto someone—take Delray Greene, for example. Our first case as a partnership."

"Tell me about Delray Greene."

"Sure. He wrote and recorded a tune in 1958 called "The First Time You Spoke My Name." At that time the record company conned him into signing away the publishing rights to the tune. It was later recorded by a major black artist under the title "Whispering My Name," and subsequently has been recorded by at least twelve other national groups. We're talking major royalties here.

"Bruce came across the original agreement where Delray had signed away the rights. That contract—identical to a similar contract that had lost a California Supreme Court battle—had long since expired, which meant Delray Greene was owed all back royalties, including interest on the back royalties. The problem was that no one could find Delray Greene."

"Which is where you came in," Scott said.

I nodded. "Bruce and I went back a long way. He had helped me to get a few of my songs in front of important people. At one time we had knocked around the idea of putting together our own publishing company. He knew I was looking for some decent money, work that involved the music business but not necessarily gigging every night, and offered me the job of trying to find Delray Greene. On these blind tries—jobs where he dug up the connection to back royalties—Bruce decided he would take a set twenty-five percent of whatever royalties he could recover. That's the deal we would offer a person like Delray if we found him. It may sound steep," I said, noticing his expression, "but we often have enormous costs to cover. Not only that, but a good percentage of the time we never do find the person we're looking for, and if we do, it's sometimes the kind of work that deserves hazard pay.

"At any rate, I went looking for Delray Greene. All we had to go on was that his original band, The Del Rays, back in 1958, had been from Cleveland."

I paused to sip from my coffee and watch a group of magpies land in the willows.

"Tell us how you found him," Scott said.

"Sure. First, I was able to locate the owner of one of the clubs they had played. He remembered a girlfriend of Delray's who was still around town. As it turned out, the girlfriend was now an ex-wife, and her old man was a dealer, and she didn't buy my story whatsoever. The whole time I'm talking to her, junkies are going in and out of the place like it's a bus terminal. They come in looking like death warmed over and kind of float back out all contented.

"Her old man had me followed. He had a good business going, and they were both convinced I was a narc. He paid some junkie a couple of bags to stick me from behind." Shirtless, I spun in my chair and pointed out the scar on my back. "I spent nine days in a hospital in Cleveland, Ohio."

His pale face was now ashen.

"The only reason I'm telling you any of this is to give you an idea of what the job's like. People sometimes get the idea that twenty-five percent is too much to charge. Should I stop? Is that enough?"

He pushed *pause*. "Listen, this is terrific stuff. Exactly what I'm looking for. Go on. Please."

I didn't like him calling my past "stuff." "You mentioned over the phone that I'd have a listen to the final edit. That still goes, right?"

"Absolutely. If you don't want it to run, we pull it. Okay?"

I nodded. He started the tape recorder again. "So I decided to stay away from the ex-wife." I grinned. "But in our conversation she had implied that one of the band members was now a bartender over on the waterfront, so I went looking for him. He was working nights at a strip joint that catered to longshoremen. I greased him with fifty bucks and he suddenly recalled hearing that Delray had played in a band in Pittsburgh for a while. Name of the band was The Heaters.

"So off I went to Pittsburgh."

"Jesus."

"I had plenty of incentive, mind you. Delray Greene was owed over one hundred sixty-five thousand dollars in back royalties and interest. Prior to this I had been taking home seventy bucks a night as a bassist in a soft-rock band. My cut alone would come to something like twenty thousand. I was willing to go to the ends of the earth to find Delray Greene."

He smiled.

"At any rate, by the time I got to Pittsburgh the lead singer for The Heaters was working a car wash by day and playing with the band on weekends. I had some more trouble there—it cost me a broken rib, new stitches, and some bruises that looked like modern art, but I came away with a good lead. Delray had called and had offered this guy a job in a Tex-Mex band in Lopedo, Texas.

"One thing about the music business," I continued, "is that it's really one huge family. Players travel from town to town, pick up work here and there, and everyone eventually knows everyone. The guy in Pittsburgh had worked a session once with a drummer I knew. That kind of thing comes up all the time. That's why you send a musician to find a musician. A typical private investigator would have a hell of a time with it."

"I can imagine."

"The coffee's getting to me. I'm making this too long. The bottom line is that when I finally caught up to Delray Greene, I found him praying to the porcelain god in a shit heap of a roadhouse, ten miles north of Lopedo. At that point he was living on straight Mescal. He was jaundiced and looked like a watermelon had lodged where his liver was supposed to be. He had a half-a-gram-a-day habit, and to look at him you would have thought he was only minutes away from death itself.

"He came up out of the toilet. I introduced myself. He looked right through me, like I wasn't there, left the can, and stumbled up on stage. Went right on playing. The guy had a monster voice, unbelievable rhythm guitar work, and knew about four hundred songs. The place was packed with Mexicans, and this band was as authentic Tex-Mex as thcy come. I ended up getting into the Mescal myself." I remembered the night and smiled. "The upshot was it took me four days of literally living at this bar to get my message through to Delray. Finally one day he turns and looks me in the eye—his eyes were yellow—and says, 'Say, ain't I met you before?'"

Scott laughed.

"I repeated my rap—God only knows I had it memorizcd—and he stared at me like he had heard it for the first time. And he probably had. He hugged me. He stepped right up to me and hugged me. He was running a fever something terrible and I recommended we get him to a hospital. He wouldn't have any of it. He wanted that money. We were on a plane in two hours flat. He never even told the band he was leaving. He drank the flight out of tequila and started working on the vodka. By ten o'clock that night we were in a meeting with Bruce."

I watched the magpies in silence. Memories have a funny way with me. From time to time a single thought can transport me back. It's so real I can reach out and touch people, I can smell the cigarettes and hear the music thumping in the background.

"Whatever happened?" he asked.

"Bruce and I both have this righteous side to us. There was no way we were going to turn that kind of money over to a man in his condition. So Bruce put strings on it. Delray could get the cash, but only after a month at a dry farm. Delray Greene had never seen that kind of money in his life. Most people would have agreed to swim to Hawaii for that money. Not Delray. He had some precious words for us and demanded his return airfare. Bruce paid it, reminding him the money would be here for him collecting interest."

"He turned it down?"

"He said he was going to hire a lawyer and sue us. At that point Delray Greene would have had trouble hiring a cab, much less a lawyer," I added. "Besides, we'd been totally aboveboard on the whole thing. He didn't need a lawyer, he needed a doctor.

So we held the money in escrow and waited him out." My coffee was cold. I'd been talking too much. "To make a long story longer," I said, "Delray Greene showed up two months later looking really bad. He agreed to the drunk tank and he dried out."

"Incredible."

"It doesn't have a happy ending," I told him. "Bruce settled with him. Delray stayed sober for about two days. Then he evidently went out of control. At least his car did. They found him in a brand-new Cadillac, dressed to his teeth, a busted bottle of mescal on the floor and a half-ounce of coke in the glove box, at the bottom of Topanga Canyon."

"Oh God," Scott gasped.

We were quiet for a time. I said, "I've often wondered what would have become of old Delray if I'd left him alone."

"Same thing," Scott assured me. "Different state is all. He would have died in Texas instead. You probably gave him one of the best weeks of his life. He probably thought he had died and gone to heaven."

"I hope that's what he did," I said.

We talked for another half an hour. Talked until the tape ran out. I told him a couple more stories that had happier endings. Delray's story was too depressing for a segment. He then asked me about Brenda Catiglio, the subject of the article in the *Express.*

"Brenda was an unusual case. I seldom do missing-person work. I stick to what I know and love, which is giving down-and-out musicians money they are owed, and a chance at a new life. Nine times out of ten it's very fulfilling despite the personal dangers that seem to pop up a little too frequently. Missing-person work is another deal entirely. I say I seldom do it, and that's true, but now and then something comes along that I feel compelled to help out with. Brenda's case was that way. I can't give you the details. Suffice it to say that Catiglio, despite what the press might have you believe, has been legitimate for years. Bruce had worked with the man on a number of occasions and thought very highly of him. Catiglio found himself in what might best be called a pressure situation, involving some former, now disenchanted, associates. He needed some help locating Brenda."

"Kidnapping?"

"No comment. This isn't for the show, Scott. It was a bad situation made worse by drugs and a porno-video ring. Very bad. Putting it in the show won't do anyone any good. Like I said, I don't do missing-person work very often. Only when I have free time, and it's something or someone," I said, thinking of Nicole, "that really grabs me. Only where and when I think I can be of some help that otherwise can't be found."

He left a while later enthusiastic and grateful and I realized the interview had been what I needed. Sometimes I have to hear myself talk in order to remind myself what it is that motivates me. I have to reshape and reform my thoughts continually in order to understand them. Nicole needed someone to help her, and unwittingly, I had just volunteered.

●

The police station looked like an aluminum-sided garage. A lonely brown Dodge with RID 1 on the plates sat in the loose gravel, blocking one of two hitch racks that flanked the freshly painted steps leading to the door marked SHERIFF. I knocked and let myself in. The plastic nameplate read KAY COLLINS. Kay was in her late forties, wiry, with big eyes, small tomboy breasts, and farmer's hands. She wore cowboy boots, faded jeans, and a white button-down Oxford. She wore almost no makeup and looked healthy enough to live to be a hundred and ten. Her voice contradicted the image: she obviously smoked. With each word it sounded as if she were rasping soft pine. "May I help you?" She suddenly beamed and stopped her work with a Bic pen. "Say, didn't I just see your mug in the local rag? Sure I did."

"Chris Klick."

"Kay Collins. Nice to make your acquaintance. Don't follow rock 'n' roll much, but then again, I don't suppose you follow C and W, do ya? Dudn't much matter, though, does it? Want to see the boss?"

I nodded. I could have corrected her on my tastes in music—but why bother? It's good to take a few knocks now and then, even if undeserved.

She spoke faster than any person I'd ever met. And I'd met a few. I wondered if the coffee cup to her right had something to do with it. I thought not. She was nervous, maybe. I'm getting used to people becoming nervous around me. It's a disquieting feeling, one of the negative aspects of being abnormally tall and large. Size is a curse. Like any curse, the worst thing about size is that once you've got it, it's hell getting rid of the image that goes along with it.

More publicity was coming out now about my efforts. *Time* had called my friend Lyel—owner of my house—and had asked about me, though they hadn't run a piece yet. With each added bit of publicity, the world through my eyes grew smaller and smaller. One of these days the whole damn thing would fit into the living room of Lyel's guest cabin under the watchful gaze of the Man With Blue Hair.

Sheriff Dean Hudson had the narrow-set eyes of a primate and rough, coarse skin from his years in the unforgiving high desert sun. In the saddle was more like it, according to the yellowed black-and-white photos on the office wall. He'd ridden broncs and he'd wrestled steers. His stubby fat hands confirmed his years on the rodeo circuit: the middle finger on his right hand was missing, lost no doubt between a rope and a saddle horn many years before. He was barrel-chested to the point of stretching the buttons on his extra-large uniform shirt when he inhaled. His voice made him sound like a mountain lion who knew the language. "You're a lot taller than I expected," he began.

"Six-five," I confirmed.

"You look more like six-seven. What, two-fifty, two fifty-five?"

"Two thirty-seven." He gave me the impression he was sizing me up to decide if he could take me or not. Like fame, size has its drawbacks. It's something The Man With Blue Hair will never have to worry about—and another reason I like him—he isn't very big. "Chris Klick."

"I know who you are. And if you can read, you know who I

am," he said, motioning toward the plastic name plaque on the front edge of his clean desktop. "Why don't you sit down?"

I obliged. There are very few chairs that are comfortable for a man six feet five and two thirty-seven. This one was no exception. I rocked my knees open and leaned forward.

"What brings you in, Mr. Klick?"

"Paul Russell."

"Figured as much. Read in the *Express* how you find people for a living. Russell's wife was in here yesterday. Cute little thing, isn't she? Got herself all in a froth about her husband straying. Tell you the same thing I told her: If I went chasing down every bull that busted through a fence, I'd have my butt in motion twenty-five hours a day. You follow that? Long as there's wet green grass on th' other side of that fence, these longhorns 'll bust it down when the home pasture dries up on 'em. There's nothing like a young filly slick between the legs. Isn't that right, Mr. Klick? Nothin' quite as satisfying as knowing you can still get a woman wet, is there? And the young ladies like the ones up in Snow Lake are just dying to show you they can get that way. Nice comfortable fit is what it is—but it don't make it no easier on the wives, I suppose." He laughed, more like a bad cough, and spit into his handkerchief, which he quickly pocketed. "This shit's been going on for twenty thousand years. No reason for it to stop now."

I wasn't buying his Western act, no matter how sincere. He seemed dyed in it, but it still didn't fit. Like his shirt. Hudson was crass and obnoxious, but beyond that, he was dangerous. I had felt it the minute we had locked eyes, and the feeling grew darker with each passing minute, like oversteeped tea. And like the tea, it left a bitter taste in my mouth. "So you aren't investigating?" I asked.

"What's there to investigate?"

"Paul Russell," I told him, and he didn't like it.

"You know, we don't stop people from moving into Ridland. But it doesn't mean we gotta like 'em."

"Paul Russell's not one of the family, so why try very hard? Is that it?"

"I do my job. Same for you as for anybody. This here's an

elected position in this community. I don't do the job right, I don't get reelected."

"And how many terms have you served, Sheriff?"

"None of your damn business."

"It's a matter of public record, isn't it?"

"Two terms," he said, huffing. "This is my fifth year. Proud of it."

"And how many missing-person reports do you get?"

"This here thing didn't become a missing person report until late yesterday afternoon. A minimum of twenty-four hours is needed. Around here I like to give it more like thirty-six. We got guys that go off hunting and show up late. Farmhands that get a little drunk and pass out under a rock for a couple of days. Even women who head down to Twin Falls and run into a traveling salesman with an expense account. You get so you can feel your way through a job like this, Mr. Klick. I don't expect you to understand that, but that's the way it is around these parts. You mark my word, that little lady's husband 'll come slinking back home, tail between his sore legs soon enough. Nothin' to get too worked up about."

"She's pretty worked up."

"What's your interest, Klick? You got your eye on her or something? A fella can't help but notice she's put together about as nice as a thoroughbred. What makes you give a damn?"

I felt my spine go rigid and the muscles in my upper back and chest tighten to the point they hurt. I caught myself holding my breath. I was probably red in the face. Anger is a funny thing. I get the most angry when people get the closest to the truth. If he had been anyone but a cop, Dean Hudson and I would have already gotten to know each other better—I was that close to reintroducing myself. "I give a damn, because no one else seems to." I stood.

"Ain't that big of you." Hudson leaned back in his chair. "I made a couple of calls earlier, if that makes you feel any better. The little lady give me his registration number and social security number—same as a driver's license in this state, in case you didn't notice. I wouldn't get all in a sweat until we know a little more, Klick. And I wouldn't make too big a deal of it."

"I noticed."

"Get outta here."

I did. I passed Kay Collins on my way out. She gave me a bug-eyed smile and offered a glimpse of her tobacco-stained teeth. I had a feeling there was more between Kay Collins and Dean Hudson than triplicate forms. My sweet little town was going sour on me.

And it pissed me off.

I drive a 1960 Ford three-quarter-ton pickup that has seen better days. About ten years ago someone replaced one of the rear leaf springs with that of another model. As a result the cab and bed lean toward the driver's side, giving one the impression that the driver must be obese. The door opens with a squeak and if you turn on the radio, it blows a fuse that controls the fuel and temperature gauges. Like the Billy Joel song, I Loved It Just the Way It Was, a dull, scratched orange with white bumpers and grille. I've never named it. No need to. It's one of a kind.

Karen's Hair Care sits on the main-street side of the Video Best rental store. Since they share a common door, the effect is disarming. When shopping for a good movie to watch, you have to put up with that distinct and unpleasant odor that only hair salons offer; when getting a haircut, the sound track of *The Terminator* or *Top Gun* fills the room, making each snip of the scissors feel as if it might end your life.

I wear my blond curly hair fairly short, considering my former profession, fairly long compared with the residents of Ridland. It is styled, though not terribly. I knew that a single session at Karen's would wipe out what forty dollars had bought me two weeks earlier on Houston Street on the north edge of

SoHo, but next to cabdrivers, hairdressers know all the latest gossip. And there weren't any cabdrivers in Ridland.

●

I took a seat on a worn couch with too little room for my legs between the couch and the coffee table littered with dog-eared back issues of *Glamour* and *Farm Wife News*. The walls were the same color purple as Nicole Russell's leotard; the ceiling spray-textured; the floor black and white linoleum squares. Next to the cash register was a rack of nail polishes in a rainbow of shades, and behind it, shelves of hair coloring, shampoo, and conditioner. All the women looked over at me as I sat down. They all smiled simultaneously as if choreographed. Karen, the owner, beamed at me enthusiastically and asked, "Can I help you?"

"In a minute, thank you," I said politely and thumbed my way directly into a brassiere ad in *Glamour*. Destiny. It reminded me of Nicole soaking up the sun. Karen trundled back behind the register and tried to appear busy, though she was engrossed in a *People* magazine. Probably not a back issue, either, I thought. My purpose in delaying her was the desire to eavesdrop on the three gals snipping away in front of me. I was two signs into the horoscopes for three months ago when I picked my coiffeur. She was quite round, pudgy-faced, and smothered in rouge. I figured her for Kay Collins' distant cousin by the speed of her mouth and her eagerness to share every detail of information she probably didn't have any right discussing. Just what I was looking for. On the mirror in front of her chair was the name Rita Roosevelt. I stood up and banged my head on a pot that held a dusty silk begonia, stopped it from swinging and approached Karen. "I'd like a trim from Rita, if that's possible."

"Rita?" Karen asked quietly, deeply surprised. She had figured me for the young and busty Helen, no doubt. No doubt Helen could give one hell of a shampoo, by the look in Karen's eyes.

"Yes," I said.

She checked a schedule. I assumed it was a formality—how could Karen be booked up? Much less Rita? I was told it would be an hour's wait. Stunned, I decided to wait it out, returning my gaze to the mindless magazine, my ears alert, intercepting various conversations, storing bits and pieces for future use. By the end of the hour, three tidbits remained strongly in my mind: Gerry Clark was three months pregnant, and Bill Clark hadn't been anywhere near Ridland three months ago (for some reason I couldn't catch that one), the rumor line had Greg Sweetland in the sack with Gerry, according to Rita. Helen, of the well-endowed chest, must have picked up on the mention of Greg Sweetland, for I had overheard her say what a tragedy it was that Greg had been killed in the hunting accident. The Ridland *Express* is a weekly, and living quite a ways out of town, I had heard nothing about a hunting accident. The third bit of gossip that I had retained out of the volumes I overheard was that "those new folks" were having marriage problems. It seemed that Kay Collins had confirmed to Rita that Nicole Russell had paid the sheriff a visit. I was proud of my decision to go with Rita. She seemed to have the latest on everything. Except hair technique.

I didn't fit in the reclining chair that they used for shampoos. I had to arch my back and spread my legs apart to hold a position. Rita had nice fingers and a good sense for water temperature. She shampooed me twice, gave me a conditioner/creme rinse, and rinsed me for a full two minutes with a nice steady massage. It was already better than my forty-dollar experience in the heart of New York City. I got her talking halfway through the second shampoo. I started her out on light subjects and tried to seem impressed by her knowledge when it seemed appropriate. It worked. We were into her social life by the creme rinse and by the time I took the chair I said, "I bet you know more about this town than about anyone."

"Damn straight," she said, smiling at me in the mirror. She lowered the chair as far as it would go. "Jeez, you're a big one, aren't you? Hey, Helen," she called out, "take a look at this." I watched her in the mirror as she opened her arms, scissors in one hand, comb in the other. Helen knew exactly what she was saying.

"Don't have him scootch down," Helen advised. "It'll kill his back." She jerked her head, wiggling her bosom like semifirm jello. "I got a little stool in the back I use for Peter. Try that."

"Peter Sweetland's our basketball star," Rita informed me. "Back in a shake."

When she returned I had my opening. "Is Peter Greg's brother?"

"Second cousin, I think. You hear about Greg?" she wondered.

"Just that there was a hunting accident."

"Killed him dead, poor man. Though we get what we deserve, isn't that so?"

"He deserved it?" I tried to sound horrified. I gave myself a B-plus.

"Greg was a nice-enough kid, but he took chances, if you know what I mean. Greg liked to live high on the hog. A big appetite. A big appetite for a lot of things, if you hear what I'm saying."

"Don't go spreading no rumors now, Rita," Helen interjected.

"Who, me?" Rita cackled. She began to work on my hair. I could tell immediately it was going to be a disaster. I reminded her three times that it was only a trim, to cut less, and she did her best to accommodate my request.

A few minutes into it I said bluntly, "What do you hear about the Russells?"

Rita sucked air between her teeth in disapproval. "The new folks? Not good, from what I hear. She's so young and pretty and sweet. He's got to have twenty years on her and none of the charm. You know she's loaded, don't you?"

"No, I hadn't heard that."

"Oh, sure. Loaded to the gills, I hear. Some say he got one look at her bank account and sprung on her like a fox in a chicken house. He don't work a bit. Not one bit." She leaned in close. I could smell a faint trace of cheap perfume. "He made a pass at Helen one night over at the Dollar when a band was playing. Christ, he even offered her *money*. Can you believe that?" I looked at young Helen in the mirror. I could believe it. I didn't tell Rita that. She said, "Puts away liquor like a horse puts away grain. And not only liquor, according to Rita."

I put on my best innocent voice. I'm not very good at it. I gave myself a C-minus. "Drugs?"

"Just grass," Rita told me. "Offered Helen some grass."

"And how old is he?"

"If he's a day he's forty-five. Maybe fifty."

"I'll be damned."

She leaned in again. "Not that grass is any big deal. I mean, I've tried it before. Most have, right?"

I shrugged, which reminded me of Nicole Russell and her patented shoulder lift.

Rita warned, "Still, I don't give that marriage long, I'll tell you that. Thank God there ain't no children. I hate to see couples like that have children."

I asked, "You have children, Rita?"

"Four of the little buggers," she told me proudly. "Best damned thing that ever happened to me was becoming a mother. Didn't do much for my body," she said, patting her midriff. "Used to have a figure like Helen's"—she pronounced figure as *figger*—"if you can believe that."

I couldn't. "I bet you did," I said, hating myself for the lie, loving myself for making her feel so good. "But just making a pass . . ." I said, leading her on.

"Not only that. There ain't nothing between them. I can tell when there's something between two people, and there ain't nothing there with them. Maybe there was once, but it ain't there no more. Ten'll get you twenty they don't spend Christmas together. There's a short fuse burning on that one. I'd put money on it."

It confirmed my initial suspicions and backed up what Hudson had told me. The haircut—the butcher job, actually—cost me nine dollars. I gave her a two-dollar tip, and it so surprised her that she brought my attention to the fact that I had overpaid. It returned some of my faith in Ridland, which I had lost after my meeting with Sheriff Hudson.

I didn't want to see Nicole Russell again. Not knowing what I now knew. I carry my sympathies to extremes sometimes, and I worried where they might lead me. I also wondered if Greg Sweetland had really died in a hunting accident, or had Bill Clark tapped into the rumor line of who had hit on his wife? And that made me wonder about Sheriff Hudson and the law of the land in God-fearing Ridland. Would he look the other way when moral justice was involved? I didn't doubt it, and that didn't sit well with me.

I walked out of Karen's with a silly haircut and a lot of questions. My telltale sky had turned partly cloudy. And so had I.

4

One of the advantages of having a little money is that bankers treat you better. For years—well over a decade, actually—I maintained a balance of less than a hundred dollars in my checking account at all times. My hand-to-mouth existence tolled harder on me than on my bank—but just getting service was something of a godsend, getting advice or help was next to impossible. The manager was always busy.

In Ridland the manager is rarely busy. She sits behind a large oak-veneered desk in an L-shaped alcove with a fine view of a Xerox copier across the room. As I entered the bank she shuffled some papers around and then looked up, but I knew from earlier visits to the teller window that nine out of ten times she inspected arrivals through a window that faced the parking lot and knew exactly who was about to push through her doors.

My account is healthy and active, especially by Ridland standards. Unlike those earlier years, I can get service now. I look different than native Ridlandites. I stick out. My size, my taste in clothing (which runs on the expensive but informal side), and my tan stamp me *outsider,* though, as more and more out-of-towners settle in this fine community, this will no doubt change.

"Good afternoon," I offered in my most congenial voice,

taking an uncomfortable seat that blocked Mrs. Bookman's view of the copier. She had a rather mousy face, liked to paint her eyelids blue and cheeks red, wore earrings that dangle and clothing that hid her excess baggage. She withdrew an amazingly long and narrow cigarette from a gold paperpack and tapped it twice on the face of her wristwatch, tamping down the tobacco. She puckered her mouth as she performed this rite, and smiled upon the accomplishment, placing the filter between her colored lips and trapping it in a vise of lipstick-coated dentures. As the tip blazed to ember-orange, she inhaled happily. No smoke escaped her mouth until she was well into her second sentence. I shuddered at the thought that the lining of her lungs most likely resembled the flat tar roof of my old grammar school on a hot summer day. It's her life, I told myself. But not for long.

"Good afternoon, Mr. Klick. And how are you enjoying our Idaho Indian summer?"

"Very much, thank you. My last job ran a little long. I arrived expecting to dig out my boots and long underwear. You can imagine my pleasant surprise to discover it was still shorts weather. Even so, I've been getting my wood in."

"So have we. What a chore! Now, what can I do for you?"

I lowered my voice for the sake of drama. "I have a rather peculiar favor to ask of you, Mrs. Bookman." She blushed, which struck me as somewhat odd—what went on in the vapid mind of Cecilia Bookman as she wiled away the hours with her copier and long cigarettes?

"I'll try," she said, cocking her head and smiling unnaturally.

"I've run into some very nice people," I explained. "The Russells. Do you know them?"

"Certainly. She's such a pretty one, isn't she?"

"Yes, she is."

"And so charming," she added between drags.

"Well, the thing is, they've made me a little business offer and it seems rather attractive, but I'm hesitant to get too involved without knowing a little more about them, if you know what I mean."

"I sure do."

"And I know you can't give out specifics or anything—and God bless you for that"—I knew she was active in the church—

"but I wondered if I were to count on them for, say, a forty-thousand-dollar partnership, would I be safe in assuming they could cover their share, or would I be foolish?"

She looked me over and chewed on the inside of her lip. "Without a doubt you would be about as safe as a person could get, Mr. Klick. I would say you have *absolutely* nothing to worry about, if we understand each other. I would say they could be your partners many times over, and you'd still be safe."

I grinned at her thankfully. "And would I be wiser to get Mr. Russell's signature on the papers, or Mrs. Russell's?"

She hesitated because she knew I was hanging on her answer. "Mrs.," she said. "Mrs. all the way."

"You've been a tremendous help, Mrs. Bookman."

"Not at all."

"I hate to make stupid business deals."

"I certainly hope you'll entertain the idea of letting us handle the account for you." She drew on the cigarette and shed its ashes absentmindedly into the ashtray.

"I wouldn't consider anyone else. I'm sure you'll be the first to know if we come to terms. Oh, and by the way, I'd appreciate it if you didn't mention this to the Russells. I promised them I wouldn't tell a soul. I wouldn't want to compromise the chance of a deal."

She batted her eyes and grinned somewhat greedily. I stood. "Good day, Mr. Klick," she said.

I had to think on that a moment. A good day? Not after my talk with Hudson. "Thanks again," I said, and then left, knowing full well that Mrs. Bookman was watching as I climbed into my old pickup and turned right onto Main.

●

She was waiting in her Wagoneer at the top of my drive, listening to Mozart's Piano Concerto in B-flat. I invited her in, and she followed me down the half-mile gravel lane that led to the secluded log home. Aspens with yellow-and-black autumn leaves swayed in the afternoon breeze. Red rose hips adorned the fence line. I rolled down my window and tried to get Mrs. Bookman's tobacco out of my nose. The air smelled like sandalwood. I pulled into the garage and was pulling down the door when I heard her say she was sorry for bothering me.

I told her she could have come on down to the house. She didn't have to park at the top of the drive waiting. "Just think what the neighbors will say," I said, kidding her. She didn't appreciate the comment. She looked down at my feet and I saw her arm begin to tremble. It wasn't cold enough to tremble. It was downright spectacular out. I tried to keep my heart out of this, but my heart and my mind don't always see eye to eye. I took another step closer and she came into my arms eager for the comfort.

"Oh Jesus, I'm scared," she blurted out.

I took a deep breath. It had been a while since someone warm had buried her head in my chest, had pressed herself against me. I reminded myself of her situation and then wrapped my arms around her anyway and pulled her tightly against me. I reveled in the sensation, drinking in the scent of her hair and absorbing the strength of her delicate arms. "No reason to be," I assured her. "Nothing to be afraid of here."

She pushed away suddenly and self-consciously. "Sorry," and for a moment I feared she might leave without another word. She pawed the gravel with her foot and then dragged her face on her sleeve. "Sorry about that," she repeated.

"No reason to be."

It made her smile. She looked into my eyes. Hers were suede brown and expressive. "Thanks."

"How 'bout a cup of coffee?"

"How about a bourbon?" came her reply.

"My kind of girl," I teased, gesturing toward the front of the house. A moment later we were inside and I was fixing her bourbon. She didn't feel like a married woman to me. I wasn't treating the situation that way in my mind, at any rate, and I wondered if it was because of Rita Roosevelt's gossip or my own primitive instincts.

"Who's he?" she asked, pointing up to Blue Hair, who appeared quite confident today.

"My deity. I burn incense and pray on a mat twice a day. He keeps my insurance rates down and guards the front door."

"You ought to market him," she said.

"He's his own man. He won't have anything to do with it."

"Who's the artist?" she asked, deciding not to play anymore. I told her and she said she had heard of Ms. Scott. I handed her the drink and then found a green Girl in the fridge. I opened the bottle carefully and moved into the living room, taking one of the overstuffed chairs across from her. She had on khaki slacks and a pink silk blouse. A gold chain hung around her neck, with a matching one clasped about her wrist. She was altogether first class.

"I don't normally drink in the middle of the afternoon," she apologized.

"I do," I said quite frankly.

She looked back up at Blue Hair and then again over at me. "Have you thought any more about helping me?"

"Yes, I have been thinking about it."

"And?"

"You said you were scared. Why?"

"The radar detector."

"What?"

"I found the radar detector under the seat. Don't you see?"

I shook my head no.

"First Harper, now the radar detector. It just doesn't make any sense. When Paul drove anywhere, except on errands into Ridland, he used the radar detector. He's a fast driver, the roads are boring, and he can't afford any more tickets without losing his license. He never took Harper unless he went hunting. I really don't think he even liked Harper much. If he went hunting, then he probably would have headed east, up the Bell Mountain road toward Crystal Creek. But the Audi is missing, and he wouldn't have gone in the Audi. He would have taken the Wagoneer. See? He *never* went hunting in the Audi, that is unless he intended to meet someone and go in their truck. So it doesn't make any sense to me. And quite frankly, it scares me. Three nights now. If he was going hunting with friends, why haven't I heard from *them*? See?"

"I think I need to know more about your husband." The beer was cold and delicious.

She nodded somewhat grimly and spoke to the ice cubes floating on her bourbon and water. "Yes, I suppose you do." It took her nearly a minute before she continued. "It's no secret that we haven't been getting on too well. It won't take you long to discover that. Not in a town this size. The marriage was a mistake. I know that now. Paul's one hell of a salesman. He swept me off my feet, as they say. I was vulnerable. I didn't see what was going on until we'd already been married several months, and I'm so damn hardheaded that once I saw it, I refused to believe I couldn't turn it back around. Make it work, you know. Get something out of it.

"What you'll hear if you ask is that Paul was after my money. Even I've heard it. I'm probably the only one who waited so long to believe it. He's twenty-one years older than me, Mr. Klick—"

"Chris. Or Klick. But not 'mister.' "

"He's had a dozen jobs in as many years. He's young at heart, a little crazy, and very much a man. For a girl in her mid-twenties suddenly without family and nervous about who was after her for what, he made a wonderful haven to hide in. Looking back, it may have been by design. I don't want to believe that, I guess." There was a long pause. "I don't love him any longer. I did for a while, but it hasn't been so great since we got married. He lives it up a lot, mixes with some strange people I don't go in for. We haven't seen much of each other since the beginning of the summer. He spends too much of my money and tries to impress. He's restless. Constantly restless. I don't think he's been unfaithful, but I wouldn't put it past him. So maybe I should be rejoicing that he's missing . . . I can see it in your eyes. That's not who I am. That's not Nicky. Maybe I'm still hoping to work this out. Still hoping to find what the two of us had those first few months. Even if we were both acting, we can learn to act again, can't we? It's all right to act a little bit, isn't it?" She was crying, and nothing I could say or do was going to help. This was a solo. I let her play it without accompaniment. I listened and studied, like the good friend I wasn't but wanted to be. That was a lie, of course—and somewhere inside I knew it. I wanted to be more than her friend. Much more.

"I need to know what's going on, Chris," she added. "If it's another woman, then so be it. But I don't think it is."

"I'm getting crossed signals from you, Nicole. I hear you say that you don't love him, and yet there is an urgency in your voice which contradicts that. I think you're acting for me, and I'd like to know why." She looked away and the sides of her petite neck scalded. "What is it that really's bothering you? Is it jealousy? Do you know who he's with?"

"No!"

"Did he catch *you* with someone? Has he taken Harper to get back at *you*?"

"Don't be absurd."

"That doesn't qualify as an answer. I'm not being absurd. You are a stunning woman, Nicole. If you weren't hit on several times a week, it would surprise me. We all give in eventu——"

"Not me! Wrong. Wrong, wrong, wrong." She rose, now quite angry. "I came to the wrong person. My mistake. My apologies for taking up your time."

"That's it, isn't it? He caught you with someone." I had stood too. This was the confrontation I hadn't expected. I was as angry as she was, though I wasn't sure why. I knew one thing: I hated being called the wrong person. I was *not* the wrong person. If her husband could be found, then I could do it as well as the next guy. I told her so.

She said, "I don't think so."

"I think you're keeping something from me, Nicole. I think you're intentionally keeping something from me, and what the hell good will that do? When a person like me gets involved in something like this, he has to know the full picture or he can get into a jam he can't easily get out of. You're not giving me the full picture." I put my hand on the door. She was on the front porch. "Please."

She stopped and faced me. The silence was long and heavy. Her shoulders slumped forward and her face relaxed to a more honest sadness. "Fifty thousand dollars," she said, "that I know of. It could be more—much more. It evidently started about six weeks ago. I let him do the books. He signed onto the accounts. I didn't want him feeling like a gigolo. What was I supposed to do? *Sooo* stupid. He withdrew it in bits and pieces, some withdrawals as large as six and eight thousand dollars, some as small as a few hundred. But it's gone, Chris, and so is he."

Behind her, sheets of amber shag weed moved in elegant

waves driven by the wind. My neighbor's horses fed on the low green stubble of summer grass that remained. An irrigation ditch bubbled with ice-cold spring water drawn from the slough. A magpie flapped its wings, then glided; flapped, then glided; followed by a red-shafted flicker. Both birds landed in the willows, though well apart. The flicker appeared nervous.

A few more shotgun reports far in the distance. More ducks, I assumed. The slaughter continued. "I can ask around," I told her in my best businesslike voice. Then, changing to a more honest tone, I said, "Don't go."

I wondered why, even to me, my voice sounded as if I was pleading with her.

5

Snow Lake is an ever-expanding tourist village nestled in a horseshoe of jagged mountains that reminded me of an open shark's mouth. The town looked as if it might be swallowed at any moment. Even in September the tips of the towering peaks were frosted white by early flurries. I thanked the Man With Blue Hair that I was fortunate enough to be in a place this naturally beautiful. There is a resonance in the mountains that heightens one's appreciation of life, like the clear, ringing tone of a single sustained note from a French horn. The same can be said for the sea: a vast expanse of churning waves with a windy white-noise connecting one point with another. But on that day, as I drove north, it was the mountains dominating the skyline that took my breath away and caused me to switch off the radio and roll down my window despite the morning chill. I was alive.

I was beginning to think Paul Russell was not.

•

My second haircut in as many days corrected what damage Rita Roosevelt had caused. If I kept this up, I would have no hair whatsoever. Again, I waited on a couch for a few minutes while determining which of the four women in this new establishment would be the most vocal. I ended up in the professional care of Judy—a bright-eyed, shapely woman in her early twenties who had all of the latest styles down. The shampoo was outrageous—thoroughly stimulating. Twice she gently brushed my ears, and I felt it clear down my spine. "This was just cut, wasn't it?" she asked, sitting me up and drying my curls.

"You're hired for damage control," I informed her. "Just yesterday I looked like a human being."

She giggled musically and led me to a soft chair that went low enough for her to work on me comfortably. "You know a guy named Paul Russell?" I asked, deciding on the direct approach.

"Sure. He lived up here before he got married. Everybody knows Paul up here. Why?"

"I just met him for the first time last week. Seems like a nice guy. He sort of implied Snow Lake could be a fun town if you knew the right people."

"That's for sure. That's Paul. He's a good, hard-core partyer. A lot of fun. You just move here? Seems like I've seen you around."

"I've visited Ridland several times over the past couple of years. Met them both last week. His wife doesn't seem the party type."

"Her? Not hardly. Paul parties alone these days—well, not exactly alone," she chortled, "but not with *her*. She's not exactly the party type from what I hear. She knows Paul had a scene going here before she arrived and I think she's pretty jealous of it."

"I lied," I told her. "I didn't meet them last week. I've known Paul for a couple of years. I owe him some money and I'm trying to reach him without contacting his wife. That's the way he wanted it. You wouldn't know someone who might be able to put me in touch with him, would you?"

"You try calling him?"

"That's out. His wife knows my voice. He doesn't want her knowing about this."

"I might know someone," she said, working on the back of my head. She looked in the mirror and smiled at me suspiciously.

She whispered, "But I got a feeling it isn't money you've got for Paul. That's why his wife can't be involved, right?"

I whispered back, "What are you, a detective?"

"Hardly," she joked. "I just know Paul, that's all. We didn't nickname him Bird Man because of his beak, you know."

"Because of his altitude," I told her.

"I like you," she said, snipping by my ears. "What'd you say your name was?"

"Chris."

"Right. I know an old friend of Paul's might know how to reach him. They're still pretty close."

I assumed Judy would take a slight pass as a compliment. If I guessed wrong, all was not lost, and to come right out and try for the name might seem too pushy. "Are *you* close with anyone at the moment?"

She tapped me playfully on the back of the head. "That's a hell of a question."

"That's not an answer."

"You're big and gorgeous," she said. "What makes you think I might be interested in you?"

"Who said anything about me? I asked about you."

"Not at the moment," she said, stopping what she was doing and looking at me in the reflection. She went back to work.

"How about a few moments into the future, like this evening?"

"The calendar's clear. What did you have in mind?"

"About seven-thirty seems good. How 'bout for you?"

"Dinner?"

"And drinks."

"The perfect couple," she said, obscuring her meaning.

"Oh, your friend," I said in my most surprised voice. "The one who might know how to reach Paul . . ."

"Debbie," she said. "She's an artist. Owns a gallery on the corner by the liquor store—Portraits West. If you don't find her there, try the Crystal Creek condos on Creekside. Last name is Benton. Second floor, I think."

"Debbie Benton," I repeated. Judy nodded. We spent the rest of the haircut sizing each other up. It took longer than it should have—the haircut, that is—and several times she pressed warmly against my arm as she hovered over me, clipping away. My mind was still on Nicole.

I tipped her ten bucks and told her it was the nicest haircut I'd about ever had, which it was. She scribbled down a phone number and an address and confirmed seven-thirty with a girlish giggle and an all-knowing batting of the eyes.

Portraits West Gallery occupied an alcove off an upscale clothing store that was already displaying winter fashions. I priced a skisuit at five hundred dollars and then carefully avoided touching anything else in the store. Debbie Benton wasn't in. Her "gallery" consisted of eight watercolors, mostly of ducks or geese, priced in accordance with the skisuits and fur coats. Fur boots, too. And fur earmuffs. And young, young women with million-dollar smiles and centerfold figures there to encourage you to buy. It was this commercial side of Snow Lake that made my friend Lyel look forty minutes south in the agriculture belt of Ridland. They hunt bucks here, the green variety, not elk or deer, and it's always open season. You are sized up in a single glance; net worth is everything. And then they take shots at you, very carefully camouflaged to give you the feeling of genuine hospitality, but shots nonetheless. If they're successful, they bag a credit card or a couple "hun" in cold cash and hand you a bag stamped with a brightly colored logo containing something you may never use. One of my recurring nightmares is having to tip-toe through a field scattered with unseen land mines. Walking down the quaint streets of Snow Lake, this phobia returned.

Crystal Creek Condominiums had a good view of the ski mountain, the trails dusted with snow, the lifts immobile, chairs rocking in the wind. I parked in the area marked "Guests" and climbed the heavy timber steps to the second floor. The door knocker was a brass-plated skier—his skis hit the mogul and alerted Debbie Benton I had arrived. "Judy warned me you might be coming over," she said as she opened the door.

She was just under five-five and wore her hair short. Other than that, I thought I was speaking to Nicole Russell. The resemblance was uncanny—her brown eyes, her perfect figure, even the sensuous mouth. She asked me in and shut the door. Her pants were tight and she moved them very well as she led me into her well-appointed living room/dining room. We walked through and into the small kitchen, where an easel held a partially completed watercolor of ducks *and* geese. She pointed to a stool, which I accepted gratefully. I had feared another uncomfortable chair. "I don't know you," she said.

"No."

"If I don't know you, then chances are Paul doesn't know you."

"Chances don't always prove right."

"Judy said she told you Paul and I were close. That was a long time ago. I just wanted to get that straight."

"Clear as a bell." I noticed a dry dog dish hidden partially under an overhang created by the lower kitchen cabinets. My eyes kept wandering over to it. There had been no smell of dog as I entered. There were no dog hairs on Ms. Benton's slacks and no scratch marks on the inside of the back door. "I have something for him," I told her. "I was hoping you might be able to help me find him."

"Did you try his wife?" she asked sarcastically, picking up her wet brush and working carefully on a wing. Winging it.

"This doesn't involve his wife. He'd rather I not involve her."

"I see." She tuned me out while she completed the wing and then asked, "What is it you have for him?"

"That's between the two of us."

"Judy said money. I don't believe that."

"Then you have seen him recently."

My comment stopped her. "No," she said sternly. "It means I think you're trying to bullshit me, Mr. Klick, and I'd like to know why."

"Maybe I have a key of smoke."

She laughed. "That's more like Paul."

"But I don't," I added.

"You a narc?"

"No. Are you a user?"

"A user? That's quite an expression. You sound like Jack Webb. You *are* a narc. I think it's time you leave, Mr. Klick."

"Not a narc. I'm a musician."

"That's where I've seen you. You're the guy they wrote up in the *Express*. The bounty hunter."

"It's not my favorite term."

"What the hell's going on here?" She stopped painting. "I think you should go."

"He's missing, Miss Benton, but I think you know that. I'm trying to find him."

"Can't help. Sorry."

"Is that Harper's bowl?" I asked.

She saw the bowl and couldn't keep the blood from flooding her face. "No way."

"But you know who Harper is?"

"No, I ah . . ."

"I think you do know, Debbie. The difference between me and the police is that I don't work for the public. I don't talk to the press. This is a small town. I imagine some things that go on between two people are better left secret." I paused for effect. "You've been having an affair with Paul, haven't you?"

"Get out of here, Mr. Klick. Your invitation just ran out."

"If something's happened to Paul, if he's in some sort of trouble, wouldn't you rather I find him sooner than later?"

"I don't believe you," she said.

"I didn't say anything had happened."

"Time to go, Mr. Klick."

I stood. "He may be in trouble, Debbie. No one's heard from him. Nothing you tell me goes out of this room." I added, for the sake of drama, "I can't do this alone. Finding people is not something one can do alone."

"Leave me your phone number," she said. "I'll ask around."

"Harper's missing too," I informed her while I scribbled down the number.

She bit down on her lip.

"I'll be waiting for your call, Debbie. I *need* your help."

"Enough. I got the message, okay?"

"Time is usually quite important in situations like these, Debbie."

"Please!"

I left. The mountains were still there when I stepped outside. That's one thing I like about them.

There was a note taped to my front door. CALL ME was written in boldface on the back of a gas credit-card receipt. It was signed "Nicole"—not Nicky, I noted. She answered on the first ring and asked me over.

Her house was a ranch-style log home on a secluded piece of property along the river. The semicircular driveway was gravel and wrapped around a kidney-shaped berm containing immature aspens staked with wire against the wind, their trunks wrapped with a thick paper meant to keep winter rodents, trapped under the snow, from chewing off the bark and killing the trees.

The house itself was made of unusually large logs—a massive two feet in diameter instead of the customary eight inches. The cedar-shingle roof maintained a steep-enough pitch to shed the tremendous amounts of snow, but was low enough to maintain the ranch look. A formal brick walkway, bordered on either side by annual beds now tilled brown and readied for spring, led to a sheltered veranda that connected the main house to the garage. Several cords of wood had been stacked against the wall there, next to a black gas barbecue on wheels. Hanging from the barbecue was a pot holder, mitten-shaped and colored like a rainbow trout hanging from its side. As I was admiring the pot holder she came through the kitchen door behind me. I heard it open, heard the screen door thump shut, and I didn't want to turn around. Part of me didn't want to see her, didn't want to experience that combination of sensitivity and charm. I wanted to think up some excuse why I couldn't keep working on this for her, but at that moment I was tongue-tied.

She wore jodhpurs and shiny black riding boots that held her calves tightly and reached to just below her knees. Her black shirt had imitation mother-of-pearl snaps down the front and a string tie around the collar with a large piece of turquoise set in silver suspended from it. Her lips were a soft, fleshy red, and her brown eyes seemed bigger than a harvest moon. She had her glossy hair pinned up into a bun, tiny silver studs in her ears.

"You look beautiful," I said.

She blushed and looked away, her eyes darting about the spaces left in the stacks of cordwood, her thumb nervously rubbing her index finger. "Thank you," she said in a quiet voice I had never heard. "Please come in," she offered without looking at me.

The jodhpurs were tailored of a stretch fabric that hugged her tiny, tight backside magnificently. It didn't occur to me until too late that she might have used the reflection in the panes of glass on the kitchen door to catch me staring. And I was staring. Desiring. Hoping for another moment of weakness when she would seek comfort in my arms.

The kitchen was small, the countertops and floor done in two sizes of square Mexican tile. The divided sink was stainless steel, the cabinets contained beveled glass panes that looked in on gorgeous kitchenware. The hardwood floors of the dining and living rooms were covered in part by hand-loomed rugs in red pastels. A 1918 Steinway held the far wall, a handsome stereo outfit was on the shelves at the far end of the room. The opposing fireplace occupied the near corner, an adobe chimney boldly reaching through the exposed roof. I struck a C-major on the Steinway and then arpeggioed with both hands to either end of the keys. It was in spectacular condition. The action on an old Steinway is something one has to experience to appreciate.

"It's nice, isn't it?" she asked knowingly.

"Wow," was all I managed to say, which embarrassed me.

Sometimes I didn't know myself. Nicole Russell had ways of affecting that in me.

As if she'd overheard my thoughts, she said, "We have to keep this business, you know." I realized she hadn't overheard my thoughts, she had recalled my compliment outside her kitchen door and had decided to deal with it. I admired that in her immediately: her strength to say what must be said, her determination to stay on course. Again I wanted to quit, right there and then. Again, I did not.

"Agreed." I was absorbed by the couch as I sat down facing her. Instantly, I felt myself relax.

"I'm attracted to you, Chris. But I can't allow myself to be." We locked eyes. For a moment my entire body tingled. I was with her. I felt positively gleeful. "You understand." It was a statement. I nodded silently. She blinked.

"What's up?" I asked as if the conversation started there and then, my mind reeling with possibilities. Could we make love on the couch, right now, passionate, wild-abandon lovemaking? Would we ever make love? Or was that the beginning and end to it all from the tender lips of the married Nicole Russell? I was torturing myself, and I couldn't seem to stop.

"Sheriff Hudson called me," she said, and I was returned to the hard face of the rodeo veteran I had met two days earlier. The spell was broken.

"And?"

"And that's why I came looking for you. A phone number would help."

"Four-four-three-four."

She looked out the living room windows at the pond dotted with circular wakes from the noses of stocked trout as they rose to autumn flies. I guessed they had to be several pounds each by the size of the rises. She said, "He claims that Paul was stopped for speeding in Hill City on Tuesday night."

"Claims?"

"I don't believe him."

"Why? He told me he made some inquiries. It would seem that somebody got back to him."

"The radar detector," she reminded. "And Harper. Why would he take Harper? It just doesn't make sense to me. And speeding in Hill City? Come on! Those railroad tracks would bottom out a moon vehicle. I've driven through there with Paul a dozen times, and not once—not once!—has he sped through that town. And that's *with* a radar detector. Someone's not telling the truth."

"He was heading south?"

"I didn't have to ask that. That much was implied. I'd sure like to know who handed him that pack of lies and why."

"Then why don't you ask?"

"You can't be serious."

"Call Hudson and ask who he spoke to. Tell him you want to ask the guy some questions."

"Like what?"

"I'll write them down. You ask them. Are you game?"

"Sure I'm game."

●

"He sounded surprised," she said, after hanging up from Hudson.

"I think I'd like to listen in. Is there an extension?"

She motioned through a small television room. "One in the bedroom," she said.

I entered the bedroom reluctantly. A white down comforter with lace edges covered the queen bed. The windows were blocked by lavender Levolor blinds. An antique rolltop desk dominated the far corner. "I'll wait for your signal," I said through the two doorways, dropping down onto the firm bed. "Tell me when it's ringing." I looked around. I could feel her here. Almost could see her. Some framed photographs sat atop a wooden dresser. Family. And Harper with a dead duck gripped proudly in his mouth. I could smell her dark hair against the fresh pillowcase. Hear her giggle.

She waved and I picked up the receiver. A minute later she was speaking with Sheriff Cochran. I saw her read from my list.

She introduced herself and immediately got down to business. There was an appropriate amount of dissatisfaction and rage in her voice. "I'd like to know by whom and what time of night he was stopped, Sheriff."

Cochran had a heavy cowboy accent. "Was me who cited him, ma'am. But if you want the exact time, I'll have to look that up. It'll take a minute."

"Thank you, Sheriff, it is important."

He grumbled and said, "Just a minute," and I could hear him holler out an order in the background. We were put on hold. Nicole looked at me from a distance and shrugged for my approval, which I gave with a hearty nod. She was doing fine. The line remained dead for a long time. Too long, it seemed to me. Finally the line clicked. "Wednesday, two A.M., ma'am," said the sheriff.

"You're certain?"

"That's what it says on this here citation. Yes, ma'am. I knew it was late, but couldn't remember exactly how late."

"And he was headed south?"

"Toward Twin, yes, ma'am."

"Can you remember what he was wearing, Sheriff?"

"Wearing? Well no, I can't quite recall exactly."

"And was anyone with him?" she asked. I had written the question that way purposely. I didn't want her clueing in the sheriff until the next question.

"He was alone," Cochran said after a long pause.

"No dog?"

"A dog?" The sheriff was frustrated.

"You don't remember a dog in the front seat?" We had labeled each of these questions as optional, as we had several others. Only if she saw an opening was she to explore these areas. She was as good at this as many professionals. I looked in on her and saw the concentration she commanded.

"Ah . . . could be, ma'am. We stop a lot of people down here. Don't exactly remember."

"Sheriff," she said, ad-libbing, "it was only two nights ago."

"Yeah, I know. There coulda been a dog in the front seat. Couldn't say for sure, though."

"One last thing, Sheriff . . ."

"Go on."

"Did he pay you that night?"

"Sure did."

"And how did he pay? Check or cash?"

"Cash," Cochran answered quickly.

"So you must have a copy of a cash receipt?" she asked.

"Sure do."

"Could you mail me a copy of that, please, Sheriff Cochran? It would be a tremendous help to me."

"Sure, we can do that."

She gave him her address. I crossed quickly through the television room to her side and scribbled a note. For a moment we were actually touching   she at the phone, I bending to write on the pad. I was very aware of the contact. And I thought she was too. Reading my note she asked, "Oh, Sheriff?"

"Yes, ma'am." He was annoyed.

"How often do you pull the swing shift?"

This time Cochran waited much too long before answering, "Whenever I have to, ma'am. More often than I'd like."

She thanked him and hung up. Having returned to the bedroom, I followed suit. She called toward me, "Now do you believe me? A," she said, making a mental list, "Paul's got night blindness. He can drive but he tires easily. There's no way he would have been driving alone at two o'clock in the morning. B, he never—I mean *never*—let Harper into the front seat. And C . . . I forget what C is."

"C is for Sheriff Cochran," I told her. "He's not a very good cop."

"Then you believe me?" Her enthusiasm was impossible to miss.

"Yes, I do."

Scott Shearson dropped the edited radio interview off. As I changed clothes I listened to it and didn't like it. He had done a fair job with what he had to work with, but all chopped up it didn't make much sense, and it painted the wrong picture of what it is I do. I'm sensitive about that. People often misunderstand my work. Instead of Robin Hood, they picture me a bounty hunter. This can be quite annoying. I decided to reject the edit politely and suggest we try another interview in a week or two.

I picked up Judy a few minutes late. She was dressed informally, but precisely. She was animated and nervous. I was wondering what I was doing there. She lived in the left-hand half of a duplex on Warm Springs. The other half was dark behind closed blinds, and leaves had collected on its gray concrete porch, indicating the vacancy there. Judy bubbled pleasantly in the seat alongside of me, and if I'd had any sense at all, I would have focused on her and made a go of it. Her body language and casual air invited me to share in her. As I studied the situation further she seemed almost desperate for companionship, the way a cat will force its way into your lap, doggedly vying for attention.

There wasn't much to say to Judy. My mind was on Nicole. My heart was with Nicole. I wanted to be with Nicole. But then, like a man who remembers what he was trying to remember, it occurred to me that I was here to forget Nicole, and all at once my attitude changed. I heard her say:

"The athletic club is the real *scene* in town. There are certain hours, say from five till nine, that it seems like the whole town's there. That's where everybody meets. You were asking about Paul earlier today. That's where I met him for the first time. He has a pretty good body for his age. You must work out. You look like you're stronger than an ox."

"Paul's disappeared," I told her.

"Debbie called. She told me. Doesn't surprise me, if you want to know the truth. Paul's a romantic. He tends to see himself as acting out a role in a movie. That's it exactly, he's an actor." She paused. "So why did you lie to me?"

The silence in the truck hurt. "I don't have a good answer for that, Judy. I didn't want to scare you off and I needed some information."

"So you lied."

"I prefer to see it as stretching the truth. But I suppose you could call it lying."

"You don't strike me as the kind of guy who lies a lot."

"Thank you."

"Don't go patting yourself on the back. First impressions can be deceiving." Then she smiled and giggled and pulled over across the seat and sat close to me while I drove.

"What a great old truck. Nineteen sixty?"

"Right," I said, somewhat surprised.

"Straight eight, with enough room under the hood to have a party."

"A catered party," I added and she giggled. "You know cars?" I asked incredulously.

"Think all I'm good for is cooking meals and lying on my back?"

I didn't touch that comment.

"My brother's a gear head," she explained. "I inherited some of it through osmosis. I can clean a carburetor, change the oil, check and bleed the brakes. I'm not much with timing or with valves, and once you crack open the block or gearbox, I'm helpless. I've adjusted a few clutches in my time, though installing them is too tough for words."

"I'm impressed."

"You were meant to be. I'm really not very good at all, but if you're ever knocking around on this old girl, I'd love to help out."

"Deal." I hesitated. "Tell me about Paul and Debbie." I pulled the truck into a space and parked.

●

We were sitting down at dinner in an old tavern that overlooked a creek. From our table we couldn't see the creek, and with the windows closed we couldn't hear it. But it was a good thing the windows were closed: it was snowing lightly. Some Windham Hill piano trickled through the small speakers. The candlelight made Judy's skin glow, and for some reason forced us both to talk quietly and privately. She was growing on me, like certain foods you've tried for the first time.

She said, "They were an item for nearly a year. It was a funny match because Debbie is health-oriented, and even though Paul goes to the club, for him it's more because of the scene—he likes to girl-watch, and there's no better place.

"But since he met *her,*" she continued, "he's kind of fallen out with the old crew. He made friends with a bunch of the younger guys in Ridland. They've been hanging out together up here for a while now. This town is pretty cliquey, and the guys from Ridland are kind of hicks. Paul should have known better."

"What's the drug scene like in this town?" I asked.

"Why do you ask that?"

"Curious."

She said offhandedly, "Same as anywhere, I suppose. Probably more of a thing here than other places, actually. Lots of money, lots of people with free time. A lot of hitting on other people, and part of that is always trying to impress, and that usually means having the best stuff."

"Coke?"

"Sure. Though less so these days. People are back into grass.

There was a big thing with Ecstasy when it was still legal, but since they clamped down on it, it's been hard to find. It used to be really hard to find quality grass in this town, too, but in the last year or so that's really changed. It's everywhere. Really good stuff and at prices better than California. You smoke?" she asked somewhat anxiously.

"Very infrequently," I said, not wanting to disappoint her, or label myself. It was another white lie aimed at preserving the illusion of my youth. It had been at least five years since I'd smoked anything—not out of any great moral or legal conflict, I realized, just something I'd grown out of.

"It doesn't agree with me," she admitted.

"How about Paul?" I asked.

She looked at me curiously and didn't answer because right then a bottle of Médoc was poured and we both sampled it enthusiastically. I felt a shoeless foot rub up my shin. "This is fun," she said. And there was something about the way she said it that implied there was more fun to come. I agreed with a grin, the sensation of her touch reverberating up into my groin. I disallowed the pleasure of that sensation.

Somewhere through our entrees she moved us onto the topic of money, and then, quite unsolicited, said, "I think Paul's sick of it all being her money. He might have taken off for good. He might just be out somewhere trying to hustle a quick buck."

"Nicole's money?"

"Nicky, yeah. You know, he has a big ego—thinks a lot of himself—and she controlled the purse strings. I've heard through Debbie that he's not real happy with that situation."

I thought about the missing money. I mentioned it and asked, "Where would he go?"

"Jackpot. He liked to gamble, though he wasn't no good at it. Vegas, maybe. He spent some time in Vegas. I heard it got bad for him down there. That was before he moved up here—a long time ago—but the rumor around town was that he had done some sort of business deal with the wrong kind of businessmen and had nearly gotten himself killed. That kind of thing can happen down in Vegas. It's a weird town."

I thought of Paul sitting in some windowless casino in a nameless Nevada town trying to make money with money, hoping to return to his wife with her borrowed fifty thousand plus a pile he had made from gambling it, which he would then keep for his own. Or had he just taken off with the money? One thing became more clear to me. Chances were that Paul had left town—even though there were conflicting reports of how, when, and in what condition. Maybe he had taken the dog to buy himself some extra time, leaving Nicole to think he'd be home any minute. Maybe he'd even gone so far as to create the impression he had disappeared on a hunt, or had had a hunting accident. Maybe he had taken her money and run, and had set up a nifty mystery to leave everybody guessing while he secretly bought himself time in which to steal across the Mexican or Canadian border.

"Seems like I've done all the talking," she said well into dessert. "I wanted to hear about you."

"Not much to tell."

"I can read a person's face. You have plenty to tell. You've been a lot of places and you've done a lot of things."

"All that from a face?" I asked.

"There are other parts of a man's body that tell you more," she said without the slightest embarrassment. In fact, she smiled at me, and then signaled the waitress. "Coffee," she told the woman. "Two," she added, holding my gaze. "We'll be up awhile, won't we?"

Back in the truck, she snuggled up against me to fight off the cold that had invaded the town without warning. She threw her arm around me and let her other fall to my thigh, and then she rambled on about how much she liked skiing, and did I ski, and had I ever done any mountaineering? By the time we reached her duplex my pulse was keeping up with the RPMs of the engine. I knew I didn't want this. I knew it wasn't right. But she was working me into a pliable state, like a strong potter with hard clay. She molded me into a desirous condition. It was something that bothered me, for I felt out of control and under the spell of another—not a sensation I'm comfortable with. I like to have the reins. I like to be in control. When she asked me if I'd like to take a hot tub in the middle of a snowstorm, I turned her down. She didn't seem too surprised or disappointed. I offered to see her to the door, but she grabbed my arm, pecked me on the check and said, "I'm fine," and hurried from the truck.

I got out anyway. Set in the light skim of snow were twin tire tracks. I stared down at them. I felt the hair on the nape of my neck stand on end. It was the gas. I could smell it from where I stood.

"Wait!" I hollered. But I was too late.

I saw her standing there in the doorway, slender, shapely, arm extended to trip the light switch. She turned quickly toward me and raised her other arm to wave good-bye. It is one of those images that is engraved deep inside the files in my brain. It is etched on some tiny bit of protein and water, trapped in a vault of cells that serve to remind us.

She threw the switch, and if it were possible to slow it all down to milliseconds, I suppose the lights went on. But the tremendous explosion, the blinding, erupting ball of orange that mushroomed up into the black sky, lifting the roof and most of the second story with it, came so quickly I never saw the lights go on. I saw her backlit by that fireball, saw her lifted off her feet and thrown out toward me like a weightless puppet. The glass of the windows exploded behind the deafening boom. I picked up a piece in my right shoulder. As flames stole through what remained of the duplex, and the world became that frightening shade of amber, I crawled over to her. She was unconscious, miraculously still in one piece, her entire backside blackened and stinking of burned cloth and flesh. Frantically I began shoveling the cold snow onto her skin. It melted as quickly as I could get it onto her, but I would not stop. I knew the cold was the one thing I was capable of administering to her. I scooped up snow and piled it thickly onto the back of her legs and buttocks. In the distance I heard the sirens grind to an eerie cry and grow ever louder. I covered her badly burned back, refilling several spots where the snow melted and slid off. I had cleared two big patches of snow from the lawn. The spreading fire began to grow too hot. I didn't want to move her without professional help; there was no telling what had broken in her flight through the air and subsequent crash onto the frozen earth. Finally I saw the pulsing lights of the fire trucks and emergency vehicles. A policeman saw me shielding her from the heat. He yelled to the others.

My wounded arm had spilled blood down my right side. Judy lay beneath me covered with snow.

A combination of images flooded my mind. I was heading into shock and didn't know it. Judy, backlit, lifted by the explosion. A pair of wide tire marks cut in the snow as we had pulled up. I could see them clearly now—the fat rubber of a four-wheel-drive vehicle or three-quarter-ton pickup. The tracks loomed before my eyes as Judy was put on a litter and whisked away. A fireman wrapped a wool blanket around me. Someone had been here while we had been having our romantic dinner.

Someone had done this to Judy. And to me.

Me, I thought. This had nothing to do with Judy. Somebody wanted me dead, and Judy had just been handy.

I arrived at Debbie Benton's condominium a little past eight-thirty in the morning. She wore a soft white terry-cloth robe with broad pastel stripes running vertically, a wide pocket on either side. Her hair had been brushed hastily, but even so, she looked remarkably pretty. She smoked a cigarette, and when I reached the small kitchen, I saw that she was drinking a screwdriver. She offered me orange juice and I accepted. When she hoisted the bottle and looked at me curiously, I declined with the wave of a hand. I could tell immediately that this was not a regular habit for Debbie, and one she was suddenly ashamed of. She put the bottle away. When she knelt down to access the cabinet, the robe hugged her tiny waist and hips, and in spite of the preceding evening—perhaps because of it—I marveled at the ability of the female to stimulate me. I nearly told her so, but decided it had better wait.

"I came as soon as I hung up," I said, trying to get things going. The doctor had suggested a sling for my arm. I had refused. Now I was having second thoughts. A day or two in a sling might have been a good idea.

She turned around and leaned what little there was of her against the strong oak cabinetry. As I looked into her eyes, there was no mistaking that she had been crying recently. She wore the dreary, slightly bloodshot, sagging face of grief. I had missed it the first time. "How is she?"

I shrugged. It reminded me of Nicole. "They flew her out to Salt Lake City. There's a burn center there. They claim she's not too bad, all things considered. She dislocated her hip and shoulder. She sustained the burns on her back. Her face is fine—"

"Thank God."

I had wanted to say more. I was eager to hear myself speak, to reinforce the fact that I was still alive. I could have talked for a long time if she had let me.

"They were after you, weren't they?" she asked with a frightened expression on her face.

"Who?" I had entertained thoughts about the same subject for most of a sleepless night.

She dragged a hand across her face and drank more of the screwdriver. I had the impression she might cry again. Somehow with this one I was in no mood to be the shoulder she did it on.

"I should have been up front with you yesterday. Judy would still be fine."

I was tempted to try and draw more out of her, but I sensed it was coming. I decided to keep her busy. Busy hands . . . and all that. "Coffee?" I asked. "Would it be too much trouble?"

"Sorry." She waved a hand in the air. "No trouble at all."

"Espresso or drip?" she inquired.

"Drip's fine."

As she fixed me a cup using a separate super-hot water tap, she spoke to a window that looked down the valley. "I probably should have called the police, but I don't trust them and I wouldn't have known what to say. They can't act on hunches, can they? And besides, they don't seem to care about Paul the way you do." She turned abruptly. "Why do you care, incidentally?" she asked as if it had just occurred to her.

"Nicole," I answered honestly.

"Oh, *her*," she said in an acidic voice.

Her tone offended me. "What is it that is so god-awful about Nicole Russell? Judy talked about her with that same tone. What the hell is it about her?"

She rolled her tongue slowly in her mouth and then arched

her eyebrows up in self-realization. "Probably jealousy." She half-frowned, half-smiled. "We're a small town. A transient town in a lot of ways. A woman like Nicole Baxter comes along—all the looks, lots of dough, plenty of virtue, and good at *everything,* and it throws too much competition in your way. Not only that, but Paul is everybody's friend. He's been around a long time. Likes to party. Nicole snatched him up and moved out of town. We're a family here. You kind of grow on one another. Like anywhere, I assume. There's an old crowd of us that's been around since the mid-seventies. Paul was very much a part of that crowd. He's older than most of us, but with him you don't notice it." She hesitated. "With me it's more than that." She mopped the bottom of the coffee cup off and handed it to me. "Milk, honey?"

I declined the extras but accepted the cup like a wino reaching out for his bottle. I was dead tired. *But not dead,* I reminded myself. "I'm listening," I said, deciding to prod.

"She stole him away from me. Sort of. Judy and I are close. I suppose that explains her disdain. We've never really talked about Nicole. Some things you don't talk about. Some things you just know."

I nodded. The coffee was strong but good.

"We met at the athletic club," she said. I knew she wasn't talking about Nicole. Her mood had changed to one of reflection. I thought if I could get close enough I might be able to see images on the surface of her eyes. "Not exactly true. We'd known each other *years.* We became interested in each other at the club. Funny place, the club. We all dress in as little as possible and show off to each other. The guys go for bulk and brawn. The gals go for shape and slenderness. But there are more reasons than that that we all go. We go to show what we've got, and all the routines show that and more. We spread our legs and open our chests, and perspire and groan and pant and collapse. It's probably a holdover from courtship rituals. The men strut their stuff. The women flap their wings and tighten up every inch of their bodies. Hell," she said, somewhat disgusted with herself, "we shave ourselves so we can wear stuff that shows as much as possible. How crazy is that?" She had conjured up a fairly vivid image. I half expected her to swing open her robe and show me.

She shook her head. "How'd I get off on that?" She looked at her nearly empty glass and that seemed to provide her with an explanation—or maybe that glance was intended to give me the explanation. I was tired and wasn't thinking well. Judy had aroused two of the more primitive instincts in me, procreation and fear of death. I was still caught somewhere between their mutual stimulation, much of which seemed centered in my groin.

She continued, "We'd socialized together for years, but the club did it. My long-term crush on Paul came to a head. I wonder if the fact that he had just married her entered into my interest in him. I think maybe I wanted to prove something to myself. He'd shown interest a few other times, and I'd put up the friendly wall of refusal."

Judy had implied that their relationship had begun prior to the marriage, but I didn't question the chronology. Friends covered for friends all the time. And at this point, I didn't see how it mattered.

She said, "Paul comes in and out of money, like a lot of us up here. You have good seasons and bad. Good years and bad. He's kind of a jack-of-all-trades and has his fingers in a million different pies. Of course I assume it's her money that he spends on me. And maybe that's why I'm so agreeable to have him do it." She finished the cocktail and proceeded to mix herself another, her initial self-consciousness melting away behind the warmth of the vodka. I noted that she poured this one strong. If the first had been that strong, I was about to have one looped cookie on my hands. Her body weight couldn't take that many ounces of booze, and I could tell by her healthy look and the way she handled a bottle that this wasn't a regular practice. "God only knows why I'm involved with him." She sipped the drink, raised her eyebrows, and sought out a spoon with which to stir it. It seemed to help. She took a few good pulls on the concoction and then placed the glass down.

She said, "It got hot and heavy fairly quickly. We had to start making excuses for him. Figuring ways to see each other. He always has the club as an excuse. We get to see each other evenings for a little bit that way. Trouble is, we both like the club, and neither of us is willing to do away with it altogether. So we had to think up new ways to be sly.

"Paul came up with a good one. He's like that: clever and devious, you know what I mean? He decided he could do away with hunting. It meant he could leave early, early morning and join me up here and talk past lunch."

I didn't make a joke about *joining* her, though in other company, I might have. I wasn't in a joking mood. In fact, my mood was lousy. It grew worse as she lit another cigarette. "Is that what happened Tuesday?" I asked. "He came up here to see you?"

"No, not Tuesday."

"The reason I ask is that he left all dressed up for hunting. Even took the dog."

"Harper," she said, looking down at the bowl. "That was his touch. He brought Harper along with him most times. When you noticed the bowl yesterday, it really put me uptight. I could see in your eyes that you knew what was going on. You knew, didn't you?" I sensed in her a regret at having told me all of this, and felt I might lose her if I didn't justify it for her.

"I knew," I lied. Suspicions were all I had had.

"I knew it." She inhaled on the cigarette and then drank from the glass. When she spoke, blue vapor escaped her mouth. "Tuesday he had some sort of business meeting lined up. I'm sure of it because we talked about it."

"Maybe it got canceled, he decided to pay you a visit."

"I wasn't here Tuesday," she said a little too quickly. "A watercolor show went up at another gallery in town and they asked me to help hang it. I was out of the house at seven."

Her comment reminded me to check with Nicole on when Paul had left. "What kind of business?" I asked.

"I don't know." She looked away in the same manner a child avoids a parent's eyes. She knew, she just wasn't telling. She hid behind the cigarette and broke the silence with a heavy exhaling.

"I think you do," I told her.

"Paul had all sorts of deals going. No telling what he was up to."

"Who was he supposed to see?"

"How would I know that?"

I decided to play hardball. She was getting too loose for me. She was making me mad with her avoidance. "Judy is lying on her stomach in some Salt Lake hospital at this moment wondering if she'll ever wear a pair of shorts again, or even a short-sleeved shirt. Did you ever leave a piece of chicken in the pan too long? That's what she looked like when I saw her last. It was ugly, real ugly. Someone was trying to kill me, and I've only talked to a few people about Paul Russell, so I have to put you pretty high on my list of someones. Now maybe, just maybe, Paul *did* have a meeting on Tuesday. And maybe that has something to do with his disappearance. But it won't do me a bit of good if I don't have a name."

She was shaking her head the way a drunk woman shakes her head. She was pissing me off. I walked over to her, took the cigarette out of her hand and doused it, by pouring the remainder of her drink over it, into the sink. I set the wet, disgusting butt and the empty glass in the sink and took Debbie Benton by the shoulders. "I'm scared, Debbie. How do we know your place won't be the next to blow up?"

"Get out of here."

That was exactly what I wanted to do. I wanted some fresh air. Some new company. I nodded and released her. "Fine," I said. "You've been a terrific help," I said as sarcastically as I could manage. "I'll say hi to Judy for you."

"Get out!" she repeated, now slurring her words so it sounded more like "gout."

I raised my hand. "I'm gone."

Our Indian summer was being pushed out of town by a determined Old Man Winter. That morning the air reeked of it. I pulled the collar of my light jacket up against a strong northerly wind and looked out in the direction I imagined Judy's duplex to be. I pictured her down in Salt Lake and my stomach turned. I am lucky enough not to suffer from many fears. Fire is one I do not escape, however. When I'm away from my house, I think of it burning down with no one there to save it. When I go to sleep at night I review every appliance, heater, and stove in my mind, assuring myself I've left nothing on, nothing that could set fire to the cabin and burn me to death in my sleep after making me unconscious with its fumes. I check my smoke detectors regularly and replace the batteries even before the machines tell me too. I'm that paranoid. Where Judy was now seemed to me a living hell. Like a recurring nightmare the image of her blackened back was chasing me around like the stinging wind I had turned my collar against.

Debbie caught me by surprise as I was warming up my truck. She stood in the robe, hands tucked under opposing armpits, forearms pressing her breasts flat. "I'm sorry," she said.

I looked at her with what had to be an annoyed expression. "Not good enough," I affirmed.

"He was going hunting on Tuesday. It had something to do with business. He made a couple calls from my place on Sunday."

"Who?" I asked. "Who with, Debbie?"

"A guy named Greg, I think. I'm pretty sure it was a guy named Greg."

"Sweetland?"

"Don't know." She was shivering. "Greg somebody, I'm pretty sure. They were going hunting out Bell Mountain, out by Crystal Creek."

"How much of Paul's business involved drugs, Debbie?"

She glared at me, turned, and ran for the stairs in her slippers.

"I'm not in the book," I yelled. "It's four-four-three-four, if you need me.

She turned from the steps and stared at me.

I put it in reverse and backed up. The gearbox whined.

9

The valley is about twenty-five miles long. Snow Lake sits in the narrow north end, where the sharp, angular mountains form a huge bowl, with the ski area on the western side. A pass through the mountains leads north. In the winter the snow depth averages seven feet, and this pass is often closed. Seventeen miles south of Snow Lake lies Butte Peak, and ten miles farther, Ridland. The railroad ran a spur into this valley a hundred years ago and left these small mining towns a way to move their ore. The mines have long since closed, but the towns remain. Butte Peak had become a service community to Snow Lake, its economy inexorably linked to the seasonal swings of tourist activity at Snow Lake. Ridland is less fortunate, simply too long a drive for the waitresses, the bartenders, the mountain-lift operators, the housecleaners, and the myriads of others to make on a daily basis. Passing through Butte Peak, I noticed the banner stretched across the wide road announcing INDIAN SUMMER DAYS, a chili cookoff and town softball championship scheduled for the upcoming weekend. Main street was lined with pickup trucks, housewives and children in tow. Except for the bank and a co-op department store, the architecture remains much as it did when the valley was first settled—stone and brick buildings with Western facades bearing hand-carved and -painted placards, proclaiming BARBER, PHIL HUFF INSURANCE, RADIO SHACK, and BROYLE'S DRUGS. The valley's only true movie theater is located in Butte Peak. Others have been built in Snow Lake, but not real theaters. Not like the Liberty. It boasts a large marquee with bold black letters announcing the evening's two films. It has a real ticket window, and inside, a balcony and a forty-foot ceiling.

When I'm eager for a night out, I often take in a dinner at Gurney's Steak House and catch a flick at the Liberty. Butte Peak is a small community. I spend more time there than in Ridland, despite my proximity to the farming town. I recognize faces now, and people wave when they spot my truck. It's one of the somethings I appreciate about the pace of life out west: There's still time to wave. Still time for a chat on the sidewalk outside the market. Butte Peak is in no great hurry.

I reviewed my talk with Debbie Benton as I continued south to Ridland. She had filled in a few of the missing pieces. It didn't tell me about Paul Russell's whereabouts, but it showed me some reasons that might be behind his disappearance. I stopped at Nicole's and sat inside the truck, motor running, wondering if I really had to do this now—or did I *want* to tell her about her husband's infidelity? There are at least two people inside of me, and much of my life is spent with these two people in conflict, each arguing one side of an issue. I remember Jiminy Cricket sitting on a shoulder in a Disney cartoon whispering into a young boy's ear. I think a devil was on the other side, countering everything Jiminy suggested. This is how I move through life, comments coming from either shoulder, either ear, and I feared today the voice that had won out was the voice of the devil. I no longer trusted my motivations.

She was on the phone. I knocked and she waved me inside into the kitchen. She wore tight blue jeans, cowboy boots, and a faded plaid cotton lumber shirt with breast pockets. Her sleeves were rolled up and the kitchen smelled of cinnamon rolls and fresh-brewed coffee. She hung up and explained, "A neighbor of mine isn't feeling well. I offered to bake some rolls for her kids." She pulled the tray of sticky creations out of the oven and quickly went about icing them. When she was done she left three rolls out on the chopping block and said, "Coffee's over there.

See if these are any good, and I'll be right back." She hurried out the door, not even bothering for a coat. I watched her from behind as she ran up the drive and disappeared around the berm.

I had consumed half of my second sticky bun when she returned only minutes later. "All done," she said, closing the door behind. I felt an easiness with her I had longed to experience for many, many years. This woman felt like home to me, and for all the obvious reasons that both excited and frightened me at the same time. She poured herself a cup of coffee, freshened mine, and collapsed into a creaking antique chair with a heavy sigh. "How are they?" she asked, picking a piece from the one that remained.

"Mm," I approved, chewing.

"Good," she said radiantly. And then she stared at me. She planted her elbow on the table and stared, happy brown eyes drinking me up.

My heart started to dance around. The irregular fast rhythms were something I associated more with the adrenaline of fistfights than a woman staring at me. I couldn't look over at her. I felt heat creep up my neck and I knew I was blushing, but she didn't back off. She continued to grin and stare. When I finally managed the nerve to confront her, she didn't look away as I had expected. She grinned even wider.

"So," she said, still staring.

In my nervousness I continued to stuff my face. "So," I muffled out.

"It's good to see you, Klick."

"You too." I nodded and slurped some brew.

"What have you found out?"

"What makes you say that?"

"I'm a quick judge of character, Klick. Something's different in you. Yesterday if I had stared at you like this, you would have stared back. Why the change?"

"You haven't listened to the radio this morning, I take it."

She shook her head. I filled her in on my evening with Judy. I made it sound more life-threatening for me than it really was. I was already too involved emotionally in this case. I try to detach myself from my work, but inevitably I fail. With Nicole Russell I was beyond failure: I was making things up in order to make myself look better, to keep my iron in the fire. What fire? I asked myself, but it didn't change the way I stretched the truth. The fire was inside the woman in those blue jeans and brushed cotton shirt, and I was eager to feel even more of its warmth.

I explained my assumption that the explosion had been rigged with me in mind. Nicole reached over and grabbed hold of my wrist. I'm big-boned, and her tiny, delicate hand only reached partway around. "Are you sure?" she said with a good deal of concern in her voice.

"Pretty sure," I said, hoping she'd never let go. She released her grip immediately and steepled her hands beneath her chin in concentration. "Then we'd better speak with the police. We'd better stop whatever it is we're doing."

"I've talked to the police. They were less than enthusiastic about my explanation. They think a breeze probably blew out the pilot light in the central heater. That's their explanation. Heaters are being fired up for the first time all year—that's their back-up explanation."

"And you don't think so?"

"Did the same breeze create the tire tracks I saw? No, I don't think so. I don't buy it. It was intentional. We're lucky Judy's still alive. Which reminds me . . ." I made a couple of calls and found out where they had transferred her. When I got off the phone with Salt Lake, I told Nicole, "Better than I thought. Second degree mostly. They said that with some good plastic surgery and a lot of time, she may not be badly scarred. Can't be certain this early, I guess."

"I think we should forget all about this. He's left me. I should have recognized that in the first place."

"There's more," I told her, regret evident in my voice.

"What do you mean?"

I told her about my talk with Debbie, though I didn't mention any names. I told her about the affair, about how they worked it out between the athletic club and the hunting. She stared at the table and nodded continually. About to cry. I saw the first lonely tear tumble down her cheek, and her lips pucker in anger. She just sat there nodding. I tried to cushion the news as best I could. Or did I? I couldn't be sure how it sounded to her. On hindsight, an hour or so later, it seemed to me I had tried pretty hard to make him look bad. Real bad. I'm not usually like that—and this revelation bothered me greatly. I caught her up on the theory that he might have gone hunting on Tuesday with a guy named Greg.

"So who cares?" she asked. She didn't look at me. She stood and walked very slowly into the back bedroom. I sat at the table for several minutes hating myself. I listened to the shower run for a long time. Then the blow dryer. There were other ways to break such news. I had made it sound somewhat cheap—which perhaps it was—but I had broken a heart and there was no excuse for that.

"Klick," she called softly.

My heart began to pound again. Somehow I knew without knowing.

"Would you come here a minute, please," she added.

I rose and walked through the small television room to the bedroom door. It was cracked slightly. The shades were drawn tightly inside and the room was quite dark. "Come in," she invited.

I stepped into the room. She was standing by the big bed, dressed in a gossamer nightgown that only shaded her flawless body from view. A very low amount of rosy light illuminated her, like the blood-red shadows cast by sunsets. She reached out her hands and I accepted them inside of mine.

"Will you make love to me, Chris?"

I pulled her into me and wrapped my arms tightly around her. She began to sob. Her fingers clawed at my back. Our hearts beat together in different times. It's like jazz, I thought. Improvised and stimulating. "No," I whispered into her perfumed hair, which was only slightly damp. She cried harder.

"May be your last chance," she tried to threaten.

"Then I miss one of the great experiences of a lifetime."

She tried to talk as she sobbed. "Don't be so sure. Don't be so sure. He obviously didn't think so." And then she unloaded. I had to hold her up she cried so hard. We stood in the artificial twilight for who knows how long, she making my shirt wet, me growing ever more tempted to take her up on the offer. I felt like crying too. It's not something I'm accustomed to, not something I'm good at. In my adult years I've cried only a handful of times.

I didn't pity her, I knew that. I think I was reminded of a similar incident in my own life, one I had never fully come to grips with. I think I was a part of Nicole Russell—or Baxter—at that moment. I think somehow I had moved out of my own body and into hers. I was experiencing what she was experiencing on the exact same level and it nearly trashed me. She began to laugh. Then we were both guffawing in unison and she was beating her head playfully against my chest.

"Oh, boy. I really made a fool of myself this time, didn't I?"

I lowered my head and kissed her. It was a long, tender, loving kiss. She stood on tiptoe and ran her fingers through my hair, sending shivers down my spine. I don't think any kiss anywhere has ever been quite so perfect. When it was over she hugged me again and asked, "Where did you come from, Klick?"

"Over there," I replied.

She nodded, still hugging me, neither of us knowing what I meant. "Who cares about him," she wondered softly.

"Not me," I told her, and she chuckled, wiping away her tears.

"Thanks, Klick."

I held her away from me and looked at her, rocking my head up and down in acknowledgment. It was a many-layered thanks. I knew that. Now I was tempted again to make love with her. Now it was all right. Now she had seen what she needed to see. Now it made total sense. But now it was impossible.

"We have to find him, you and I. We have to find him," she said.

I looked at her curiously. The "you and I" I liked very much.

"I want that money back," she said. "I want every last penny."

I nodded.

"Half of every last penny," she corrected herself. "Half goes to you, no matter what you say. I don't *need* the money. It's the principle of the thing."

I shook my head. I didn't want her money and that bothered me.

It wasn't because of her generous offer that I stuck my hand out toward her in agreement. It was because of those last few minutes spent together. Something had changed. Or at least I convinced myself it had.

She took my hand. It was more than a handshake. Yes, indeed.

We both knew it. And we both smiled.

I caught up to Sheriff Hudson in the Silver Dollar Café. He was sitting with a bunch of leathery good old boys in their dozer caps, three of them smoking, all drinking coffee. When I pushed through the door, a bang of laughter echoed from their table. The odd assortment of waitresses wore blue-and-white-checked dresses with white waist aprons and hair nets. They each wore one of those annoying have-a-nice-day faces pinned to their aprons.

They made their rounds and then attached their orders to a wire carousel and rang a bell for the cook.

The people of Ridland are good-natured and happy despite the apparent depressed economy. Everyone knows everyone's business, and it has been that way for generations. Old Mac McGreggor was sitting at the counter holding court with a couple of the dirty-faced welders from the metal shop across the street. Mac was eighty-three years old and didn't look a day over sixty. He had more stories than most people had hair, and every single one of them was true—something that couldn't be said for all the stories that circulated around Ridland.

One of the waitresses couldn't have been a day over thirteen. She looked uncomfortable in the uniform with her unshaved, pale legs, and she hadn't learned how to carry a tray yet. She took a lot of grief from old Mac, who was never afraid to tell you a better way to do whatever it was you were doing. This morning he was an expert on carrying trays. He kept demonstrating to her, holding an imaginary tray way over his head and shouting across the restaurant at her. The guys from the metal shop were amused, as were the men with Sheriff Hudson.

I walked straight over to the table and said, "Sheriff, wonder if we could have a few words." He looked up at me slowly, as if I'd disturbed a poker hand. "You again, Klick?" He cocked his head, indicating a table in the far corner, and kept me waiting a full seven minutes. I counted each one as if it were an hour.

On the walls behind me were reproductions of black-and-white photographs depicting the town of Ridland in the late 1800s, when the streets were mud and manure and the few buildings that lined main street looked like props in a stage play. Hudson's eyes were red with fatigue. He held his coffee cup awkwardly, the irregular stub of his fourth finger resting against the handle's white porcelain hoop. He said softly, "Heard you were involved in that mess last night. Tough bit of luck for the girl." His cowboy twang, his steely eyes and sun-toughened skin bothered me. He was a cold man, way down inside cold like the dark, damp bottom of a mining shaft. He held his hands around the cup to warm them. His teeth had undergone a lot of gold repair. It looked like a jewelry store in there.

"What can you tell me about Greg Sweetland?" I asked.

"His family's deciding what to do about a service. What is there to tell?"

"I think there's a chance Paul Russell planned to go hunting with Sweetland last Tuesday."

Hudson's brow furrowed. "Is that so? What put an idea like that in your mind?"

"Just the way it figures," I said, attempting language he could understand.

"Something you heard? Listen, Klick, lotsa rumors in a town this size. Wouldn't go by any rumors."

"It happens to make sense, that's all."

He didn't like my tone. "You thinking maybe Russell killed

Sweetland?" he asked, twisting my words. "I suppose that might account for his being seen in Hill City at two in the morning."

"Maybe someone else shot Sweetland and Russell saw it. Maybe Russell shot him by accident and panicked. Maybe they had a fight and Russell shot him. Who knows?"

Hudson sipped his coffee and stared blankly at the young waitress making her rounds. He looked quickly at me and then back into space. There was no way to tell what he was thinking— if anything. He'd been a cop too long. He was well practiced.

"What was Sweetland like?"

"Like? He's an all-right kid—*was,* I guess I should say. Listen, Klick, thing of it is, this here is a real small town. Always has been. Back sixty, seventy years ago, men didn't have all that big a selection of women to chose a wife from, what with disease and hardship. Some o' the folks around here is a little too related to one another, if you know what I'm saying. And, well, the Sweetlands, they've had their share of troubles. Been a lot of intermarrying over the years.

"Fact of the matter is," he continued, "the Sweetlands didn't have all that much schooling, what with the way their daddy worked 'em. But schooling ain't everything. They're all-right folk just the same. Not a better hand in the valley with a young horse than Greg Sweetland. Could break any goddamned bronc he set his mind to, and make him gentle as can be. Not a better hand anywhere.

"Thing is, old Grandpop Sweetland made the shine for a number of years at their ranch out there. Think the most of the family has inherited some of them problems that go along with that. Greg was a big man. Get a couple of drinks in him and he'd go plum crazy. No telling what he'd do. And with women! Jesus! Never seen a man get in so much trouble over women in my whole life. Swear to God. There's one stud been mounting mares since he first got stiff. Tell ya that. Got himself a real reputation for it among the ladies, if ya know what I mean. Ain't been a lonely lady in this town for years on account of him.

"If he weren't a big sucker, he'd a had the shit kicked out of him long time ago. Might a been a good thing, too. Last I heard, he was jumping Gerry Clark. That's one hell of a woman, I'll tell you that. Good God Almighty, that's lean beef. Who can blame the boy?

"If I had to make a guess, I'd put my money that it was Bill Clark that blew the kid away. That Billy's got a temper worse than Greg's. Might be like you say. Might be Billy Clark heard Greg was going hunting and decided to take advantage of the situation. They been enemies for years. Was Billy stole Gerry from Greg in the first place. Don't think Greg ever forgive that one. Could be that's got something to do with it."

I asked directions to the Sweetland place. The sheriff flashed me an odd expression and asked, "What the fuck do you want to go out there for? No way," he said. "A stranger, a guy like you, as big as you are. No, sir. You been listening? I'm trying to tell you, these Sweetland boys is short upstairs. Dusty in the attic. You leave them be, Klick. You hear me? You leave them be."

I told him I planned on paying them a visit, asking a few questions, with or without his blessing. It was the wrong thing to say.

"Listen. What I'm trying to tell you, the Sweetlands aren't known for their hospitality. They keep to themselves, and expect others to do the same."

"Who's the coroner in town, Sheriff?" I asked, holding my hand over my cup as a grandma came by with refills. Hudson accepted a "warmer." I wondered how any stomach could endure six cups of that stuff. Not to mention taste buds. Not to mention nerves.

"*County* coroner, not town. He's up to Butte Peak. Bates is his name. It's an elected position, you know? What is this, a joke?" He sounded angry.

I shook my head no.

"He's my brother-in-law," he explained.

I tried to cover my surprise. "Does he do the autopsies?"

"Hell no," he said. He seemed relieved. "A doctor does the autopsy. All Bates does is the paperwork. That's all."

"And there's no question it's Sweetland? Couldn't be any mistake?"

"Goddamn, you got an imagination on you, Klick. Mistake? Hell no. It's Greg Sweetland, all right. His own family identified the body, for Christ's sake. You would think they ought to know, right?"

I nodded.

"Unless maybe you knew him better than we did."

"And you trust the doctor?"

"Amos Cole? What's wrong with you, Klick? You see, that's what's wrong with you city types. You come bustin' into a place like Ridland and start distrusting everyone. Before you know it, 'cause of you, and people like you, no one's trustin' no one. The whole spirit of the place is shot to hell. Don't take many of you to wreck a town like this. Far as I'm concerned, we don't need you here, Klick. Far as I'm concerned, you can go back where you come from and take your suspicions with you." He stood up, bumping the table. "You got a lot to learn about the way people live together out in these parts, mister"—he bumped the table again, spilling some of the coffee—"a hell of a lot to learn." He looked down at me. Glowering and intimidating. "I'd leave this alone, if I were you, bucko. This ain't got nothing to do with you. None of your goddamned business." He was talking loud and several heads had turned. "Some of us got jobs to do, and we going to do them. You want to play Dick Tracy, go back to your friggin' city and do it there. I, for one, don't need your help." He snatched his hat and stomped out of the café, making as big a scene as he could.

Everyone was staring at me. No one looked particularly friendly. I got the feeling the sheriff had plenty of support in this town.

I raised my hand for the check. It took me another ten minutes to get it.

11

Mac McGreggor told me how to find the Sweetland place. It was
a good seventeen miles out of town toward Crystal Creek, up a
narrow valley—a drainage—that looked out over the "triangle":
a half dozen cultivated sections bordered by three state highways, which formed an enormous triangle of flat farmland. The
Sweetland ranch was in the foothills. I guessed that if you went
directly up and over the range to the west, you'd tumble down
the other side into Ridland.

The pickup began to bounce badly on the washboarded dirt
road that ran the last five miles out to the ranch. I slowed down.
I could see some of the Sweetland pasture up ahead, improved
land cut in a large wedge into the rough, sage-covered Bureau of
Land Management—BLM—range. I thought of the tireless
hours required a hundred years ago to till such land with a team
of horses and a strong back. So far we had come, it seemed. And
yet now, burdened with land payments, and machinery costing
hundreds of thousands of dollars, the small farmer was a vanish-
ing breed. Perhaps they should scale down, return to horse and
oxen, I thought, wondering if that would make any difference. I
decided it wouldn't. The economics of farming, complete with

subsidies, interest rates, and government loans was far too complex an issue to solve with a single simple-minded idea.

As I followed a creek around a gradual turn in the hill, it struck me that all of Sweetland's fields were empty. Not only were no cattle or sheep or horses visible, but the land itself had gone fallow. The few irrigation hand- and wheel-lines I could spot were partly swallowed by vegetation, indicating a complete lack of use. A few of the fences had gaping holes in them from collapsed posts, victims of dry rot, and none of the fence was in good shape. I wondered what kept the Sweetlands going, living twenty miles from nowhere, up an isolated canyon in central Idaho.

As I pulled into the ranch, crossing under what remained of a sign that had once named the property but now hung broken in half from a rusted chain, I noticed at least six small children playing what looked like a game of soccer or kickball out behind the worn house. I passed a dozen paddocks, each with a pair of fine-looking horses in them.

A row of farm implements looked something like museum pieces along the near side of one of the three huge barns. Two of the barns were relatively new, the third a relic from past generations of Sweetlands. A narrow-eyed woman with big hips and broad shoulders crossed toward a toolshed, eyeing me briefly, but hurrying too quickly to wave. She didn't want to wave, I realized as she slammed the door behind her. I parked the truck and climbed out, standing by the vehicle's door, like a child stands by his parent's legs for security. I looked over for the kids, but they were gone, summoned perhaps by the only adult Sweetland I had seen. I heard a screen door bang and turned to see a man of about thirty approaching. He was as big as me, but had a heavy protruding brow of bone, narrow pinpricks for eyes, and a jutting jaw. He had at least forty pounds on me, and carried it effortlessly.

"What you want?" he asked in a husky voice.

"Wanted to talk to somebody about Greg." His belt buckle winked at me. It was silver—"Larry" engraved in gold rope lettering across its center. Unscratched. New. Expensive. The kind of extravagance only Lyel and a few people in Snow Lake could afford. What was this guy doing with it?

"Get out of here."

"Larry!" came a strained high voice from the house. "You leave the man alone."

Larry glanced over at the gray-haired withered woman and said, "Yes, Mama," in a childlike voice that made me go cold. He trundled off with his head low to the ground and found his way to the same shed into which the younger woman had previously disappeared. The toolshed had to be living quarters. Instinct told me to climb back in my truck and make tracks. Hudson had been right.

I noticed his snakeskin boots from behind as he opened the door. The leather soles were that pale color of yellow that can only be found on a new pair of shoes or boots. These were fancy boots, not the kind of thing to wear around the barnyard.

"I'm Emma," the high but strong voice said from behind me. "Don't mind him, child. He's not much on strangers. What can I do you for?"

I generally don't take well to being called child, son, or boy, but this woman was the exception. I had the impression she had been playing mother since Moses rafted from the bulrushes. "Child" was just fine with me.

"Don't mind Larry, child. Larry give the sunrise a bad time if he didn't have nothin' else to do. Don't pay no 'tention to him at all. I think I seen you before. Maybe in the *Express,* ain't I?"

"Yes, ma'am."

"You're a big man. Just like my boys," she said proudly. She fished some glasses from her sagging chest and, putting them on, tried to look at me. She took them back off. "Every time I put them bifocals on, I can't see nothing but fuzz. You're a damn good-looking man," she cracked out in her high voice. "Good-looking men plenty welcome around here. Don't get some of these children married off, we best be turning another shed into a bunkhouse." She grinned toothlessly. "Run outta sheds one of these days. Come in, child."

She turned and led the way. "Girls," she hollered as she opened the door to the farmhouse, "got a good-looking one here, get yourselves presentable."

I felt myself blush. I heard what sounded like a stampede above us on the second floor. She led me into a dirty and cluttered kitchen and motioned for me to sit down. The ceiling was low. I didn't fit in the chair. She put some water in a kettle and put the kettle on to boil. Then she took a chair herself and said, "You come about my Greg, I figure."

"Yes, ma'am."

"What is it you want to know?"

"Well, I . . ."

"Greggie was a good boy, bless his sweet heart. My daughter Julie's boy—she died in a range fire in sixty-five. I raised him like my own. Same as all the rest here. Long as I'm alive, I'm in charge."

"Yes, ma'am."

"Lost my man to the war," she told me with sorrow in her voice. I had no way to judge her age, and so had no idea which war she meant. Probably World War 1, by the look of her. He had probably died in a trench, lungs burning up with mustard gas. "Had to run this place all by myself," she added.

"I understand Greg was good with horses," I tried.

"Good? Whoever told you that's a damn liar. Greggie was the best for miles and miles. None better than my Greggie. He had an eye for good stock. That was his real talent: breeding 'em. You and he about the same size. I bet you're good with horses."

"I like to ride, ma'am, but a trainer I'll never be."

"Greggie did a fine job. Fine job." Her eyes glassed over and I saw her swallow. "Crying shame we lost him so young. Crying shame."

I nodded, but couldn't tell if she could see me or not. She tried her glasses periodically but then set them back down in disgust.

"How many of you live out here, ma'am?"

"How many? Oh, my. I lost count a long, long time ago. Too many to feed. That's what I keep telling the young ones, but do they listen? Ought to geld them, is what we ought to do." She grinned and showed me her gums again, pink, black, and empty. "We ought to geld them is what." Then she hollered, "Girls!" and I heard more stampeding. She clucked her tongue against the roof of her mouth and looked at me as if she'd never seen me before. Then she puckered her mouth into a knot of wrinkles and seemed to remember. "Yup, Greg was good with horses."

Her hands were bent by arthritis. A wedding ring was trapped by a knotted knuckle, never to be removed without a jeweler's saw. Her right eye, blue from a cataract, twitched. At first I thought she was winking at me, but I quickly realized it was uncontrollable. Seeing her reminded me that if we're lucky, this was how we all eventually end up. What kind of luck is that? I wondered.

"Would you happen to know who Greg went hunting with on Tuesday?"

"Hmm?" she asked, and I repeated the question. "Tuesday last?" After some thought she said, "Don't know who. Can't say who." Her eye winked at me again. She held a bent, wrinkled finger to her lips and hissed, "Shh. Can't say who, Mother."

Her behavior confused me. Was she repeating something said to her, or was she just wandering off into a spongy part of her aging brain? I took a good look into her eyes. Another cataract was forming on her left. No wonder the bifocals weren't doing much good.

"Shh," she said again, and then yelled, "Girls!"

The stampede started afresh and I could tell by the acoustics that a number of people were running down the stairs. They clearly moved into the room behind me and then I saw Grandma give the nod and a line of them paraded into the kitchen, one by one, as Grandma made the introductions. There must have been seven or eight young women, all under twenty. I lost count when I saw the third-to-last was pregnant. Each of the girls had bad teeth, hairy legs, and hairy armpits. Two of them had crossed eyes. I tried my best to smile, but the combination of the worn but clean clothing, the inherited angry eyes, and their apparent eagerness to have me like them or find one of them attractive turned my stomach. I felt dizzy for a second. More would be made pregnant before too long, I feared, the sad victim of a brother or an uncle or even a father. It was something I didn't understand, and had no desire to confront. Yet something that happened everyday. In my mind I heard the dim hollow echoes of these girls, screams of fear and hunger, screams of unchecked appetites and uncontrollable moods, screams of innocent longing and screams of ultimate forgiveness as a tender twelve-year-old smile twitched to satisfaction. All this inspired by the peculiar lack of life in these girls' faces. Girls numb to the world around them. Or numbed by it. My stomach twisted again and I tried to smile, but my eyes were stinging.

Granny dismissed them and they giggled and ran away. They seemed more like a pack of kids than young women. They probably were.

"Pretty girls, aren't they?" Her eye twitched again.

I was feeling claustrophobic. I ran my fingers around my loose shirt collar and pulled for air. Why had I come out here? I couldn't think what I had hoped to gain by coming out here. Greg Sweetland, I reminded myself. Paul Russell.

"Would any of the others know who Greg might have gone hunting with on Tuesday? Larry, maybe?"

"I wouldn't be speaking with Larry if I was you. He's real upset about his brother. Larry's *real* unpleasant when he's upset. Nasty." She rubbed the back of her neck and pulled at a knot in her thin gray hair.

"How many brothers does Greg have?" I inquired.

She shook her head and looked at me through that fogged left eye. "What's your name?" she asked.

I had lost her. One minute she had been there, the next she was gone. "Klick," I told her.

Suddenly lucid, she said, "Mr. Klick, my grandson didn't do nothing wrong. Nothing wrong at all. We Sweetlands are private folk. Never did nothing to harm no one." It sounded memorized.

Through the window I saw the edge of a satellite dish. "You get television way out here?" I asked.

"Oh, yes. Now we do. We like the TV. Don't you?" I saw no reason to crush her, so I nodded.

"I used to love the *Dukes*," she said. "Don't know why they took them off the set. At least we've still got *Dallas*."

Right then I heard a child screaming. I looked out into the hard dirt driveway and saw a boy of about five or six take another whack on the tail from a woman in her early twenties. There were too many people around here. And they all looked the same. The woman noticed my truck and paused. I saw her stuff something into her back pocket and thought little of it. The boy broke loose and ran toward us, storming into the kitchen and heading straight for Great-Grandmother, whom he called Mother Sweetland.

"Where'd he go, Mother Sweetland? Where'd he go?"

Before she had a chance to answer, the child's mother had caught up with him. She hurried through the door, nodded at me, and yanked the boy by his arm. She cracked him across the butt again, looked me in the eye, and dragged him off into the house somewhere. His crying faded. I noticed I was clutching the table, my knuckles white. It was just the kind of thing, way out here, one didn't stick one's nose into. The mother had a sharp beauty about her: the same haunting eyes as most of the others, long dark hair that touched the belt loops on her faded jeans, and an exceptionally thin and well-shaped body. There was something earthy and sensual about her. An image of her lingered in my mind, like the pleasant aftertaste of a fine wine. I wanted to speak with her. I wanted to ask what she had stuffed into her back pocket. She knew something.

"Greg's wife and son," Grandma said.

And I nodded slowly. Yes, she knew something. But I would never get close to that one. Never in a thousand years.

12

I drove away from the Sweetlands' ranch feeling uneasy. The truck lumbered through the potholed road, jostling me from side to side. In my rearview mirror I saw two or three more Sweetlands whom I had not seen on my visit. They seemed to crawl out of the woodwork. I don't have a sixth sense—don't claim to. But I've done enough of this work that I've sharpened my sense of curiosity; like a barber stropping a straight-edged razor, I know when it's ready to cut. I had received crossed signals at the Sweetlands'. Curiosity aroused, I wanted another visit.

On my way out I paid particular attention to the surrounding terrain, watching for side roads or animal trails. I sought access to the ridge that overlooked the farming compound, hoping for a spot to leave my truck well hidden. I wasn't even sure I would be back—I had not yet convinced myself it was worth my time—yet I was preparing for that eventuality. The Sweetlands had stirred something up in me. I couldn't be sure if it was the blatant incest, the grandmother's confused babble, or the young woman's lack of grief. Perhaps a combination. One thing ate at me consistently: these people showed every sign of being dirt poor—fallow fields, farm implements overgrown by weeds, dilapidated fencing—yet they owned an expensive satellite system and one of the brothers had been wearing two-hundred-dollar boots and a three-hundred-dollar silver belt buckle. The satellite system was not all that unusual. Many families in Ridland, regardless of income, had managed to beg, borrow, or steal such a system. But the boots and buckle were incongruous. There were, of course, any number of viable explanations: buckles, at least, were often offered as prizes for horse or rodeo competition, and the Sweetlands were supposedly known for their horsemanship; perhaps the brother had a day job, his own income, and chose to spend it on flashy items, like pink Harlem Cadillacs. I told myself to discount the fallow fields. After all, the horses could have brought the family into money. But I still wasn't buying that explanation. Something back there had tickled my curiosity, and I wanted to know why.

The drive back into Ridland was beautiful. One of the added benefits of living out here was the endless, everyday beauty of the surroundings. The shifting light and colors made each piece of scenery constantly new to the eye, like randomly lit alternating backdrops on a large stage. Each day the sun's path changed angle slightly, catching the jagged peaks of the highlands or the round, balding hills of the lowlands in a new and different light. On this day, as I made the final turn into our small town and aimed up the valley at the bowl of peaks surrounding Snow Lake, far in the distance, it was nothing less than spectacular.

As I stepped up onto the covered porch between Nicole's garage and main house, my heart began to pound heavily, and it had nothing to do with hormones or unscratched itches in the groin of a man quickly approaching middle age. It had to do with the drops of blood on the flooring. For a brief moment I actually staggered. My knees felt weak and I grabbed for the screen door. "Nicole!" I attempted to shout, but it came out as more of a gasp. "God no," I said as I pushed through the door. I shouldn't have left her alone, I told myself. Not after the apparent attempt on my life. Not after her husband had disappeared. Why had I left her alone? I didn't call out again. I moved slowly, following the thin red trail across the hardwood floor, apprehensive and prepared for either an encounter with her assailant or sight of what was now the anticipated horror of a mutilated corpse. My right fist was clenched tight, and I was moving stealthily on my toes. I heard running water and I pictured her lying face down in the bathtub, water spilling over onto the floor. My vision blurred, and I realized I was close to crying. Me, the man of no tears. What had this woman done to me?

I moved through the small television room and pushed open the door to her bedroom/bath, prepared for the unexpected. But not prepared for what I saw. She was bent over the black, matted hair of her Labrador, the sink faucet hissing above her. Several Band-Aids were strewn about the floor. She had apparently pulled off the bandage and opened the wound.

She looked up, unsurprised by my intrusion, mascara streaked down her pale face. "He's been shot," she said.

•

The Valley Animal Clinic was constructed of a rough-wood stained siding with a sturdy shake roof. It smelled like a mixture of a dentist's office and dog biscuits. A bearded vet whom Nicole knew as Mark took Harper into an examination room and placed him on a stainless-steel table. I led Nicole back to a vinyl-padded bench and the emergency surgery began. I assured her that Harper would pull through, though I doubted it. The dog had quite obviously traveled a considerable distance—I had noticed that his normally leathery pads were worn raw. That he was still alive at all seemed something of a miracle to me, though I thought that if I were shot and dying, I, too, would exhaust every last synapse of energy in order to see Nicole one last time. In this way the dog and I were no different.

She leaned her head against my shoulder and I didn't dare move for fear she would change her mind. "I heard a whimpering on my porch. I ran to the door and there he was: he was dragging his rump, only his front legs seemed to work. I removed the bandages . . . I don't know why. He started bleeding. He looked up into my eyes and lay down at my feet like everything was fine." She began to cry again. It had been off and on for the past half hour.

Again I told her that the dog was going to make it, although this time I cushioned the statement by adding that Harper had obviously lived a full life and that all things come to pass, even dogs.

Bitterness filled her voice as she said, "You heard what Mark said: he's been wounded for days. Did you see those Band-Aids? Band-Aids! Why didn't someone bring him to a vet earlier? Anyone could see he wouldn't make it without surgery. He's riddled with buckshot, for heaven's sake. How stupid can you be?"

"Maybe not stupid," I said, sitting up and causing her to do so as well.

"What do you mean?" she asked inquisitively.

"Maybe the person who found Harper didn't know any better."

"I have a hard time believing that."

"What if it was a kid? That would account for the Band-Aids."

"A child?"

"There's something else, Nicole." I reached down and took her cold hands.

She held mine reluctantly. "What?"

"Someone tried to shoot Harper while he was running away. That's why he was hit in the butt." She nodded. "I think it's time you start preparing yourself for the possibility that Harper wasn't the only victim."

"Paul," she said softly, a great distance between her and her words.

13

I found the Clarks' double-wide on my third try. As it turned out, I had driven right by it twice without knowing it. The trailer was tucked down an alley surprisingly close to the back of the Silver Dollar Café. A cord of wood had been stacked and covered with a thick black plastic. A tricycle with bent handlebars lay kicked over at the base of the small steps that rose to the nearest door. The trailer itself sat beneath a separate peaked roof, constructed to shed snow. A similar shed roof perched over the steps. I ducked to avoid hitting my head on a beam and knocked.

Gerry Clark was a pretty, pale woman in her middle twenties with platinum hair that looked real, blue eyes, tiny bones, and what might be called a decent figure. She appeared about six months pregnant, stood duck-footed, wearing an apron with a gold-and-red flower print. She had white teeth that could have used braces a few years earlier and moist, sensuous lips. She spoke with a Western twang that I was accustomed to. "Howdy," she said, eyeing me.

"Hi." I made my introduction and she hers. We shook hands. She had a surprisingly strong grip, and short nails. She invited me in and I ducked again and moved into the small living room, which smelled like fresh-baked bread.

She took a seat on a well-used couch, legs spread open, hands on her knees. She exhaled. "One in the oven," she said, chuckling and patting her abdomen. "Takes a lot out of you."

I didn't know what to say, so I nodded.

"You selling something, I got to tell you that we ain't able to buy nothing right now, no matter what it is. Had to cancel cable last week, and believe me, ain't nothing as important to my Bill and me as our cable." She tried on a smile that didn't fit. "Damn tough going these days."

"Not selling," I informed her.

"Real good then. That's a relief. Buying? You here about the snowmobile? I could show it to you, exceptin' it ain't here. Bill took it over to Heston's for a going-over 'fore we tried to show it off."

"No, not the snowmobile," I said. "I'm here about Greg Sweetland."

She looked mean. "Think it's time you left." She struggled to her feet.

"Hear me out. I'm not with the police. It's nothing like that. I only have a few questions."

"Whole damn town thinks this baby is Greg's. Well, that's not true. Ain't true one bit. There wasn't nothing to us the way everyone says. Now he's gone and gotten himself shot and everyone's looking at Bill like he pulled the trigger. This is a small town, mister. Sometimes I like to feel like it's about to smother me for good. Now state your business or get out."

"I'm trying to find a man named Paul Russell."

"Well, that's a relief. Never even heard of the fellow. So I ain't gonna do you no good, am I? Now if you don't mind leaving me alone, I got some baking to do."

I stood, required to duck. "All I want to know is where your husband was the night Greg Sweetland was shot."

Her eyes looked less than convincing. "He was right here. Right here with me watching TV."

I looked down at her. "I don't mean to be prying, Mrs. Clark. But didn't you say the cable was shut off last week? I'm asking about Tuesday night."

She bit down on her lip and looked perplexed. "You just get out of here," she said, exhausted.

"Does your husband hunt?"

"Everyone in Ridland hunts. What of it?"

"Does he own a shotgun?"

"Birds? Hell, Bill don't waste no time shooting birds. He hunts for the freezer. He hunts to feed us. He shoots a rifle, not a bird gun."

"Then he didn't kill Greg Sweetland. Where was he Tuesday, Mrs. Clark?"

"I told you where he was. Now just get the hell out of my home 'fore I call the sheriff."

I ducked on my way out and heard the door slam behind me. Through the thin wall I then heard the oven door squeak open. I was beginning to get frustrated. I have a high threshold for frustration, but this town and the people in it were pushing me toward the edge. Everyone seemed to have a story to cling to—and not one of them convincing. For a brief moment I toyed with the idea that they were all in something together.

Then I realized I was getting paranoid. It was time for a six-pack and a little investigative work.

I turned left up a hilly drainage, still a good three-quarters of a mile south of the Sweetland ranch. I chose twilight for my trip, when the air goes gray, because I think it's the most difficult time of day to see at a distance. Overhead a red-tailed hawk scouted for dinner, reminding me that out here in this seemingly empty high desert, filled with sage and wild grasses, dozens of species of rodents, rabbits, and other half-pint quadrupeds and snakes foraged for food and a meager existence.

I kept my eyes open for the snakes. I don't like snakes.

I parked the truck behind a rock outcropping about a quarter-mile up the drainage so that it couldn't be seen from the dirt road below. The sky was not yet to sunset colors, but I could tell it was going to be a dandy the way the clouds were patterned like a checkerboard.

I climbed through the sage, winded immediately by the effort at this altitude. The bottom of the valley is over five thousand feet above sea level, and even the slightest exertion serves to remind you of this. The footing was not good: scree and crushed-granite gravel. The sage smelled magnificent, perfumy. Pungent. It scratched at my jeans. I stayed this side of the ridge, careful not even to glance over the top. I knew the ridge ran parallel to the road and that I had a good distance to cover, so I moved on at a steep angle, occasionally pausing to catch my breath as the slope continued to climb.

The view improved with every step. I glanced back down at the first lights of Ridland, well behind and below me. The sun continued to set and the first flush of color reddened the underside of the weightless clouds.

I hurried on. I had hoped to use the slow twilight to my advantage. I knew that once full darkness fell, there would be little to gain from watching the Sweetland ranch—if there was anything to gain at all. I was driven more by curiosity than suspicion.

After ten minutes I edged up to the lip of the ridge; only then did I realize I'd left my binoculars in the truck. I went down on hands and knees to sage-height. I was still a hundred yards short of the ranch compound. I backed up and continued on the far side of the ridge, away from view of the compound. Above me the clouds began to bleed with color. My jacket looked red in the light. I moved through another drainage and up the other side and when I crested this hill from the rear I knew I was on top of the compound. Again I edged my way up to the top of the ridge, and this time sat down next to a good-sized sage where I would be impossible to notice.

I could see down into the house where a blue television haze flooded the floor and furniture. I couldn't see anyone from this angle, and couldn't be sure how many might be watching. I heard low voices from a shed on the far side of the compound. A couple of the girls were milking cows by the sound of it.

Then I noticed that I could see down into the other shed that had been converted into living quarters. Through the dirty window I saw a young woman doing dishes, her arms up to her elbows in soapy dishwater. I couldn't be sure, but I thought she was the first person I had seen here earlier in the day. Some equally feminine arms reached in and stole a pan from the wet hands and a towel engulfed it and the arms disappeared. Two young boys came from a grain silo pushing an empty wheelbarrow. They went over to the long stack of bales of alfalfa, brought down two, loaded them onto the wheelbarrow, and headed off toward the first paddock. As they began to feed the horses, I thought I heard a feminine giggle. My eyes roamed the various shadows but I couldn't find where it came from. It was amazing how the sounds traveled such distance with little or no loss in fidelity.

It was during this search for the giggle that I noticed an unusual phenomenon. Light escaping from both of the large barns switched off simultaneously. I hadn't even noticed that any lights were on in these barns until they shut off. But the synchronization startled me. I waited to see at least one person leave each barn, but none came out. What coincidence, I thought, not used to such feelings. How strange the lights should go off at the same time and yet no one leave either building. Then I realized what had happened: Someone had tripped a breaker, or a pair of breakers, most likely from the house. It made sense—if you needed to go out to the barn late at night, you could turn on the lights from the house and give yourself something to steer toward.

I heard the young giggle again. It sounded vaguely sexual. And then I spotted a junked truck moving slightly on its leaf springs and my mind filled in the blanks. Such is the way young sisters end up pregnant in places like this, I thought, grimacing with the thought. The noble white-knight side of me felt tempted to interrupt the goings-on. But I didn't. And I hated myself all the more for it.

The feeding of the horses continued, paddock to paddock. My eyes and attention kept shifting between the living room window of the main house, the kitchen window below me, and the controlled chaos of the old truck cab.

I saw Grandma appear briefly in the blue light of the television. I saw an electric skillet being washed by the long thin arms and hands. Then I saw and heard a woman in her thirties come out of a trailer over by the barn and start calling for Margaret. The movement of the truck cab stopped immediately, and I knew the identity of at least one of the pair in the truck. The woman continued to call for Margaret, but finally gave up and returned to the trailer. Within seconds one of the girls I'd met, a woman no older than sixteen, scurried out of the cab of the truck, snapping her jeans shut, and sneaked around low, through a paddock, careful to avoid being seen by the one doing the dishes. A moment later a large man climbed out as well. Larry. The brother with the shiny belt buckle and new boots. And in this family, he was clearly old enough to be her uncle—or father. He tucked in his shirt and buttoned up his fly, hidden by the cab from the compound.

I heard the one behind me much too late to react well. But if I hadn't reacted at all, I reflected later, I might have spent the last few minutes of my life overlooking the Sweetland ranch. He had to be a Sweetland; he had the same empty eyes as Larry, though he was wirey, not broad. He must have grown careless on his final approach, for some rock moved beneath his feet, giving me just enough time to roll to one side and kick backward. I connected with his knee and he went down, dropping the rifle and somersaulting over his back. But he was fast. Before I fully registered what was happening, he was up and on top of me. He drove a hard fist into my gut and then took hold of a piece of rock and hammered it toward my skull with all his weight behind it. I jerked out of the way, tossing him off me, and rolled to get to my knees in time to block his next attempt. We were both well aware that the rifle was there somewhere, but the odd, orange-red sky homogenized everything around us. The red hue covered everything, blending it together, hiding it, like fruit in a bowl of cherry Jell-O. I caught his forearm on his next try. He thought quickly enough to release the rock anyway and it fell onto my head, cutting and bruising the area around my right eye and partially blocking my vision. I leveraged myself well and propelled him off balance with all the strength in my legs. He rolled down the scree slope. I took two large leaps, slid, and fell on top of him. I hit him twice, very hard, just below the V in his rib cage, connecting fully until my elbow locked behind the punch. The twin heart punches left him breathless and unable to move. I had used the hit before. I knew he would not function well for several minutes. I used one bootlace to tie his wrists behind his back. The other bootlace secured his ankles together. I tied my red handkerchief around his head and mouth as a gag and left him. If he tried hard, he could get over the ridge in twenty minutes or so. An hour at the latest. By then I planned to be long gone.

And I was.

15

I fixed myself a stiff drink and built a fire. My bones hurt and I was rattled. I come out to Idaho between jobs to relax. Moving through the has-beens of the music world can take you to some seedy, nerve-rattling places. I like it better here. I should have kept all this in mind on that afternoon only a few days earlier, when Nicole Russell walked up onto my deck and stood blocking the sun. I should have said no despite her charm, despite her looks, despite her predicament. But I didn't. Here I was nursing wounds with a double shot of eighty proof and trying to lick my ego free of the realization that I had nearly been buried on the Sweetlands' hill because of slow reactions.

I saw the headlights coming down the drive and did not move an inch. I knew those headlights. The left is angled down slightly from an accident that bent the grille and nearly ruined the entire frame. As a result, most of the time he drives with brights on, despite the fact that the right light basically blinds you from head-on.

Lyel is bigger than me. He has a rounder face and he's wider at the waist. His eyes are reminiscent of a basset hound. He has a broad sweeping forehead with three distinct lines which can indicate everything from boredom to exhilaration. He keeps his hair short, emphasizing the enormity of his head and the thickness of bone. He wears specially tailored clothing to fit those shoulders, and many men's shoes would fit entirely inside of his. His full name is James Chandler Wilshire Lyel III, but for as long as I've known him it has always been Lyel. He is "dependently wealthy"—as he calls it—clipping coupons and managing family money that could be delivered in dump trucks. But he doesn't show it. He dresses down and has little of that telltale aristocratic posturing that grows tiresome. He and I travel in a pair for some reason that still eludes me. Probably because I house-sit several of his abodes. When I'm at his place in New York, or Los Angeles, Lyel has a way of suddenly materializing. And if he doesn't materialize spontaneously, then he is at least "on call."

"Howdy, Klick," he said, greeting me, breezing through the front door and approaching the lower cabinet, which serves as a bar.

I don't remember where I met Lyel for the first time. He's one of those guys who has been around forever. He has a keen knack for finance and the ways of the world. He had a wife once, quite a while ago, and even I don't ask questions. Since then he likes to chase young women around. Snow Lake is perfect for that, and Lyel has the chasing down to a science. He is one of the most socially "busy" men I know, or ever will know. All this activity has given him a reflective, spiritual side that contradicts the manager-of-funds side. Looking at him, you might think he had once been a professional basketball player—and you would be right. In fact, that might have been where I first met him.

"I killed off the remainder of the rum," I told him.

"Selfish of you," he said, examining the label of one of my lesser-priced spirits and returning it politely to the rear of the shelf. He found something that appealed to him and poured some into a glass to which he added ice cubes and soda from the refrigerator. "Who got your eye?"

"An inbred about your size and height. He tried to match me up with a bullet. I was lucky, as it turned out. No match."

"Are you going to tell me about it?"

"Where have you been anyway? A lot's been going on around here."

"Steelhead have been returning early up north. Went with Tim and tried my luck."

"And?" I knew Tim. He was a local charter pilot.

"Don't ask. We were up there two weeks. Tim did fine. He says I'll get the hang of it. Of course that's what you say, too. I don't know. Sometimes I think I should give up fly-fishing altogether." He came over and sat on the floor, leaning up against one of his overstuffed chairs that don't hold him comfortably. He spends a lot of time on the floor. Not much furniture is built for a guy six-six and two-seventy. He clings to the hope of someday being a world-class fly-fisherman, a sport that, like golf, defies perfection. Lyel is much better at golf. "You were going to tell me about it."

So I did. I started out with Nicole Russell's arrival that late afternoon. When I told him that her car had scared away two mergansers, I heard him make one of his patented clucks. Lyel, too, has grown to appreciate birding, and he knew the disappointment of losing two diving ducks on a clear fall afternoon. The main house—hidden from the guest cabin—has a wonderfully close view of the slough.

I went on about Paul Russell's disappearance, my two trips to Snow Lake, and Judy's injuries. When I reached the part about Harper's miraculous return despite a butt filled with buckshot, Lyel excused himself to make us both another drink. Since I was out of rum, he made me something with vodka in it and told me to pretend. A few minutes later he interrupted me.

"It's your Prince Charming syndrome again."

"Don't remind me."

"That thing is chronic in you."

"Please."

"And the thing about it is that every time you get this notion to save someone like this Nicole, you do it not only at your own expense, but often with great risk. Why is that, do you suppose?"

"Let's not analyze me. Not tonight."

"Maybe it comes from something in your childhood."

"We're way off subject."

"And now here you are again. Does Bruce know? Is there any money involved at all?"

I had neglected to tell him about her offer. Once I had explained, he said paternally, "Why didn't you say so? I take it all back. Twenty-five thousand, eh? It's a perfectly *wonderful* case to be involved in, and you don't even have to hang around smoky bars until two in the morning to get a lead. Imagine that! Be careful, Klick. This one may spoil you."

"Sarcasm I don't need."

"The point is, you are often led around by your heart or certain other anatomical parts instead of by your wallet or your brains. I hope you grow out of it. When you and Bruce are on to something, you're at your best. As someone who sits on the bench and simply observes you, I'd say this is one of those things worth bridling. The younger women will one day begin to take advantage of your kindliness, and where that might lead is anyone's guess."

"You would have done the same thing."

"No. Not I. Have I ever, even once, attempted one of your noble gestures? Not I. I am a semi-retired individual content to move through life with one eye on the Dow average and the other on the bond market."

"You're getting drunk."

"Nonsense. What makes you say such a thing?"

"You're talking about you. You never talk about you."

"I had a few with dinner tonight." He sipped his drink. Even a small sip for Lyel took the drink down considerably. "I'm nursing my way back from my failure with those damn steelhead. And you're nursing your wounds from your struggle at the Sweetlands'. May I offer an objective reasoning of the facts you've put forth? I have this feeling that Nicole has eliminated the opportunity for any objectivity on your part."

"I would welcome it gladly. Please. Be objective, my friend. What the hell is going on?"

It may be a result of his privileged position in life. Or perhaps something to do with his intimidating size. Whatever the reason, Lyel has the ability to step back and make summations that rival those made by the best attorneys. I value his friendship for all the usual reasons, not the least of which is an occasional bit of profound advice.

"Three obvious things come to mind. The first, and I'm sure

the most difficult for you accept, is that Paul Russell may have seen a very easy way to a very large amount of money. He could be long gone, Klick, gambling and whoring his way through God knows how many thousand with the greatest of ease. First thing I'd do is have *all* her accounts audited. He may even return and apologize, and, if you really want the truth, your Nicole may just take him back. It would not be the first time. Or she may never see him again, that is, unless you get extremely busy and quite lucky. But on the top of the list we put SCAM, because that seems the most obvious."

"And next on the list?"

"One footnote, if you please." He stopped for another sip and moved to warm himself more fully by the fire. "Miss Debbie Benton could well be a part of this whole contrived disappearance, and, if so, then should be watched carefully. If they were in this together, then, depending on Mr. Paul Russell's shrewdness, she may be summoned to join him at a point in the near or distant future, to share in the wealth—if you will—and revel in the glory of victory. Even as little as fifty thousand can be made into a considerable nest egg if one has the right advisers."

"In the case of Paul Russell, I have the feeling the fifty could be gone in a week-long poker game."

"Less than that if he has no talent for the game."

"Very little, I'm told."

"All the reason to watch Miss Benton even more carefully."

"I think we better keep thinking. If he has the money and is gone, then that's that. It doesn't help explain the other unexplainables, however."

Lyel asked, "What if it wasn't Greg Sweetland who was killed? Bear with me. What if it's a cover-up? It gives Sweetland a way out. With Sweetland believed dead, Clark doesn't try to find him and avenge his wife's pregnancy. And who does he use in place of himself? Russell. Sweetland ends up with the fifty thousand dollars, which may explain some of the recently added wealth out at the ranch. If Russell was a big mouth, as you have indicated he might have been, then what's to prevent Sweetland from finding out about Russell's intentions to fleece his wife? Fifty thousand dollars is a lot of bait. He blows Russell's face off and when he goes to take the money, the dog gets away. He tries to kill the dog. What was the dog's name again?"

"Harper."

"Yes. It would explain Harper's wounds."

"What would?"

"The buckshot. Hasn't that occurred to you? No, I can see it hasn't. That's because you and I don't hunt. The season is only open on deer right now. The bird season was delayed until Fish and Game can determine the effects of last year's drought. Haven't you been reading the paper?"

"Meaning?"

"Meaning that you don't hunt deer with shotguns. You hunt with rifles. And the dog was wounded with a shotgun. Why? The thing about rifles is that they don't confuse medical examiners. They don't destroy faces. Not like a shotgun can. I believe if you place an inquiry with the local medical examiner, you will discover that the corpus delicti suffered a shotgun wound to the face, and that the shot will match at least in composition the shot removed by the veterinarian from the hindquarters of your lady friend's canine. You're the one who doesn't like coincidences. A shotgun wound to the face, a shotgun wound to the dog? It's only a hunch, mind you, but it adds up."

He was definitely drunk. I must have looked at him with astonishment, for he gave me a queer look. I had hypothesized many of these same ideas, but I had not connected the role of the shotgun.

"No reason to be smug."

"There's every reason to be smug," he told me. "I've been drinking and I thought of something you overlooked. It's a perfect time to be smug. I'd like another," he said, handing me his empty glass. And he grinned at me. So I fixed us both drinks, stoked the fire, and sat back down. The wind was really blowing now, and I could hear it whistle through the log walls. The fire sparked with the new wood and Lyel moved back a few feet because of the heat.

He said, "If Sweetland's not dead, then he has an awful lot to protect."

"Message received. Though we can't be sure we're even close."

"Fifty thousand reasons to be careful."

"And maybe even Debbie Benton. She strikes me as the kind who could have played an intricate role in all of this if given that many reasons."

"I know Debbie, indirectly, and I can't say that I agree with you there. She and Paul Russell were for real, I have the feeling."

"Maybe, but I'm told Greg Sweetland had—or has—his own special way with the ladies."

"And horses, you said. I'm beginning to dislike Sweetland," Lyel said.

"You should meet his brother," I added, touching a sore bruise.

16

I drove up to Butte Peak the following morning, the approaching winter in evidence as a tangy chill. The truck warmed up finally and I turned the fan on high and pulled out the knob to defrost the windshield where my breath had been collecting as a faint gauze on the inside of the curved and tinted glass. I appreciated Lyel's visit. In the back of my mind I continued to search for excuses to visit Nicole, but realized I would rather have results than excuses. I am used to a single kind of investigation, where finding a person consists of tracking him or her down, usually with the help of the musicians' union, often sobering up the individual and then spelling out the nature of my visit in terms of a cash offer. The Russell affair was a different sort of thing. Few of us enjoy having our envelope of self-belief stretched to limits. I am no exception. I like to think of myself as someone who can get the job done, who can stick with it and reason his way to completion. This job was beginning to chip away at my confidence, and if there is one element you need to stay healthy in this line of work, it is confidence. If often doesn't matter if you're right, as long as you believe you are. Belief can carry you the distance.

After two attempts, I found Paul Bates holding court in

Butte Peak's Sears outlet. The mail-order store contains a bare minimum of inventory, just enough of the more popular items to catch an occasional impulsive buyer by the wallet. Bates had a round face and dark eyes. He ate well and spoke with conviction. The woman in front of me at the counter couldn't have been over five feet, and the difference in our heights made me feel uncomfortable. Excessive height is not everything it's cracked up to be. Sometimes you feel like a carnival act.

When she turned around to leave she must have been looking somewhere below my shirt pockets and the sight of me startled her. She stared up into my eyes with a degree of fear on her face, forced a smile, and hurried from the store with tight little steps and the sound of her shoes scraping the vinyl tile. An annoying electronic buzzer sounded as she jerked open the door and left.

"Help you?" asked Bates.

"Are you Paul Bates, the county coroner?" I asked.

"That's me."

"I had a hard time finding you."

"Got to earn a living, friend," he said. "What can I do you for?"

"I wondered if I could have a look at Greg Sweetland's body?"

He carried a pair of expressive eyebrows on his forehead, and I had the impression he was trying to control them as they twitched once in annoyance.

"You must be Klick," he said in that country way where people seem to be talking to themselves but allow you to overhear. He had slipped up, and his face confirmed it. The statement proved someone had spoken to him about me, something I took as indication that I was doing some good after all.

"That's right." I held out my hand. "Chris Klick."

He had no choice but to shake my hand. His palm was damp. We squeezed each other's hand tightly—a ritual of the West that goes beyond common courtesy and approaches a kind of macho rite. I looked into his dark eyes, still unable to tell what color they were. We released our grip on one another and he said cordially, "Pleased to meet you. The sheriff said you asked after me. Told me to help you in whatever way I could." His explanation was well conceived but too late to cover that first twitch in the eyebrows. He continued, "'Fraid I can't help you with Greg, though. Cremated the body the day it came in. Between you and me, it was an ugly mess and there weren't no way to salvage it. The doc and I recommended that the family have the body cremated right away and save some storage expense. Death has gotten expensive in the last few years, and the Sweetlands . . . well, there are sure enough of them and they don't need no more expense."

I hadn't expected this response. I had been prepared to argue my way into seeing the body. Now there was no body. "You know the Sweetlands well?"

"Know them? Hell, I'm related to them somehow. Half the people in Butte Peak and Ridland are related one way or another. This guy's daughter marries that guy's son, and they have a kid who later marries his mother's cousin's kid. Small populations, that's what does it. Hell, I'm a second cousin or something to Greg. My mother's cousin was a Sweetland. Died of a fever back in the thirties. Truth is, I don't know them very good. They live way out east of Ridland toward Crystal Creek and stick pretty much to themselves. Greg's made a name for himself with his horse breeding. His brother has tried his hand at it, but ain't done no good. Greg will be missed though, by golly. He'll be missed for certain."

"And you're sure the body was Greg's?" There wasn't any other way to ask it and I was tiring of this man's country-cousin attitude. He had turned on a twang in his voice and I felt like a one-man audience. It was the same feeling I had experienced with Hudson.

"Of course I'm sure. Hell, it wasn't me who did the identification anyway."

"Amos Cole?" I asked, remembering the name from my talk with Hudson.

"No, not Amos either. Amos got called out of town. Doc Kupps did the autopsy. As good a doctor as Amos. Just as thorough. Hair color matched. Same height and weight as Greg. The sheriff dug up some fingerprints and they checked out—"

"He had Sweetland's prints on file?" I noticed Bates blush. He quickly said, "Ain't a kid in this valley ain't brushed up against the law at least once. Couple too many beers, that sort of thing. Sheriff cools them off for a night and runs them through the mill to remind them that he's serious about enforcing the law. Probably something like that with Greg. Dean's a good sheriff. Knows how to get a kid back on the right track."

He was saved by a customer who entered, sounding that awful buzzer.

"I'll be just a minute," he told me. But it was apparent that he was bent on more country-cousin talk, stalling to bore me into leaving. I obliged him by making a motion toward the door.

I asked, "Dr. Kupps here in town?"

"Over to the clinic most days," Bates said in his twang.

The door buzzed again as I left.

●

Kupps was not at the clinic. Only an overweight nurse practitioner and a receptionist with bad skin. An elderly woman in a heavy coat overheard me ask after the doctor and grabbed my attention by waving her hand as I was about to leave. She confided in me that the good Dr. Kupps was known to exercise his elbow at all hours of the day and suggested I pay a visit to the saloon over next to the hardware store. I thanked her and she winked at me. If she had been forty years younger, I had a feeling she would have made me forget all about Nicole Russell. I winked back at her and left.

Dr. Jim Kupps was at the far end of the bar watching Donahue on an overhead color set. There were five of us in all: the doctor; the bartender, a short, stocky man with thick glasses and a beer gut; a woman of indistinguishable age and shape, slumped over a mixed drink and holding a cigarette that needed ashing; a young guy, no older than twenty-two, pale with hands that shook and eyes that refused to look up; and myself. And Phil Donahue.

I knew the one on the end was Kupps. It wasn't that he looked particularly scholarly—in fact, he needed a shave and a haircut. It was his hands. They were perfectly clean, nails and all. I knew other doctors who had a fetish about keeping their hands clean, and for the life of me, I couldn't think of any drunk who would bother with such fastidiousness except a drunk doctor.

"Dr. Kupps?" I asked. He turned to me with rheumy eyes and that unfocused dazed stare that often accompanies drunks. It was as if he were searching the bar for the man who belonged to the name I had mentioned. Then it struck him that it was he.

"You're looking at him." His eyes began to focus and I saw in them a deep-rooted embarrassment. "Can I buy you one?"

It's not my practice to drink before noon. It's something I purposely forego in order to avoid joining the ranks of the Jim Kuppses. But to any rule there are exceptions, and I sensed in Kupps an opportunity that had heretofore eluded me. "A beer please," I told the bartender. The man began to recite a memorized menu of domestic offerings when I cut him off with an order for a Bud Lite draft. Always looking to keep down the weight.

"Good," said Kupps, "and I'll have another too."

I noted the good doctor was drinking a double vodka martini, up, with an onion. He attacked the drink like a man left long in the desert.

"Well, you've found me," he said. "Now, what's your trouble?"

"It's about Greg Sweetland."

He paused and pursed his lips. "Damn shame."

"Yes. I understand you performed the autopsy."

"That's right. Who are you?" He looked me over. There was no hint of the intoxication that had been so obvious only a few seconds earlier. Kupps was a good, solid alcoholic, I decided. Well practiced in the art of performance. He had probably practiced medicine on unsuspecting patients while drunk, I thought. And I shuddered as I sipped my beer.

"Chris Klick," I told him.

"The name doesn't mean anything to me," he said after reflecting for a moment.

"A man named Paul Russell has disappeared. He may have been out hunting with Sweetland on that same morning."

"He the one who blew Sweetland's face off?" he asked.

"What I wondered, and I mean no disrespect, is if with the

face blown off . . . can you be sure the body was Sweetland's and not Russell's?"

He looked at me with such indignation that I leaned back and nearly slipped off the bar stool. "Think I can't do my job?" he asked. "Look at that." He held his hand straight out in front of him. It remained perfectly still, like the marble hand of a statue. I was duly surprised. He was an even better performer than I had originally thought. "Of course I'm sure it was Sweetland. What was left of him. I resent your insinuation, Mr. Klick, and request an apology."

I apologized and offered to buy him a drink, which he accepted gladly. He requested I join him and so I finished off the draft and ordered another. Donahue was berating his guest to the audience's amusement. The woman at the other end of the bar had another cigarette going. The young man still hadn't moved. After delivering the drinks, the bartender moved to the far end of the bar, turned around and watched the television.

Kupps took in half the martini and said, "We have a small town here, Mr. Klick. That does not mean it is a town made up of small people. We are as capable as any people you'll find anywhere. More capable than most. Five years ago Ridland and Butte Peak were on their way out. Take a look now. We're resilient and our citizens have strong character. I don't know what your expertise is, Mr. Klick, but mine is medicine. Greg Sweetland died of wounds suffered by a shotgun blast to his face. We confirmed the identity of the corpse and we cremated it. That's all there is to it."

It was a good little speech, considering the amount of booze this man had consumed. But it didn't sell me. He seemed to recite it. And those eyes, which had been so suddenly strong, had returned to the dazed stare. I couldn't tell if it was the booze or something else. Like lying. Dr. Kupps had several people inside of him, and I couldn't be sure to whom I was speaking at any given moment. "I understand you don't usually do the medical examining," I said in a questioning tone.

His eyes darted about and he checked out Donahue briefly. I assumed he was preparing an answer, which I received a moment later. "Amos Cole was called out of town. Bates asked me to handle it."

"How long was Cole going to be gone for?"

"How should I know?"

"You didn't ask?" I wondered. "You just went ahead and did the work anyway?"

"Sure. I did the job. That's right. Paul asked me and I did the work. What's wrong with that?"

"But what if Cole was just going to be gone for a couple of hours?"

"No. All day. He was going clear to Boise."

"Then you *did* ask," I said, trying to confuse him, which I succeeded in doing.

He looked at me, befuddled. "No." He shook his head. I could feel him groping for an excuse. If it was there, it continued to evade him. I suddenly felt guilty for mentally tormenting this man. But I continued. "Paul Bates asked you to fill in?"

"Yes."

"And why did you cremate the body so quickly? Why not wait for Dr. Cole to return from Boise?"

Again his eyes wandered and his head rocked slowly back and forth.

I couldn't allow him time to put together an answer. I had to keep his thoughts moving, keep him off balance. "And how can you be sure the fingerprints were Sweetland's? Maybe they were Russell's."

"Fingerprints?" he questioned.

"That's right. Bates told me you confirmed it was Sweetland by fingerprints. He said one of Sheriff Hudson's deputies delivered them. Isn't that right?"

"A deputy. Sure. Fingerprints." He wasn't looking at me.

But now he had me. I had purposely lied about the deputy, but how could I be sure he had purposely lied back? With his rate of consumption it would be a miracle if Kupps could recall anything about the day before, much less something that happened nearly a week ago. And I saw the brilliance of choosing Kupps for the job. He was an unreliable witness. I had a feeling Amos Cole was cut from a different cloth entirely.

●

Amos Cole's nurse and secretary told me he was up at the Snow Lake hospital checking on some patients and waiting for an afternoon surgery. I reached the hospital just before lunch. I hoped the breath mint might hide the beer, but I couldn't be sure. I located Cole in the tiny cafeteria, beneath harsh fluorescent lights that made everyone's skin tint green. Cole was in his fifties, with the body of a thirty-year-old. He had a tightly stretched narrow face and wore heavy black glasses. His sandy hair was trimmed military-short and he had thin lips and white, white teeth. He shook my hand strongly and offered me a seat, making a scatological reference to the food he was about to eat and suggesting I don't try any.

"I've spoken with Paul Bates and Dr. Kupps this morning about the Greg Sweetland killing, and your name came up several times. I understand you were called down to Boise last Tuesday."

"Three-hour drive for nothing," said Cole disgustedly.

"How's that?"

"A screw-up in communication. I get this phone call that says I'm supposed to assist on a surgery of a former patient of mine. The secretary said my good friend Ken Rose was coming down with flu and didn't think he should operate. So I agree and head over there. It's a three-hour drive, as I'm sure you're well aware. Anyhow, I get all the way over there and come to find out Ken feels fine and there's no operation planned. They don't know how it happened. Someone messed something up and caused me one hell of a mess. I missed all my patients up here, had six and a half hours of down time; I'll probably have to work through the weekend. Next time I talk to Ken personally before jumping in my car."

"Did you speak to the nurse or receptionist who made the call?"

"Speak to her? Hell, no one was eager to take the blame for that one. You should have seen Ken." Cole smiled. "He was fit to be tied. I think if he'd found out who called me, he would have fired her right there and then."

"If whoever called you was even in his office."

"What's that?"

"You can't be sure you were even called from Boise, can you?"

He looked at me funny and put down his fork. "I suppose not. What are you driving at?"

"Just thinking aloud."

"Hadn't thought of that," he said. "Someone played a practical joke on me? Something like that?"

"Something like that. Maybe."

"You're thinking it had something to do with the Sweetland thing?"

"Let me ask you this. How common is it to cremate a body the same day it comes in?"

"You know, that bothered me, too, at the time."

"Then it isn't very common?"

"Not at all. It's almost always a few days at least. I see what you're driving at. You're implying Bates might have wanted me out of the way for a day so Dr. Kupps could take my place." He nodded. "I see what you mean. Sure. It could have been someone up here who called me. Any number of people know how close Ken and I are. But why the hell would Bates do that? He and I get along fine."

"That's something I would like answered," I said.

"You're damn right," said Cole. And he pushed the tray of food away.

17

"Come in," Nicole yelled, responding to my knock. "Who is it?"
As I walked into the room she was sitting with her back to me in
a Windsor chair. I heard the swish of her clothing as she spun
around. Her fresh face beamed as she identified me. I hadn't felt
this way since Patty Standard allowed me to walk her home back
in seventh grade. I had no idea where Patty Standard was living,
or even if she was. But on a fall day those many years before I
had sampled the first morsel of awakening, a wonderfully as-
tonishing excitement, and I'd possessed no tools, no experience
with which to interpret it. It was one of those moments of divine
innocence which, once encountered but a single time, can never
be quite the same again.

But now it *was* the same. Nicole did it to me. This was her
gift to me. She awakened a sense of freshness, of newness that I
not felt for decades. She began to rise and I motioned for her to
stay seated. It was the middle of the afternoon and sunlight now
stretched low and invasive through the kitchen windows, catching a prism she had hung there, spraying rainbow light around
the room.

I coveted her. "Hello," I said.

"Hello," she said softly and warm. Nicole didn't seem the

kind of woman to send a man mixed signals. Yet I was mixing them up quite nicely.

I carried another of the Windsor chairs and sat down close to her. "I've just visited the local coroner and a pair of doctors, and I've come away with more questions again. If I had to make an educated guess, I'd say two of them are involved in a cover-up of some sort. It's the second time I've sensed a conspiracy and it's starting to bother me."

"What would they be covering up?"

"I can't be sure. It occurred to me that this is a small town. People protect each other in small towns. Maybe Bill Clark shot and killed Greg Sweetland and Paul witnessed it and ran. There's a lot of moralizing in a place like Ridland. A guy like Hudson might be convinced to look the other way when a guy kills an adulterer, if the evidence can be destroyed quickly enough. In this case the evidence is a body and it's gone, and it is probably the only link to whatever happened, and I have a feeling guys like Hudson and Bates would do about anything to protect a cover-up once it got started, including blow up a nosy stranger like me who comes poking around. How's Harper?"

"Better." She paused, obviously thinking about what I had said. "Improving," she added. "And so is your friend Judy. I called Salt Lake and inquired. They have high hopes for her. Very little scarring, if all the grafts take."

"Well, that's a relief. I should send her something."

"Already done. I sent her some flowers this morning. Two dozen irises. I put your name on them." She caught my look and explained, "She doesn't even know me."

"You're something special, you know that?"

"It's an expression my father used to use. God, the memories that brings back." She was silent for nearly a minute, which seemed more like an hour. "Thank you," she said.

I thought of the walk with Patty Standard and nodded. Tempted to reach out and take her hand, I folded mine in my lap instead.

"Why would he just *happen* to have taken the money?" she inquired. "I don't believe that for a minute. He had the whole thing planned." She looked into my eyes. "I won't have him back, you know. But I want the satisfaction of getting back what he took from me. The money, that is," she added remorsefully, realizing he had taken much more than that. She looked from one of my eyes to the other and again I felt tempted to take her into my arms.

"I agree. I also think Harper figures into this. Sweetland was killed with a shotgun. Harper was wounded by a shotgun. Are we supposed to believe that's a coincidence? I've never been fond of coincidences."

"You think it's Paul, don't you?" She looked away. "You think Paul killed him."

I was faced with one of those awful moments. My friendship with Nicole demanded honesty, yet I didn't want to give it. "No, I don't. I think someone may have killed Paul, *tried* to kill Harper, and is now trying to cover it all up. I think the money is involved. I'd be willing to bet that Greg Sweetland is alive, and may even be living out at his ranch still. I think the sheriff knows what's going on, or at least suspects. He's protecting someone— maybe even Sweetland. I think Bates, the coroner, is involved. I think they—or someone they hired—tried to kill me once, and they'll probably try again, and that makes me worried for you. Hudson knows it was you who got me involved in this. Who knows what else he knows? I don't think it's safe for you until we know what's going on. As much as I hate to say it, I think you should leave town for a while." She shook her head. I continued, "Just until we know a little bit more. We don't even know who the players are in this thing yet. That leaves us too vulnerable. As I've already proved, I can barely take care of myself. I'd feel horrible if anything happened to you."

"I believe you would."

"Yes," I told her.

She took my hand in hers. "You're a dear, dear man, Klick. I feel very lucky to have met you."

I kissed her fingers and tried to use my eyes to tell her how I felt. I couldn't tell if she got the message. "Just a week or so," I tried again.

She shook her head. "No. I'm the one who got you into this. I'm the one responsible for that poor woman lying burned in a Salt Lake hospital. I won't run away, Klick."

"I'm not kidding when I say it isn't safe. You can't leave doors open—that sort of thing. You're inviting trouble."

"You leave your doors open."

"There are security devices. I know when a car has entered my property. I can tell if I've had any visitors when I've been out."

"Then I'll move in with you," she said matter-of-factly, pulling her hands loose from mine and hopping up. "That's the perfect solution." She paused by the door into the small television room and turned, offering me her perfect profile. She had more than a sumptuous body; she had an appealing posture that carried her breasts high and flattened her stomach, her neck stretched long and she held her chin proudly; but she also had the elegance that accompanies wealth: the fine tailored blouse, pleated to allow room at the top and yet hug her waist tightly, understated silver-and-turquoise jewelry, and perfectly manicured hands that she used like the Chinese women use fans. She was nothing less than spectacular standing there awaiting my approval. "Well," she asked. "Is that okay with you?"

"Do you hear me complaining?"

She smiled, and giggled, I think, and retreated into her bedroom to pack.

●

We locked up her house tightly. I led the way in my twenty-year-old truck. She followed behind in her sturdy four-wheel-drive. I kept checking in my rearview mirror, expecting that I had made this all up. I knew that one of these times when I checked, her rig would not be there, she would not be following me down to my place to move in. But each time I checked, there she was, and I even got the sense that she knew when I was checking, for she seemed to be in a constant smile. I wondered if I'd be able to sleep knowing that Nicole was only a room away from me. I wondered if I'd be able to leave the house, knowing I was leaving her behind. I was as nervous as I'd been in years, and the feeling was altogether disconcerting. This woman had control over me. And I had a sneaking suspicion she knew it.

The log cabin has three bedrooms, but I use one as an office, which leaves one as a guest bedroom. This is also especially convenient when people call or write and want to come visit. I can honestly reply to any with children, and/or friends, that I haven't the extra room. My time in Idaho is usually quite private. I go here to talk with Lyel and enjoy the mergansers, not entertain the world. And yet it is one of those places that attract everyone you've ever known. In the winter it is Snow Lake that lures them, and in the summer the well-founded rumor of the spectacular high mountain climate with its hot, dry days and long, long, shimmering evenings.

The guest room has a marvelous view of several hundred acres to the south, usually filled with energetic horses. Although the property belongs to a neighbor, I have long since grown to think of it as mine, just as I often think of this house as mine. The large window facing this bucolic view also faces the brick path to the house, a fact I reminded Nicole of, since at night it is easy to forget to lower the blinds, and should guests arrive, they can see quite clearly into the bedroom. "Who cares?" she said quite cavalier. "They've seen it before."

I doubted "they" had ever seen someone quite like her, but I reserved any comment to that fact. Besides, I never pulled the blinds either. With the exceptionally long driveway, you could always spot headlights in time to make yourself decent, and the view of those same fields drenched in a blue-hued moonlight, long-maned horses wandering along the fence, and the occasional swooping shadow of a great horned owl made me wonder why Lyel had ever installed the blinds at all. From this room the view seemed more like an animated full-color Ansel Adams photograph. I could tell immediately that Nicole appreciated it as much as I did.

After she unpacked I gave her a brief tour of the technical end of this quaint country cabin. I explained the bell—no buzzers for Lyel—that can be set to announce a vehicle entering at the far end of the long road that leads eventually to the cabin and on to the main house. I showed her the light and/or bell that can be engaged to signal someone stepping on either of my two welcome mats, one at the front door, one at the garage. I explained that I had wired windows and doors with sensors to indicate an intrusion, and then, after considerable debate, I showed her the location of one of the handguns I keep hidden in the house. There was more, but not that she needed to know.

"One could get the impression you're paranoid," she said, her mood changed.

"I take precautions," I explained. "The owner and I are away from the house a great deal of the time. Being this isolated, it is ripe for robbery. The trip on the gate up at the top of the road can be switched to buzz my neighbor's place. The other stuff can be connected with the police and fire." I didn't explain that in my line of work it's inevitable that you make a few enemies. All it takes is one enemy to end all the fun. I thought I might spoil hers if I told her that. My explanation seemed to suit her. Once again her mood picked up and her eyes sparkled.

"And I promise not to scare the ducks," she said.

"How 'bout a drink?" I asked.

"Please. Whatever you're having."

"Are you game to try it out on the deck?"

"To try what, Klick?" she said, biting back a smile.

I sobered. "Do me a favor. Don't play with me, Nicole. I happen to be extremely enamored with you."

"Who's playing?" she said, and let herself out onto the deck. "I moved in, didn't I?" she added before pulling the door shut. We stared at each other through the glass of the door. Then she leaned forward and breathed onto the glass and fogged it. She drew a heart and then walked out onto the deck. I watched as the fog receded and the glass became clear again. The image of the heart remained etched in my mind. I made the drinks. I poured mine strong.

It was chilly outside, not cold, and the strong afternoon light made us think it was warmer than it was. It was a little early still for ducks to be flying, but I hadn't ruled out the possibility that some might be feeding on the slough, so we faced our chairs where the slanting sun caught us from the right and yet we had a view of the slough to our left. She kicked her feet up onto the bench seat on the perimeter of the deck and settled into the webbed lawn chair. "It feels good to be out of my place. Too much to remind me of him. It's funny how quickly emotions can change, isn't it? I was really deeply concerned for him a few days ago. Now? I don't know. I don't think so. I don't want to see him. I don't want to have to face him. I think of him with her, and coming home to me, and I want to kill him. What a bastard. I don't live in any fairyland, it's nothing like that. I knew full well what I was getting into with Paul. We are not at all alike. I suppose I saw this coming way back when, but he knew how to control me. He knew how to get in under my skin and get me to do what he wanted. And what he wanted was control of the books. He played head games with me. Physically too, I suppose." She blushed. "And he got me where he wanted me. He got me to open up the accounts to him. I can see now that that's all he was after. It hurts."

We were silent for a long time. I pointed out the strange chortling sound that meant there were some ducks feeding out of view. She looked to the break in the willows waiting to see them, wide eyes held open in anticipation, the way a child looks through a store-front window at Christmas time. I admired this childlike quality in Nicole. She retained a youthful zest so many try so hard to hide and then can never find again. And she managed to control it instead of the other way around. Nicole impressed me as a woman willing to be herself. She instinctively knew when to talk and when to be silent, when to be serious and when to be light. When to flirt and when to draw hearts on glass doors. I was falling in love with this woman, and for the first time, sitting out on my deck sipping cocktails on a fall-come-winter afternoon, I had the feeling she welcomed it. If not the love, certainly the attention.

She reached over and took my hand. I fumbled to switch my drink to my left. "Do you mind?" she asked.

"No."

"I feel close to you, Klick."

"Yes."

"I don't know whether it's because I want an escape or because it's for real."

"I understand." I looked out at the leafless willows and felt her warm, soft skin wrapped in my big fist.

She chuckled. "I thought you would try to tell me it's for real."

"What's real for me may not be for you," I said more softly than I had intended. Out of the corner of my eye I saw her nod.

"When we first met, I didn't like you."

"That's one place we differ."

She laughed again and said, "You say all the right things."

I released her hand, switched my drink to my right and took a sip. "You're good company," I told her.

"So are you."

"I'm nervous around you."

"I can sense that. Why?"

My turn to shrug. "Just the way it is, I guess."

"Paul?"

"At first, yes. Now I'm not so sure."

She sighed. "I could use a diversion, Klick. I think you're my diversion. At least, you're all I seem to think about, and that hasn't happened to me in ages." She blushed again and it touched me. "What did you put in these drinks—truth serum?"

"Special formula," I told her.

"Effective," she said, finishing hers.

"Another?" I inquired.

She held the glass out to me in her delicate hand. "I'm in your care, Klick. You make the drinks, I'll cook the dinner. After that we'll play it by ear. You're the musician. You must be good at playing by ear."

"Improvising," I said.

"That too."

As I reached the door I secretly breathed on the glass. The heart was still there. It came to life and then slowly faded away.

18

The evening could not have been going better. Then Debbie
Benton called. When the phone rang I was just pouring a
Cakebread Cellars Chardonnay and admiring the way Nicole had
quickly adjusted to a foreign kitchen. She had found a crepe rec-
ipe in my *New York Times* cookbook and was dividing her attention between a wok of stir-fried vegetables and the cooking of
the crepes. I had offered to help twice and both times been
shooed away. Never ask more than twice is what I'd been taught,
so I went about setting the table and chasing down the
Cakebread Cellars. Nothing was too good for Nicole. I used
Lyel's Blue Line china, his Orefors crystal, and some family sil-
verware that dates back to the Civil War. I put a bouquet of silk
roses and irises in a Swedish crystal vase and flanked it with two
glass lanterns that burn a tiny wick and look about as elegant as
elegant can get. The table itself was dressed in a pure white dou-
ble-stitched linen, and for effect I had selected the soft-rose cotton napkins and had stood them on the Blue Line like small ships
setting sail. I dimmed the lights to a perfectly romantic sheen
(the stove remained lit by its own fluorescent, which I couldn't
wait to turn off), and I flicked on the outside flood that high-

lighted the lawn, and in the distance the thick, towering willow bushes that rimmed the slough.

The minute the phone rang I was annoyed I had not had the good sense to turn it off. There are times the phone rings and you know you have trouble, and this was one of those times.

She glanced over her shoulder and looked at me. Her expression made me feel as if we had been living together for ages. We *both* knew it was trouble. She watched as I reluctantly stepped toward the phone and then she oohed for she had noticed the table and her attention remained fixed on it, like a child infatuated with a new toy.

I answered the phone and mumbled. Debbie Benton was hysterical. I said yes three times and then hung up. Nicole looked at me. She had my apron tied around her and it had never looked better. Aprons are meant to look that way, I thought, full of curves and tight around the waist. "Debbie Benton," I said. "She's hysterical."

"We can warm it up when you get back."

"I'm sorry."

"I know."

"I'll put another log on. The library's in the television room."

"I brought something along with me. And I can get the fire. You get going. The sooner you go, the sooner you get back."

"I should have turned the phone off."

"That would have left Debbie Benton in a bad place. Go on. I'll be fine. In Europe it's fashionable to eat late."

I approached her, placed a finger gently under her chin and kissed her. She closed her eyes and her lips slid smoothly over mine and then drew away. I heard her drop the wooden spoon into the wok and then felt warm hands on either side of my face as she pulled my head down and kissed me again, staying with me longer, making me remember it. "One for the road," she said, grinning and turning back to her cooking. I wanted to wrap my arms around her from behind and hug her and nuzzle my nose into the crook of her neck, but I resisted. I kissed her on top of the head instead and said, "One for the cook."

"Hurry up, Klick. Begone."

I moved too quickly to the hook on the wall, found my way into the sleeves of my L.L. Bean flight jacket and opened the front door. "Lock up behind me," I said. She nodded and I left. I didn't notice how long it took the truck to warm up. I was plenty warm without its help.

●

Debbie Benton had the door to her condominium locked and chained. She struggled with the chain and finally admitted me, relocking it behind. Although a naturally pretty woman, she did not look well. Her eyes were puffy, she wore no makeup, and her hair needed a good brushing. She had a cigarette going and was too nervous to sit down. She offered me a beer and I accepted, wishing it was a glass of Cakebread Cellars Chardonnay instead, and that I was back with Nicole. I sat on her couch and noticed for the first time that every window had a blind or a curtain pulled.

"I'm sorry to bother you this time of night. It's just that I'm pretty scared, and I'm not sure what to do about it, and I thought you might be able to help me, and I couldn't be sure who else to trust." She sucked hard on the cigarette, inspiring the red ember, and looked at me with pleading eyes.

"Why are you scared?" I asked.

"I didn't think anything of it, at first. I mean, why would anybody be watching *me,* following *me?* But I'm sure they are— someone is—and I don't know what to do. I've seen a million cop shows, you know, and for the life of me I can't think what the hell I'm supposed to do. I'm sure as hell not going to confront the bastard, I'll tell you that. And I keep thinking I've lost him and there he is again."

I suppressed a smile. "You know what he looks like?"

"Not exactly. A white pickup truck is all. Same truck every time. Here, at the gallery, even outside a dress shop: That's the creepy thing about it. It's just like he's keeping an eye on me."

"Is he out there now?"

"I'm sure he is. Out there somewhere. Looking. Waiting." She raised her voice. "What the hell does he want?" Her ash tumbled to the carpet and splashed into a small gray puddle.

"He probably wants you to lead him to Paul."

"Me? I don't know where Paul is. I have no idea where Paul is! Paul? Oh my God, what have I gotten myself into?" She collapsed into an overstuffed chair facing me and snuffed the cigarette out in a crowded ashtray.

"There is a growing group who assume Paul may contact you sooner or later and ask you to join him. Whoever that is out there must want him as badly as his wife does." I paused to let this sink in and then said, "I think the best thing you can do, Debbie, is tell me everything you can that might help me put some of the pieces together. I don't give things away for free. I can help you, but you've got to give me something first. You've got to show me you're willing to play along."

"How chivalrous of you."

"This is my job, Debbie. I don't do this to be chivalrous."

"So I noticed."

I waited for her to start talking. I was eager to be back in my little cabin, and this was one evening I wouldn't be strung along by anyone. At that particular moment I didn't care about Paul Russell, or Sheriff Hudson, or Debbie Benton, or even the money. At that moment all I cared about was a brown-eyed angel who was waiting for me with lukewarm crepes and a well-chilled Chardonnay. I'd played my final card and stood. My head bumped a mobile of humpback whales that hung from an exposed beam. The whales swam though the air frantically.

"Wait!" barked Debbie Benton.

"I already have," I told her. I took a step toward the door.

"Paul was a dealer. Small-time," she said.

I stopped and turned. She motioned to the couch and I sat back down, avoiding the whales, who had settled down.

"Nothing big. He acted as middleman a couple of times on some out-of-state runs. It's how he kept himself alive for the last few years. Until *her*. He'd package a couple of keys and then break them out into ounces and sell them in pounds and half-pounds to others around town."

"He ever deal in coke?" I asked.

"No. He did a little himself from time to time, but nothing heavy. He dealt in grass. This whole town smokes grass. It's a party town and the market is steady and strong. Paul has been in on it for years and years. He made a nice little income that allowed him to play most of the time. Paul likes to play. Likes to gamble. Cards, horses, it doesn't matter. When he married Nicole, he did less dealing. Didn't need it anymore."

"But," I added.

"But when we started hanging out together, when we started *seeing* each other, he decided he wasn't so sure he would stick with Nicole."

I didn't like that term "*seeing* each other." They had been sleeping together, and even that was putting it mildly, for I doubted they had once slept while together. No, they had been having sex with each other, copulating, committing adultery behind Nicole's back, and I resented this woman horribly for it. "And?"

"And then he started talking about a big deal he had in the making. A whole new thing, with lots of potential. He flew down to Vegas a couple of times. The last time was maybe a week before he disappeared. He seemed all excited."

"And you made plans."

She paused to light another cigarette. Once she had it going, she said, "Yeah. We made some plans. But not like you think. I wasn't going to meet him someplace or anything like that. He was going to come up here and pick me up. Tuesday. He was supposed to pick me up Tuesday afternoon. We were going to fly down to Vegas, do a little business, and then head down to Cancun for the winter. I swear that's the way it was going to be, only he never showed up. I didn't think much of it. Paul isn't the most reliable person in the universe, and these deals have ways of not coming through when they're supposed to."

"And what about Greg Sweetland? What did he have to do with it?"

"I swear, that's only a name to me. He might have mentioned the name Greg a couple of times. I thought he hunted with the guy. That's as much as I know. I never met him and I don't know what he had to do with Paul. Paul never gave me any of the details. He knew I didn't approve of his dealing, and I warned him about getting involved with anything big. He claimed he was through with dealing, that he had something better going. That was for my sake, I think. I told him it was stupid to get too big. He had a nice simple thing going up here. Made enough to pay the bills and ski. He should have left it at that."

"Who did he work with in Las Vegas?"

"No idea. None whatsoever. Claimed he was dealing with a whole new class of people. I think maybe he was lying."

"Did you know he stole at least fifty thousand dollars from his wife?"

"What? You're kidding! Fifty *thousand*? Jesus Christ!"

"That's privileged information, Debbie."

"I understand."

"She'd like it back. I don't think she much cares about getting her husband back."

Debbie nodded, deep in thought. Her brow knitted and she took another drag of the cigarette. I was beginning to get a raw throat. I drank half the beer and waited for her to say something. "Maybe it wasn't grass," she said. "Maybe it had something to do with something else."

My head was swimming with possibilities. I tried to look at Paul's taking the money from a variety of angles. "What about Harper?" I asked. "He took Harper with him on Tuesday."

"I don't get that. Unless he *was* going hunting. Maybe the deal, or whatever, fell through, and Paul was just killing a day. He liked to hunt when he got uptight. It was his way of relaxing."

"He wasn't coming up here?"

"Not for that. Not that way." She blushed. "He would have at least called me. Besides, he knew I was working at the gallery on Tuesday. That's why he was going to meet me late afternoon. He wouldn't have taken Harper unless he was going hunting. He didn't like the dog much, but evidently Harper was both a good pointer and retriever."

"Maybe he just wanted Nicole to *think* he was going hunting," I thought aloud. She ignored the comment.

"What am I supposed to do?" She looked at me again with a frightened face. "God, I can't even sleep knowing somebody's out there keeping an eye on this place."

"How do you know they're still there?"

"Peek out that window. I'll bet you anything there's a white pickup truck over by that corner." I moved over to the window and split the curtains. "Through the trees, you can just make it out. Parked on the corner in front of the brown condos. Is it there?"

"Yes."

"When I drove out last night, I noticed someone sitting behind the wheel. When I came back an hour later, the truck was gone. When I was heading to bed I pulled the curtains, and there was the truck again. It has a perfect view of this apartment."

"It has a good view of several of the condos. You can't be sure—"

"I'm telling you, he's keeping an eye on me. I know he is. And I don't know what the hell to do about it."

"Okay." I stood.

"What are you doing?"

"Leaving."

"Well, thanks a lot for nothing."

"I'll have a talk with your friend in the truck and explain he's bothering you. He doesn't have a view of the parking lot. You take my truck up to the Lodge and take a room. Make sure the brights are on. He won't be able to see inside the truck if the brights are on. Leave me your keys. If I'm successful I'll drive your car over to the Lodge and switch back to my truck."

"What name do I register under?"

"I'd suggest Debbie Benton. It'll make it easier for me to find you. This isn't *Simon and Simon,* Debbie. You're only going to be there one night, and you probably know the desk clerk anyway."

"Okay. Okay. I get the message."

"Your keys," I said. "Mine are in the truck. I want you to wait five minutes. I may be able to take advantage of the truck leaving." She dug her keys out of her purse and handed them to me. "Is there a back way out of here?" I asked.

"Only the balcony," she said.

"That'll do." I opened the sliding glass door and stepped out onto the balcony.

"You're going to jump?"

"I'm going to drop. Remember, give me a five-minute lead."

I stepped over the railing and lowered myself down until I was hanging from the floor of the balcony. Arms overhead, fully stretched, I reach nine feet. It left me a little over a two-foot drop. I heard Debbie close and lock the sliding glass door.

Using the remainder of the condominiums as a block, I moved away from the parked truck Debbie was worried about. I came out a full block and a small hill below the truck in question. I walked across the street to another set of condos and now was completely out of view. I walked around the block, increasing my strides after checking my watch and discovering I only had a minute or two until Debbie would be leaving in the truck.

These condominiums seemed a bit more upscale than Debbie's group. The landscaping was well thought out and the stucco-and-beam construction appealed to me. I stopped at the third corner. The truck was parked about fifteen yards ahead of me. Debbie was right. A man was sitting behind the wheel, his back partially against the door so he could look right at her condo. The motor was running—to keep him warm, I thought—and I could hear the faint pulse of rock music even from here. He looked to be a big man, maybe an inch or two shorter than me, and for an instant I wondered if he wasn't a Sweetland.

I heard my truck start up. Engines have a distinctive sound and I knew mine well. I have an intake valve that refuses to sit just right and the resulting clatter is as unique as a fingerprint. The lights came on and my truck backed up. I saw her switch them to high and she came out of the driveway and down the small road toward the stop sign.

The man in the truck took notice. He sat up and switched off the engine. The music stopped as well.

I moved quickly, straight for his door, hoping to God he hadn't locked it. But as I reached the truck I saw the button was down. Perhaps leaning against it, he had locked it by accident. The triangular vent was not latched, however. I'd locked myself out of my own truck enough times to know how to open one up.

I rammed my hand through the vent window, dropped it quickly before he understood what was going on, and leaned forward, fishing for the handle. I touched the metal and yanked up on the handle, pulling on the door at the same time. I was quick enough, and he was slow enough, that he came tumbling out the door backward spewing some choice words.

I reached out to catch him and pull him to his feet, but he

used some sort of move on my wrist that dropped me to my knees. I'm not a big fan of fighting, though I've done enough of it to know how to keep from being sore the next day. These were the guys I feared: the ones that knew the Far East moves. There seem to be more and more of them every day, and one of these days I suppose I'm going to have to take a course to keep up with them. Once he had me to my knees, he kicked me and sent me over backward.

Free of him, I came to my feet and deflected his next effort. I've fought a few of these guys and can avoid most of the novice routines. It's the darker belts one has to worry about. This guy was somewhere between yellow and green, if I have my colors right. I'm your basic wear-them-down kind of fighter. With my size and quickness this has proved to be the winning strategy. No facial work. I don't like cutting a person and I don't like breaking my hands. I blocked another of his wild swings and hit him square in the gut. He expelled a great amount of air and buckled over briefly, looking me in the eye. A foot came out of nowhere, and if I hadn't skirted to my left, I think he would have broken my knee. I kicked the inside of his outstretched leg, however, and spun him around, dropping him to the partially frozen ground. One good gut punch and he was motionless beneath me. I grabbed him by the shoulders and helped him to his feet, slamming him against the truck.

I patted him down. No weapon. I grabbed for his wallet.

"You stupid asshole," he said. "Read it and weep." He tried to turn around to face me, but I wouldn't let him. I had to hold the open wallet at an angle to catch the light.

"You can read, can't you?" he asked.

I could, and I did, and I felt my stomach sink. The card with the photograph listed him as George Blokowski, Special Agent, DEA. Drug Enforcement Agency. "Oh, shit," I said.

"That's right," he replied. "You stepped in it this time, friend. Let go of me and get in the truck."

I obeyed, handing him back his wallet.

"Sorry," I said, once both doors were closed.

"You're going to be a lot sorrier by the time this is over. Show me your driver's license." I handed him my wallet. He asked me to remove the license and hand it to him, which I did.

He switched on the overhead light and read it. Then he handed it back. "Well, Mr. Klick, what was that all about?"

"You've been following Debbie Benton. I mixed you up with someone else."

"And what is your relationship to Ms. Benton?"

I know better than to screw around with federal agents. If they want you to be in trouble, there is little to stop them. And I didn't want to be in trouble. Not tonight. Not with Nicole waiting on my couch. I wanted to be down the road. "I'm looking into the disappearance of a man. Ms. Benton is his lover. I was hired by the man's wife. Ms. Benton called me because you had frightened her."

"You a private dick?"

I loathe that term. It makes me feel like a penis for hire. "No. It's kind of a hobby."

"I could arrest you for assault, Klick."

"I know."

"But in a town this small it would probably make the press and I can't afford that. Do you follow me?"

I nodded and then he switched off the interior light because a car was approaching. He waited until it passed us. Looking straight ahead, following the car with his eyes, he said, "Leave the investigating up to us. You'll muddy the water."

"You're investigating Russell?"

"Who or what we're investigating is none of your business. Who we're keeping an eye on is also none of your business. Was that Benton in your truck?"

"Yes."

"What did you have in mind?"

"I'm going to switch cars with her at The Lodge and then go home."

"Good idea." He waited a moment before asking, "Who did you think I was?"

"I couldn't be sure."

"Don't fuck with me, Klick."

"I thought maybe one of the Sweetlands. But not until I saw you from behind. You're big like the Sweetlands. Before that, I couldn't be sure. I was hoping to find out who you were."

"Mission accomplished."

"Indeed."

"No arrest. No charges. But it'll go down in my report, and if you screw up again, we'll bring charges against you. The kind of charges that are no fun to try and get out of."

"Your plates are Nevada. You traced this from Las Vegas, didn't you?"

"How we traced this is none of your business."

"Is Paul Russell alive? Do you guys have him? I could quit a lot sooner if I knew his whereabouts."

He hesitated. "We don't know," he said, and I believed him. "What else can you tell me that might help us out?"

"Paul Russell embezzled at least fifty thousand dollars from his wife. She'd like the money back. He was a small-time dealer in this area and may have had a big deal going down on Tuesday. That's the day he disappeared—along with the money. A guy named Greg Sweetland had his face blown off on Tuesday, and the county coroner and a local doctor seemed anxious to turn him into ashes, which is exactly what they did. I don't know how Sweetland fits in, I don't know for sure that whoever they burned up was actually Sweetland, and tonight I found out that Las Vegas may have been involved in whatever Russell had going. Now I meet an agent from the DEA driving a rig with Nevada plates who's keeping an eye on Russell's former lover. So I figure you might know where Russell is."

"I don't. We'd like to know. That's all I can tell you."

"If you find him and you find what remains of the money, don't go locking it up in a vault somewhere assuming it's dirty money. It belongs to his wife."

"And a percentage to you, I assume."

"No comment."

"Give us room to operate, Klick."

"I'd appreciate the same consideration."

"Not a chance. Go get your truck back. And if she asks, tell her she had it wrong. Tell her the truck was empty."

"I'll do it, but she won't buy it. Your surveillance wasn't exactly subtle. Nevada plates? No wonder we're losing the war on drugs."

He glared and did his best to look tough. He wasn't very good at that either.

"Any *other* ideas?" I asked.

He looked away. "We'll go in together. You'll get your keys and be gone. Looks like it's time for me to have a talk with her." He retrieved a short wave radio mike from under the dash that I hadn't noticed. "Snow Goose, this is Gander," he said into the microphone.

"Cute," I said.

"Get out of here," he said angrily, hand off the button so no one could hear.

I slammed the truck door and heard him mumble into the radio as I walked away.

19

I let myself in through the front door quietly. The front door is mostly glass and I could see her curled up on the couch, asleep under an afghan, the fading orange glow of the fire's embers reflecting off the chimney of a hurricane lamp. I knew she hadn't activated the security system, because if she had, my entrance through the property gate would have sounded a bell that would have awakened her. Then it occurred to me that perhaps the bell *had* sounded and she was simply playing asleep to see what I would do with her. I unlocked the door and headed to the security panel, which is hidden in the front coat closet. It works off a twenty-second delay—just enough time to enter the "disable" code and stop the alarms from sounding. After I disabled the house code, I punched in the numbers for the fence alarm to see if it was activated and it was. So she was either playing with me, or she had fallen quickly back to sleep.

A third of the Chardonnay remained. I poured myself a deep glass, quietly placed a small log on the fire, and took a chair across from the couch and studied her. I decided she was asleep. Her mouth was cracked open slightly and her breathing was long and regular. Her face looked peaceful and even childlike in sleep. Beautiful. A sprig of her brown hair cascaded down over her chin, and at the corners of her eyes were the faintest beginnings of crow's feet. The afghan heaved with her breaths, her hands wrapped up in it, holding it close to her neck, keeping her warm.

I sipped on my wine. I had only known this woman a matter of days. Days. And yet my heart was fully with her. I felt no urgency to hurry our friendship or relationship (I wasn't sure which it was). And though I longed for intimacy with her, I knew if it would come at all, it would come on its own time schedule. We both would know when the moment was right. There was no need to force it.

She made a sleep sound and stretched a leg. The fire sparked and crackled with the fresh log. Some lyrics came to me and I rose to find a scrap of paper and write them down. This done, I returned to my chair and worked on the wine, my attention split between the mesmerizing fire and this enchanting woman. A half hour passed. My wineglass emptied and I decided it was too late to pour myself another. I went into her room and turned down the bed. Then I went back to the couch and knelt by her. I could hear her breathing and the heat from the fire warmed my right side. I slipped a hand under the afghan and hooked her knees. She came partially awake and smiled demurely. I ran my left arm under her back and up to where I could support her head. I said, "Here we go," softly, and used my knees to lift us both slowly. She hummed and wrapped her arms around my chest loosely.

I carried her toward her bedroom, dodging the furniture, savoring the moment. Her hair brushed the Boston ferns as we passed the front door and this elicited another small grin. I lay her down on the sheets, pulled off her shoes and covered her up. She grabbed my hand as I tucked her in and, eyes closed, pulled me toward her. She pecked me on the cheek and said, "Night, Klick. Dinner's in the fridge."

I punched the electric blanket on "Lo" and switched off the light, shutting the door quietly. When I was nearly through my second delicious crepe I heard water running in the bathroom and I was glad she'd have a chance to get out of her clothes and into a nightgown. I don't like waking up fully clothed, and I've never met anyone who did.

I cleaned up my dishes, closed the wood stove, and set the

living room thermostat to 55, changing my mind then and bringing it up to 65 for my guest in the morning. I'm used to a brisk kitchen until the wood stove has warmed the house; my guests seldom are.

Within a few minutes I was in bed, lights out, eyes open, thinking about Nicole. I knew it was going to be a rough night. I have a fertile imagination, and I don't sleep well when it's active. I considered reading but decided to daydream instead. The stories I could create about Nicole and me were better than any I could find in a book. And then I must have dozed off.

I awakened when the storm began. We get fluke lightning storms in the mountains at all times of the year. I've even seen lightning in the middle of a blizzard. No meteorologist has ever explained this phenomenon to me. It must have something to do with the friction between temperature layers. This storm was as magnificent as any summer storm we've had. The activity was mostly up in the clouds—very few spikes to the ground—bright blue-white flashes illuminating the view from my window as far as I could see. I looked to my clock to see what time it was and realized the power was out. I settled back down and listened to the angry rumble of thunder as the center of the storm approached.

I didn't hear her enter the room because of the thunder. I felt the covers move and then two cold feet slid in next to mine and a soft, warm body with only a thin layer of silk or satin between us pressed up against my bare back and those beautiful hands wrapped around my chest and pulled us close together, back to front. "Cold," she said quietly, a small shudder. "And just a little bit scared."

I reached behind me and ruffled her hair playfully, my heart pounding. I felt her cheek pressed up against my back. The strobe lights continued across the lawn and the deafening cracks of thunder erupted overhead. We stayed this way, like spoons, for quite some time. There was no way I would find sleep with Nicole pressed this tightly against me. She must have read my mind, for she inched away from me and pulled me to where I lay flat on my back. Then she crawled a leg across mine and leaned her supple warmth against me, stroked my hair and kissed me long and nice. There was no holding back for me. I came open like the petals of a daylily in the morning sun. Our hands searched each other, hers like a wind across my skin, exploring, stimulating. My fingertips wandered over her, eliciting small coos of approval. We became caught up in each other's scents and pulse, blindly breaking new ground while the storm afforded us an occasional glimpse of each other. Then we became almost frantic, rolling over one another like two children playfully fighting. Kissing, groping. And then absolute stillness as we found ourselves together. A moist blissful unity overwhelmed us as the final echoes of the powerful storm slipped quietly to the south, and our eyes came alive in the dull blue light.

20

We remained in bed until a few minutes past ten. We didn't talk
'business.' It was the farthest thing from my mind. We talked
about the beauty of the lightning storm. I talked about her
beauty. She tried to talk about mine. When I left the house Nicole was still swallowed up in my maroon robe, eating a honey
bun and waiting for the espresso machine to finish making another cup. She had brushed her hair while I had showered and
we had consumed our first cup silently staring over the rims of
our demitasses and making eyes at each other. There were no
attempts at excuses, and I appreciated that. I hated to leave,
really hated to leave her, but now there was a new urgency for
me to finish the Paul Russell case. I wanted it over so I could
concentrate on more important matters.

●

Sheriff Hudson looked exactly as he had on my previous visit.
Uniforms have a way of doing that. His bulk was rooted firmly
behind the desk, his fingerless hand drumming irregular rhythms
as I entered. We shook hands, though he didn't rise and I took a
chair without an offer.

"What now?" he inquired.

"I have a few questions I wanted to run by you."

"Surprise."

"I wondered if you could tell me who the big guy out at the Sweetlands is? He's about my size, short cropped hair, a little heavier—"

"That sounds like all of them."

"New boots and shiny new belt buckle."

"Wouldn't know." He knitted his brow.

"Big son of a bitch. A little light in the brains."

"Larry. He's Greg's older brother. Six Sweetland boys in all. Five of 'em still live out there. They got families now. A couple of them got grandchildren and they aren't forty yet. Greg was second to the oldest, then Scott. The oldest boy, Larry, is a little slow, you know, and Greg has always run the show. I imagine it's Scott's turn now that Greg is gone, and that's a shame because Scott doesn't have the sense the next boy, Tommy, has. Tommy is almost as good at spotting breeding stock as Greg. Scott's got his mind in the gutter most of the time. Inherited his father's habit for the drink. He can be a mean son of a bitch when he's loaded. If you want to believe the town gossip, most of the children out there are Larry's, regardless of the mother." Hudson found this amusing. He laughed until he saw I didn't appreciate the comment. "They'd do better if they turned things over to Tommy."

"Is Tommy tall and kind of lanky? Big without looking big?"

"That could be Abe. You shouldn't a gone out there, Klick. We talked about that."

I nodded.

"That woman's seen more pain and suffering than any woman you'll ever know. I guaranfuckintee you that. You shouldn't have gone out there. I told you not to."

"I went for a hike up around the Sweetland place and one of the boys—I think it might have been Abe—tried to kill me. How do you explain that?"

Hudson leaned forward. "If you had fuckin' ears in your head you wouldn't a gone out there in the first place. Your own damn fault. Serve you right one of them boys blows your head off. Them people is real private. I already told you that.

Got the place posted real good. You get yourself shot there, the law's on their side, mister. I'd think about that next time if I were you."

Hudson scratched his head with the hand missing the finger and his tight-set eyes looked me over. "What the hell you want up there?"

"Answers. I'd like somebody around here to give me some answers. I'm not particularly happy with the way things have been explained concerning Paul Russell."

"Like I said, the Sweetlands are private folk. There are five, maybe six families in these parts like the Sweetlands. Old families that done a lot of intermixing. A lot of crossed bloodlines in those families and they tend to keep to themselves. Town folk tend to make fun of them, so they stay at their own places, off on their own. I doubt Abe was trying to kill you. But if he caught you poking around, he sure as hell would try and scare you off. Wouldn't put that past them."

"The man had a gun aimed at me from about four feet— that's a felony—and his finger was on the trigger. And something else. For all their poverty, that odd one, Larry, is wearing about a three-hundred-dollar belt buckle and snakeskin boots. And they've got what looks like a brand-new satellite dish. How do you explain that?"

He tensed. "Mighta sold a horse, I suppose. Greg was damned near God when it came to training horses. Listen, maybe I better go out there and have a talk with them boys. They don't got no phone out there. Lucky to have electricity. But I can't guarantee they won't do the same thing next time. My advice to you, bucko, is to keep the hell out of there. That's what I do, and I'm the goddamned sheriff."

"I've spoken to Nicole Russell. She's ready to go ahead and press charges against her husband for taking that fifty thousand. If the police in Hill City are right, then Russell isn't in this state any longer. Where should she file the complaint?"

"Oh, Christ. Here, I suppose. I don't mind telling you these interstate filings are one pain in the ass. She's sure he took it?"

"She didn't take it and it's gone. They're in the middle of a full audit. It's either him or the bank. What's your bet?"

He glared at me. "Send her in. We'll take the complaint."

"Thanks loads."

"Fifty thousand, huh?"

I nodded. "At least. And probably cash."

He whistled. "Hell of a lot of money."

"It certainly is."

"Send her down. We'll do whatever she wants. Even bring in the federal boys if she wants."

It reminded me of Agent Blokowski. I said, "I understand you supplied some fingerprints of Greg Sweetland for Dr. Kupps to use for identification."

"Kupps tell you that?"

I nodded.

"He drinks too much. Ought to stop practicing medicine, if you ask me."

"Is it true?"

"The fingerprints? Sure it's true. What do you think? With a face like that you gotta find a way to ID the body."

"Why did you have Sweetland's prints on file? What got him printed?"

Hudson looked at me questionably. "I sure as hell don't have to tell you that. Do I?"

"It's a matter of public record, isn't it?"

"The man's dead and gone. No sense in smearing some old shit on the walls for the sake of your curiosity, if you ask me. It was a long time ago. He was a kid. Lots of kids around here find their way into trouble at one time or another. That's all I got to say."

Ridland is a small town and it's a place people still cover for each other, so it didn't surprise me that Hudson didn't want to dig up Sweetland's past. I decided to put Nicole on it, or better yet, Lyel. A couple of hours in the back issues of the weekly tabloid would answer my question.

"I'll tell you what bothers me, Sheriff. It bothers me that Sweetland's body was cremated within hours of the coroner receiving it. There must be photos. In your records, I mean. I'd appreciate seeing them, if I could." I thought I noticed a sheen on Hudson's lip. I couldn't tell if it was nerves or simply coffee that he had failed to wipe off.

"What the hell? Bates is a good man, honest as the day is long. Not saying that Kupps isn't liquored up most of the time. And men that drink that much end up in trouble more often than not. But you got this wrong. It was the *family* that wanted the body cremated. Not us. They wanted to avoid some expense and so they had the body cremated. They didn't want no autopsy, and the cause of death was certainly plain enough to see. As for the photos . . . I haven't even seen any photos. Have to look into that."

"What about Bill Clark?"

He looked frustrated. "Bill Clark didn't do it. If you want to know the truth, Klick, I think your Paul Russell probably did it, but I got nothing that says he did, so there ain't nothing I can do about it. Otherwise I'd slap a manslaughter charge on him."

I decided to tell him about Harper. I told him I thought the dog might have been cared for by a child. Who else would put Band-Aids on gunshot wounds? I explained the scene in the Sweetland kitchen where a very young boy had been asking, "Where'd *he* go?" Something no one had wanted to discuss. I questioned why Paul Russell would shoot his own dog after accidentally shooting Sweetland. Hudson looked stunned.

"You saying the dog was found?" he questioned. "Alive?"

"Made it all the way up-valley to the Russell home," I explained.

"Well, I don't know why or how the dog took some buckshot, but I'll sure as hell tell you one thing. That connects Russell to the shooting as far as I'm concerned. That's enough to issue a warrant. You can send Mrs. Russell down if you want, but she needn't bother if she don't want to. As of this moment, Paul Russell is wanted by the state of Idaho for questioning in the shooting death of Greg Sweetland. If we put that out on the wire it will sure as hell draw a lot more attention than a husband robbing a wife." He picked up a pen and began searching his desk drawers.

"I don't think Russell killed him, Sheriff."

"So you said."

"You want to hear what I think?"

"Not particularly."

"I think it was the other way around. If I had to put money on it, I'd bet that Greg Sweetland is still alive. Paul Russell is the one who got cremated, either accidentally, or on purpose."

Hudson looked up angrily. "Good thing you ain't a betting man," he said. "Or are you?"

21

I drove my truck about half a block and then pulled off in front
of the pay phone that sits outside the Silver Dollar Café. I
phoned Lyel. On the third ring he answered in his typically
happy voice. For years I thought this voice was contrived, but
I've learned to accept it. It is the essence of Lyel: optimistic,
energetic, enthusiastic. And a touch snobby. There is no one I
know who has a better grasp of what it takes to make it through
life than he. He has built a foundation of security through
wisdom. His theory is: The more you know, the less there is out
there to frighten you. So he has spent the better part of his adult
life packing himself with information, converting the information
into knowledge, gleaning it from any available source, be it a bag
lady in New York City or the Library of Congress. He is something of a walking encyclopedia. When you match this with one
of the naturally strongest men you've ever met, you come up
with a kind of thinking gorilla—a big but tender Einstein who
can bench-press 310 pounds.

I briefed him on my discussion with Hudson, pausing briefly
after mentioning Hudson's refusal to tell me about Sweetland's
priors, so Lyel would know this was the reason for my call.
There wasn't time to fill him in on the DEA agent. I suggested

that combing the weekly rag might tell us something, since the paper lists arrests opposite "Doonesbury" each week. Lyel didn't need the nose ring. He accepted the mission gladly, pointing out the more direct route would be to go to the county courthouse and simply look up any decisions against Greg Sweetland.

"I knew there was a reason I called you," I told him.

"To further prove that your bloodlines date back to Tom Sawyer, I think, which only further supports my belief you are a fictional character living a lie. Your subtlety, or lack thereof, never ceases to amaze me. Do you have a fence that needs whitewashing as well?"

"We have fences that need stretching. But when we tried that last spring, you broke the fence stretcher, if you remember correctly."

"What do I do once I have the Sweetland info?"

"Getting fairly cocky, aren't we? Just like that, you're going to get the Sweetland information?"

"If he was taken to court, it will take me all of a matter of minutes. You say five years ago, maybe more?"

"Only guessing."

"I'll start there and work back, if I have to. Should I call you?"

"Let me buy you a drink. I'll introduce you to the mystery lady."

"She's at your place?" Lyel was always kind enough to refer to *his* guest cabin as my place. And I never missed it when he did.

"Don't make a big deal over it. It was her idea. I asked her to leave town, she asked me if she could move in."

"You're so *gallant,* Klick. So self-sacrificing and chivalrous. What a noble gesture."

"Is that out of your system, I hope?"

"I promise to be the perfect gentleman."

"Be less than perfect, Lyel, just for a few hours. I wilt under competitive conditions."

"Duly noted."

At that moment I noticed RID 1 moving down Main Street away from me, Sheriff Hudson at the wheel. He signaled and turned left onto Pole Road. I thought I knew where he was headed. "Got to go," I told Lyel and hung up.

I turned around and headed after RID 1, maintaining so much distance between us that I couldn't see him up ahead. It was only a guess as to where he was heading, but he had mentioned paying the Sweetlands a visit, and for some reason I wanted to witness the meeting. I have to rely on my urges. They fail me nearly as often as they prove valuable, but if you give up trusting yourself, who is left? I keep a pair of binoculars in the glove box because the area is heavy with birds of prey, and on any drive you are apt to chance upon a sight worthy of a closer look. There is nothing more frustrating for a birder than to catch such an opportunity and be ill equipped to enjoy and partake in it. I bought the binoculars mail-order through Edmonds Scientific. Expensive, they are worth every penny. Last time I had forgotten them. This time I did not.

From my earlier visit to the Sweetland ranch I knew the perfect spot from which to secure a good view of the compound without being anywhere near the ranch itself. A ridge of sage-covered hills flanked the far drainage, and I knew from my trips to Crystal Creek that an old mining road led most of the way up the backside of that drainage. That's why I drove past the turnoff that led out toward the Sweetlands' and continued another mile and half down Pole Road. Looking to my left as I passed their turn, I saw the feathery plume of brown dust rise behind a speeding vehicle headed out toward the ranch and I knew it had to be Hudson. I gave the old truck a little more gas, put up with that noisy valve and reached a sportsman's access road less than a minute later. I turned left down the dirt road and maintained a consistent fifty miles per hour until I saw the old mine road up ahead. I was forced to take this rut-filled road more slowly and carefully for fear of blowing a tire or breaking an axle. After about five minutes I reached the debris that had been left behind to decay following the closing of the mine and I shut off the truck. A flow of clear springwater ran from the collapsed mouth of the mine, spilling over the road and cutting a trench down the face of the near-barren hillside. I grabbed my binoculars and scrambled up the steep slope, imagining that a hundred years before, a few dozen men had tunneled miles below me in search of silver, zinc, and lead.

I reached the top of the ridge and sat down amid the shoulder-height sage, well hidden and camouflaged. The Sweetland ranch was farther away than I had anticipated. Nonetheless, through the binoculars I had an unobstructed view of the area between the house and barns. I identified Sheriff Hudson's patrol car and the uniformed sheriff leaning against its side, impatiently tapping his foot. After a moment, Larry came out of the trailer alongside the barn, his new buckle catching the sunlight. He was followed only moments later by the lanky one whom I had left tied with his own shoelaces. Hudson leaned forward, his hands behind him on the fender, and I could tell he was shouting. Then he stepped forward and pushed the lanky one, Abe, so hard that the young man fell to the ground on his butt. He was plenty angry at the way they had treated me, and I reveled in seeing them berated this way. But then something strange happened. Hudson stepped up to Larry, who towered over him, and unhooked the man's belt buckle. He pulled the entire belt from the man and dropped it into the dirt. Then he stomped on it with his boot and twisted the shiny buckle into the rock and dirt and manure. He followed this by dragging his own shoes against the new snake hide of Larry's boots, and even from here I knew the damage being done. Where did a sheriff get off doing this? I wondered. He pointed roughly in the directions of the barns, gesticulated wildly and began screaming at both men again. Abe had climbed back to his feet. Both the Sweetlands' postures implied a reluctant but accepted subservience. The sheriff continued to harangue them. He followed this by walking over to the nearest barn and I thought I saw him tug on the handle of the large barn door. It was a curious thing to do before leaving, but that's what he did. A minute later he was back in the patrol car and heading out of the ranch at a good clip.

I skied on the heels of my boots down the slope to my truck, managed a delicate three-point turn and bounced my way back on tired leaf springs toward the sportsman's access. I was back on Pole Road a few minutes later, and I knew that Hudson had to be in front of me, the speed he had been driving. I was in no hurry to catch up. I kept an eye out for any sign of a car in front of me, and drove at about forty-five.

I couldn't be sure it was Hudson's patrol car, but a few minutes down Pole Road I noticed off to my right another plume of dust rising behind a speeding car. I pulled to the shoulder and let a truck and horse trailer pass me. I grabbed my binoculars from the glove box and trained them on the plume of dust and then on the car responsible. It *was* Hudson's car. Once Hudson was out of sight, I drove to the turnoff. According to the mailbox, there was only one ranch at the end of this road, way up the drainage, with what had to be a spectacular view of Crystal Creek. The mailbox read RED CLAY RANCH. I knew of an attorney named Clay. His place? Why did Hudson want to speak to an attorney?

●

I parked behind the post office and spent about twenty minutes reading throwaways I fished from the trash can. Bored with the advertisements, I turned my attention to the bulletin board. Someone was selling a skimobile. Cordwood. A dance at the armory sponsored by the Senior Citizen Center and featuring Vintage—The Sounds You Remember. Mary was willing to iron shirts for seventy-five cents, dresses for a dollar. A couple of high school girls were available for baby-sitting. Their ad was more modern: A phone number was hand-printed repeatedly at the bottom of the typing paper and they had carefully cut between each number with scissors so you could tear the number off and take it with you. A few of the numbers had been ungraciously torn from the sheet.

I looked out the glass door and watched two young boys ride bikes past. I remembered clipping a playing card to my front fork with a wooden clothespin what seemed like a century before. I hadn't seen a wooden clothespin in years. Now the bikes had black boxes mounted to the handlebars that made *Star Wars* sounds, like laser-beam-particle guns and master blasters. My clothespin never needed batteries.

As expected, I saw Hudson coming toward me on Main Street. Then, unexpectedly, he continued right on by, missing the turn to his office. I hurried out the back door of the post office and climbed into my truck. By the time I was out on the two-lane highway that served as Main Street in each town, I was six or seven cars and trucks behind the sheriff. I followed the line for ten minutes into Butte Peak and drove right on by as the sheriff turned and parked in front of the Sears outlet. I didn't stick around to see how long he stayed with Paul Bates, the sometimes coroner of Butte Peak. I didn't dare risk it. I turned right, drove down one of Butte Peak's lovely residential streets and eventually found myself parked behind the Ore Wagon Saloon. My mind was reeling.

Kupps was at the far end of the bar on the same stool I had left him. "I Dream of Jeannie" was on the tube. "We got to talk," I said, grabbing him by the elbow. He didn't resist. If I'd been wearing a Nazi uniform, he wouldn't have resisted. He was numb to the world, yet surprisingly agile on his feet. I didn't want to risk Hudson's coming through the door and seeing me talking to him. I led him to the men's room and helped him inside. He was glassy-eyed and his lips were wet. "What's going on?" I asked.

"Damned if I know," he said, shaking his head, "this is your idea, not mine."

"I mean with Greg Sweetland."

His brow cinched. "Huh-uh," he grunted. "Don't know what you're talking about."

"If the sheriff brought you fingerprints, they sure as hell didn't match, did they?"

"He brought 'em and they matched. I already told you that."

"You're a part of this thing?"

"Don't know what you're talking about."

I don't like to use force, but in the case of a numb doctor three sheets to the wind, I didn't see a lot of choice. I lifted him off the ground by his shoulders and helped him gently against the wall, and held him there. It got his attention. A tear ran from his eye and I felt about as big as Jiminy Cricket. But I didn't let him down. "Someone, or a group of someones, are running me in circles on this Russell thing. I don't particularly care for it. In fact, I'm getting a little bit annoyed at the situation. You fit into it somehow, Kupps, and I'd appreciate a little help. They don't serve booze in jail, my good doctor. And that's where you're going eventually if you're involved in this."

Kupps tightened his brow in concentration and looked me over.

"They told me Amos was called out of town. Bates needed me to sign the papers. That's all it amounted to, I swear to you. I looked the body over. I'm sure I did," he said quite uncertain. "No question how that body died, I'll tell you that much. Sheriff arrived with the prints. I was a little shaky—you know how it is—and Bates was good enough to ink the fingers and take the prints for me. He confirmed them; I signed the papers. That's all there was to it. Swear to God. No one did anything wrong. It was straight as straight can be."

"But you signed the papers saying you had checked the prints."

He tried to shrug, but I was holding him. I set him down and he was a bit unstable on his feet. "Bates did it for me. What's the difference? It's a technicality. Not worth another thought. It was all aboveboard, I'm telling you."

"And why'd they cremate the body so quickly? That doesn't add up."

"Said that's the way the family wanted it. Nothing against the law about cremating a body. Next of kin can do whatever they want with it."

This contradicted what Bates had told me. I thought this over before saying, "But it was a *criminal* situation. The man had been shot by a gun. There should have been an autopsy. Why would the sheriff permit the body being cremated so soon?"

"Have to ask Dean that, wouldn't you? No way I would know that. But I'll tell you one thing," he said with a wry smile, "that body wasn't going to tell anybody anything. That man's days of talking were long past. And it was a damn messy sight. Shotgun couldn't have been fired from more than a few feet away. Whoever did it has what you might call dead aim. If you ask me, the family did the right thing. Another day or two, even in a freezer, that body wasn't going to look any better. I would have burned it too."

"What about any photos?"

The door came open and the beer-bellied bartender didn't

look too happy. "What the *fuck* are you doing?" he asked me, and I knew I had trouble. I'm a real genius sometimes. The bathroom was small. The bartender was big. He was blocking the door. "You all right, Doc?" he growled, not taking his eyes off me, not allowing me the first move.

"This guy's been roughing me up," Kupps said, pleading for help.

"Is that right?" the bartender replied. "Come on out of there, Doc."

Kupps squeezed past me and ducked under the stained armpit of the proprietor.

"I've seen you around," he said to me.

"No harm done," I told him.

"Bullshit, buddy. You fucked with one my steady customers. That won't do at all." He stepped into the bathroom and came at me. He had the head of a water buffalo and a chest as wide as the grille on a Mack Truck. I knew I'd be quicker—at least I hoped I would be—but I couldn't be sure which of us had more strength. There was a lot of jelly to him and I didn't know how much muscle it was hiding.

His first swing answered my question. He caught me on the point of my left shoulder and numbed it. My fingers—in fact, everything below my elbow—were missing. Everything above was on fire. I tried to lift the arm to block his next strike, but he caught the same place again, and now the whole thing was numb. I felt the hair on the nape of my neck stand up. He fought like I did: with his head. It frightened me. I had expected a television fighter. He was quickly disappointing me. His strategy was to make me useless and then go to work.

I kicked him in the groin, kneed him in the forehead as he came over, standing him back up, and then tried for a heart punch as he bounced off the door. He had too much padding where I hit him. It would have to be higher. He connected solidly into my gut and buckled me over. He lifted his knee to return the favor, but I dodged it, and belted his left shoulder as hard as I could to try and even the score. He tried to lift it, and it came up slowly. I hit him low, just at the bottom of his rib cage, and connected well. He jerked to that side and pushed me hard, sending me back against the sink. I still couldn't feel my left arm.

I had no way to guard a blow from that side and he knew it. He came in fast and low, wanting a kidney punch from that side. I moved quickly enough that my dangling left arm partially blocked the hit and I spared myself a week of painful peeing. I went for the rib again, and this time I got it good. He really felt it, and it stood him up. I faked a kick and delivered a well-aimed heart punch that sent him back against the wall. The wall rattled.

He roared and charged me with his head lowered. I moved to my right and tripped him and he speared the mirror, breaking it into a thousand pieces. The head wound bled badly and the sight of his own blood seemed to take something out of him. He was distracted now, and at least partially dulled from ramming the mirror with his head.

Someone opened the door to the bathroom and it caught his eye. My back was to the door and so I was spared the diversion. I numbed his left shoulder, blocked his next hit with the left side of my body that had an arm attached to it somewhere, and then I nailed that rib again. He really screamed this time, and I knew the pain had weakened him.

"What the fuck?" I heard over my shoulder.

I palmed his head and connected it with the side of the sink. A pipe came loose and water flooded onto the floor. He wasn't out, but I had slowed him down significantly. He was nowhere to be seen by the time I had the truck spraying gravel behind me.

By the time I returned home the weather had once again made a pendulum swing back toward summer.

Nicole and Lyel were sitting out on the deck, the two of them, he with his long legs kicked up, feet resting on the bench, she looking prim and proper, impeccable posture, beer held in hand. They glanced over at the truck in unison as I arrived. She waved. He grinned. I felt a pang of jealousy, for I knew how wonderful each of them was, and I thought that perhaps by now they knew as well. I parked the old heap more quickly than usual and slammed the door to make certain it would not need a second effort to stay shut. Lyel had returned to a famous Lyel stance: legs up, eyes closed, face absorbing the sun. From this distance, his lips moved silently and slowly as he spoke to her. She giggled as I stepped up onto the porch.

"Don't tell me you're already through with the research," I said to him.

"All right, I won't," he returned, still facing the sky. "I'll let you guess."

I saw Nicole fight back a smile and turn away to look at the slough so I wouldn't see it. Now I *was* jealous.

I've often tried to identify the cause of the occasional jealousies I feel. Why do I allow myself to unlock and open the door to insecurity that most of the time I keep well sealed within me? I know it is no one's fault but my own, this jealousy. But there are little triggers out there, just waiting to throw the switch and start me going.

"Care for another?" I asked Nicole.

"Please," Lyel said.

Nicole nodded and smiled again.

"Two beers coming up," I said. I had seen Lyel like this before, I realized, and it had little or nothing to do with Nicole. He was simply proud of the speed with which he had dispatched himself to the task at hand and was waiting to tell me something I didn't know. We compete this way, Lyel and I, day in and day out. I suppose it's our way of confirming we are needed.

I pulled up a deck chair and faced them, the sun catching the back of my head and warming my cheek. She looked too good to be true: tight faded blue jeans, a mint-green sweater with a white collar peeking out, dark hair brushed fully and changing colors as it caught the sun. Lyel looked big and dangerous and quite content in his sun-worshipping pose.

"What did you find out?" I asked him.

He sat up and grinned. He has big teeth and an equally big mouth. He was proud of himself.

"I went to the courthouse as we discussed. It took me all of about three minutes, because as I asked to see Sweetland's file, the clerk, a woman in her fifties, asked me why I wanted that and I told her. She said there was some sort of policy that prevented me from actually reading the file but that she knew it real well because due to his death it had been across her desk a half dozen times this week. So I asked her why and when Sweetland had been arrested." He paused to let this sink in, and, I think, to add some drama. "She told me Sweetland had been jailed for one night on a juvenile offense when he was fourteen. She didn't remember that one. At sixteen he was caught stealing a horse— an expensive cutting horse—and was nearly charged, but the charges were dropped because of his age. Sweetland claimed he had found the horse out in the BLM."

"So that's when he got printed," I said.

"There's more," he said. "Eighteen months ago, Larry and

Greg Sweetland were arrested and charged on a number of counts, including intent to distribute marijuana, possession and growing. They evidently had a nice-sized crop going up there and were supplying Snow Lake with their harvest."

"Interesting."

"Isn't it, though? I got the attorney's name"—Lyel never called them lawyers. He pulled out a piece of paper. "An Indian fellow. Name of Running Rain Clay. They call him Red. Lives out by the triangle."

"I *know* where he lives," I said. I recalled for them both my following Hudson out to the Sweetland ranch, to the mailbox marked RED CLAY RANCH, and to the Sears. I then filled them in on my tête-à-tête with Dr. Kupps and the resulting fisticuffs in the men's room. Lyel said, "I thought you looked a little worse for wear."

"Thanks."

"He tagged you a couple of times."

I chided him with an ungrateful smirk.

"He must be big," said Lyel, attempting to patch me up, "and fast," he added.

Nicole said, "So you're saying the sheriff is somehow involved in this? Or was he just warning everyone to shape up?"

I said, "For the time being there's no way to tell. If we take him at face value, he was just doing his job. But the visit to the Sweetlands' attorney is curious. I think I'd like to meet the man—"

"—and exchange pleasantries," Lyel contributed. "An additional curiosity is that the transcript of the Sweetlands' trial is conspicuously absent from the records."

"Gone?"

"It's a public record, as you know. So, being my thorough self, I asked to take a look at it." He paused. "Not to be found, as it turned out. When I asked how such a thing could happen, the woman had no immediate answer for me. It seemed to perplex her as much as it did me. The records may be copied, it seems, but they are not to leave the courthouse. She was a bit embarrassed by the whole thing.

"I then inquired about the judge who heard the case," he continued. "I thought he might make a good interview for you.

But as it happens, the good judge is no longer in service to the great state of Idaho. He is off for points unknown, and, according to my somewhat homely companion at the courthouse, under suspect circumstances. Something about his daughter being Sweetland's high school distributor, or sweetheart, or both. I had to extract that from her with verbal needle-nosed pliers. I am under the impression there will be no more information forthcoming from her. It would seem her proclivity for running on about cases has gotten her into trouble several times, and she is more than aware of that. From what I can tell, the county courthouse jobs are cherished and not worth losing in a valley beset with the difficulties of a fickle seasonal economy."

"You're saying the trial was less than due process," I said.

"It would appear someone got to both the judge and the transcripts."

"I can't believe that!" Nicole said indignantly. "That kind of thing is still done?"

"All the time," I said.

"So what do we do?" she asked.

Lyel changed the subject, implying nothing was to be done. "I don't like the implications of the good sheriff pushing around Larry Sweetland."

"Neither do I," I agreed.

"Why?" she asked.

Lyel answered for us. "It implies an unexplainable intimacy that is less than encouraging."

"Why should he be worried about the Sweetlands' sudden show of wealth?" I posed to her.

"The belt and the boots," Lyel pointed out. I listened. "Why did he object to the belt and the boots?" he wondered aloud. "Again, it implies an intimacy. Something about those fancy boots and that silver belt made Hudson angry. Very angry."

"The Sweetlands show signs of sudden affluence, Nicole. They're dirt farmers," I contributed.

"And that could mean your money," Lyel finished. "Although that's jumping to conclusions. It could also be something easily explained, as Hudson put forth to you, Klick. They could have sold a horse or something."

"Could have," I said.

She nodded. She understood. "Paul's dead," she said softly. "Paul could be anywhere," Lyel stated. "It could mean anything." I told them then for the first time about Blokowski, the DEA agent who had been following Debbie Benton. Lyel seemed a little put off I had waited nearly half a beer to mention this. I smiled at him. I took great pleasure in surprising Lyel.

Nicole said harshly, "DEA?"

"So, if you add up the DEA, and what I found out at the courthouse, you have a possible drug connection," Lyel contributed.

"And we have Debbie Benton's confirmation that Paul occasionally dealt grass."

Nicole shook her head, too frustrated and confused to get any words out.

I went inside and tuned in WQXR, New York, a classical music station that comes in via my satellite dish. It trickled softly from the Aurotone I had mounted under the eaves of the roof. I returned with a round of beers. Nicole had not finished hers yet so she set it in the shadow of the rough wood picnic table. The sun was still that strong. The music distracted me some, as did the jabber at the end of the pieces, but I assumed it would lighten the mood, and it seemed to be having that effect.

"How do we find out if he's dead?" she asked. "If he's dead, I think I'd like to know." There was no tone of self pity or even sorrow. Nicole wanted to conduct some business. She needed to know.

"It won't be easy," I said.

"I'd like to know," she repeated.

"So what's next?" Lyel asked, breaking the somber spell.

"Dinner," I suggested. "You'll stay?" I asked him.

"I don't think so," he said.

"Please," Nicole commented. I felt a little deflated.

"Stick around," I told him.

"Yeah, okay. I'll make a couple of calls." He pried that huge body of his out of the chair. The waffle plastic crackled as it shrank, attempting to return to the shape it had been in before Lyel had sat down. He lumbered toward the side door and let himself inside.

"You all right?" I asked her.

She pouted and nodded.

"We don't have to talk about it anymore."

"Yes, we do, Klick." She leaned forward and took my hands in hers. "We have to get it over with. I'd like to get it over with."

"I understand."

"On some level, I suppose you do. I can't tell you what I'm going through. It's not love for Paul. I don't love him at all anymore. It's more like hate, I think. It's something I'm not used to, not very good with. I don't want to get comfortable with it. I don't want to learn to live with this. I'm scared." She pulled her hands away politely and rubbed her eyes. "I have this incredible anger building up in me. If he's dead, it denies me my chance. How's that for selfish? I got all my crying done up front, most of it before I even came to see you. In the back of my mind I guess I suspected something like this. I had been told that Paul's past had been *colorful*, but I allowed myself to believe that he had put that all behind him. It's hard to get used to the idea of someone using you. He took my money. He used me." She shook. "I hate him."

I could see Lyel through the window. He was on the telephone. I was glad he was staying. I was too close to this woman. Lyel, no matter what the situation, has the ability to make light of things. It goes beyond his natural talent for telling jokes; it is more an attitude, a way of living that permeates everything he does.

"I'm not sure of what to do next," I told her.

"What did Dr. Kupps say?"

"I got the impression they used him."

"Who?"

"Bates and Hudson, probably, although I can't be sure. They orchestrated a cover-up that no one will ever prove. The good doctor is convinced it was all aboveboard. I doubt he's lying. In his pickled brain, I doubt he thinks of much more than how to get his next drink. That's a lousy thing to say, but that's the way it feels."

"It's probably true."

We sat in silence. I looked at her as she studied the deck. I had met a few women more pretty than Nicole, but none more beautiful. I wanted to take her into my arms. I wanted her to come surprise me in bed while the lightning played off the ceiling. Had I dreamed that up, or had it really happened? I felt tempted to ask her. But the lightning, the thunder had been real. I had seen the driveway's rain-stained gravel this morning. It had all been real and it was simply my problem that I didn't want to believe it, or couldn't allow myself to. I do that to myself occasionally. I deny acceptance of the wonderful things that come easily. The music world is a tough world. Nothing comes easy. Nothing. And it burns into you a fear of anything that does. You come to believe that is the way the world works: no pain, no gain. It is these stays in Idaho that are slowly breaking me of this attitude. I think it's why I came here in the first place, why I find it hard to leave.

I sensed in that moment that I would lose Nicole before I really had her. She was a confused and hurt woman, not the sort to fall into my arms and forget all that had happened. More the kind to seek retreat somewhere—disappear and lick her wounds. I feared that inevitability. As I grew closer to her, she seemed to be growing farther away from me. I wanted to reverse the trend. Was there a chance that if I moved emotionally away from her, she would be drawn to me? I didn't think I had it in me. She had captured me in that mysterious net of hers, and like any trapped animal, I saw no way out.

"I made a call for you," Lyel said as he came toward us, carrying a tray.

"To whom?" I asked.

He pulled up a chair. It wasn't a tray, it was a cutting board. He had red peppers, broccoli, and carrots, and my sharpest prep knife. He placed the board in his lap and began to work on the vegetables. "Why don't you catch us one of those native brookies?" he asked.

"To whom?" I repeated.

"One that will feed all three of us."

"I'd love to watch you fish," interjected Nicole.

"Whom did you call?"

Lyel looked up from the red pepper and slid a slice into his mouth. When he chewed down on the slice it crunched. "Running Rain 'Red' Clay," he said. "Sweetland's attorney. I was very up front with him. Told him you were curious about Greg

Sweetland. He hemmed and hawed, but I convinced him it was in his interest to speak with you. He invited you out to his place tomorrow morning."

"Why is it in his interest to speak with me?"

"Because I mentioned that certain lawsuits were forthcoming, and that forewarned is forearmed. That piqued his interest."

"I'll bet." I looked at them both. They were staring at me, as if they didn't want me there. "I think I'll go fishing," I said.

"Good idea." Lyel glanced over at her and smiled. He finished the pepper and began work on the carrots.

23

As I was preparing to tie a tricot fly onto a 6-X tippet, the cruiser arrived in the driveway. Lyel joined me on the deck. Hudson ambled up, taking his sweet time about it, and moved to within inches of me.

"You're under arrest," he said smugly. "Assault, creating a public nuisance, couple other things. I'll read you your rights now, listen carefully."

Lyel and I listened. Hudson cuffed me and led me to the cruiser and drove me away. I looked over my shoulder and saw Lyel consoling Nicole. I felt lousy. I was going to miss the evening hatch.

They didn't have time to rough me up. I had Lyel to thank for that. He arrived with an attorney—a man named Carsman—and a wad of cash before Hudson's engine had cooled.

The bartender had filed charges. Thanks to my new attorney, my hearing was delayed for two weeks. I was released on bail in time to see the sun set. Lyel drove me home in silence. For some reason I felt like a teenager being driven home by Daddy. Lyel has that effect on me from time to time.

We ate spinach pasta salad and raspberry cheesecake to the sounds of Dexter Gordon. Lyel hummed along, off key, fingers drumming adroitly in time against the beveled edge of the oak table. Before him, through the thick double-pane picture window, strong white electric light illuminated the browning lawn out to the fragile-looking willows by the slough. Somewhere out there, I thought, was a family of ducks long since asleep.

"Back to business," Lyel said a few minutes later.

"I'm listening," I replied.

"Me, too," added Nicole.

"The day Paul disappeared, you said he was driving the Audi, is that right?"

She nodded.

"You see the conflict, Klick?"

He had put me on the spot and I wanted to follow to his line of thinking, but I knew better.

"No," I admitted.

"Let's say he was intending to do a drug deal. Fifty thousand dollars will buy what? Conservatively, that kind of money has to buy at least twenty-five kilos. Probably more like thirty-five or forty. Now, we put aside for a moment where Sweetland would have gotten the grass and we concentrate on what—"

"—Paul was going to do with forty keys in an Audi," I finished for him.

He raised his brows at us. "Why not take the truck? It would have been much easier. Why fool around with the Audi?"

"So, we're back to the idea that he simply stole the money and was going to run away with it and *her*," Nicole stated flatly.

"Then why go hunting?" Lyel asked.

She said, "He liked to hunt when he was feeling uptight. Maybe he was just trying to kill some time before picking her up."

"What are you thinking?" I asked him.

"That may be right." To Nicole he said, "You certainly know him best."

"Let's theorize," I suggested.

"What if the fifty thousand was intended for something else? What if Paul met Sweetland through his dope deals—maybe Sweetland was some kind of supplier—but they found they had something else in common? Besides hunting. What would it be?"

"Horses," I said.

"Paul hated horses," she commented.

"But not money," Lyel pointed out.

"No, not money," she said.

"Horses," Lyel repeated. "If they had done other deals together, why not a horse deal? Your Miss Benton said Paul had business in Vegas. That could be one of three things: gambling, a drug deal, or—"

"A horse deal," I repeated.

"That's the way I see it," he confirmed.

"There are too many ifs," she said, frustrated. "We just don't know enough. And if we don't find him soon, say good-bye to the money. Paul could blow that kind of money in a matter of weeks if he put his mind to it."

I said, "Everyone says how great Sweetland was at picking breeding stock. Maybe he had some hot colt and Paul thought he could find a buyer in Vegas."

"It's possible," Lyel agreed. "The point is, we can't rule anything out."

"Back to the pot," I said. "The Sweetlands were busted for growing," I thought aloud.

"Right."

"But the court apparently let them off."

"Right."

"So maybe they cut themselves a deal with Hudson."

"Payola?" Lyel wondered.

"Business continues as before, only now the sheriff has a piece of the pie."

"Yes. Now we're getting somewhere."

"You lost me," she said.

But Lyel and I were too far gone to break the train of thought. I continued, "So we need to know more about that trial."

"I'll return to the courthouse and brownnose the clerk into a few ugly rumors which I'll verify at the library with my head buried in back issues of the newspaper."

"I'll take the newspapers," Nicole said. She caught my glare and said, "If Lyel drops me off and picks me up, then I can't get in any trouble."

I nodded, as did Lyel. I added, "So what it boils down to is that the Sweetlands may have never closed up shop."

"Which in turn might explain where Paul got his source."

"When I went out there to have a look at the place—the second time—it was right around sunset. The lights to both barns went off simultaneously. At the time I thought they had been shut off from a breaker inside the house. Now I'm thinking timer."

"The barns."

"You could grow one hell of a lot of pot in those barns."

"Beats stacking hay for a living," Lyel said.

"The Sweetlands use the cash to help finance their horse breeding, which in turn gives them a legitimate cover for cash flow. The perfect solution to the plight of the small farmer."

"And just maybe Greg Sweetland is as good with raising horses as everyone claims."

"A grass crop," I kidded.

"Paul doesn't know who he's dealing with. He's bought pot from them a few times—"

"Sweetland's in trouble with Bill Clark for knocking up his wife. Maybe Bill's the type to kill a man for that."

"Sweetland kills Paul, switches clothes, and lets everyone believe that he was the one killed. Hudson goes along with the switch because he's on Sweetland's payroll. He wants the money to keep coming in."

"Still doesn't explain the Hill City police stopping Paul," Nicole interjected, breaking her silence.

I said, "Maybe it was Greg Sweetland in the Audi, not Paul."

"I like that," Lyel said. "That fits."

"He was pointing at the barns," I recalled. "Hudson got pissed off at Larry for the belt and boots, pointed at the barns and became furious. Maybe they were supposed to close up shop. Maybe he thinks I'm getting too close."

"What about the money?" Nicole wondered.

"If they killed Paul, then they probably kept the money."

"I hope they killed him," she said. But she didn't mean it. She tensed and then excused herself to work on the dishes. I was about to object when Lyel gave me one of his all-knowing looks that told me to leave her alone.

"I'd like to get a look inside those barns," he said.

"You and me both."

"You and me together," he suggested.

"Tonight?"

"It may be our last chance if you're right about Hudson telling them to shut it down."

I looked over at Nicole. Lyel knew what I was thinking. He raised his eyebrows, asking me which it was going to be.

"You'll need dark clothes," I said.

He stood. "I'll ride with you."

I nodded.

"Thanks for dinner," he said. He walked over to Nicole, who was just finishing up at the sink. She looked so tiny next to him. He took her by the shoulders from behind, leaned forward and kissed her affectionately on the cheek. I admired the innocence of the kiss for some reason. She brushed cheeks with him in response. "Nice meeting you," he told her.

Lyel wore a black windbreaker. "How's she doing?" he asked.

"It's beginning to sink in. We were a little rough on her, I think."

"We have to prepare her for the possibility he's dead. I'm sure he is. In the long run it'll be easier on her."

"I've been doing that. Still . . ." I didn't know what to say.

"Have you slept with her?"

"Why do you ask?"

"I could feel it. Unfortunately it felt like a form of tension. Do her a favor. Don't sleep with her again. Not now. It'll only confuse her more. Besides, she could direct some of the blame over to you if she looks at it the wrong way. No sense in ruining something before it's started."

"I love her. I think I love her."

"Yes, I know that much. In all the years we've run around I've never seen you quite like this."

"Like what?"

"You ogle."

"Do I?"

"And I even felt some jealousy out on the porch."

"Guilty."

"I was flattered. Have I ever stolen a girl from you?"

"No."

"Would I?"

"I don't think so. But stranger things have happened, right?"

"I chase eighteen-year-olds around the warm-up huts on the mountain. I watch them work out at the club. I surround myself with youth, focusing on the impracticality of companionship."

"But you want it, don't you?"

"No. The dirty laundry I can do without. I'm too set in my ways, I'm afraid. I look at them. They humor me. Once in a great while I drink too much and find myself wrapped up with one. It's different for me than with you."

"You have more women friends than any man I've ever met."

"They know I'm harmless."

"Bullshit. You're much too big to be harmless. People like you are rarely harmless."

"I project a sexual neutrality that the young ones find attractive. They're used to the pimple-faced ones with bones in their crotch chasing them out onto the dance floor for a slow grind. They tire of it. I offer them the chance of a lifetime: a discussion. Conversation. They warm up to me quickly."

"Sexual neutrality?"

"Just a term."

"Don't kid yourself."

"I try not to."

"I think they find you a curious phenomenon, a sort of hyperthyroid teddy bear with brains and a knack for language. You're the only writer I know with an MBA."

"Privileged information, Klick. If word of that got out, I might never see another Danskin again."

"You're a strange duck, my friend."

"Yes. Quack, quack."

We rode in silence for a few minutes. The phone poles on Pole Road clipped by like the uneven frames of a silent movie. A gray mouse darted across the road.

Lyel said, "I wonder what the world looks like through his eyes. Can you imagine what this truck must look like, barreling down on him, how its wind must feel on his back, how loud the engine must ring in his ears?"

"The mice never pause to look. Not like other animals. They rush straight across as fast as they can run. I think somehow they know they've got trouble. They have a brain smaller than a snow pea and yet they seem to know instinctively that if they pause to look, they'll be dead. Maybe their eyes are different. Maybe that's why they don't freeze in the light like other animals."

"Perhaps they're running blind, totally blind. Perhaps they run flat out until they strike something."

"It's a thought," I said. "Are you trying to tell me something?"

"You always were fast."

"I'm listening."

"We're running a little blind ourselves, Klick. We don't want to make any assumptions without something to back it up. We also don't want to run so fast that we strike something and hurt ourselves."

"You're worried about this."

"I don't like the description of the brothers. I prefer it when we're bigger than our opponents. I'd prefer Denver over Atlantic City, if you'll recall."

"Those suckers were big in Atlantic City." I grinned.

"I didn't enjoy that."

"Nor did I."

"Prudence is in order here, I think. We should proceed cautiously. If we happen to have guessed correctly, then they have a lot to lose."

"A point well taken. So I'll go in alone. You'll remain behind as backup. If I mess it up, you can make a quick decision whether to attempt to help or head off for reinforcements."

"Who would I call on? Sheriff Hudson perhaps. They would certainly appreciate that."

"George Blokowski, DEA. If you can find Debbie Benton, Blokowski won't be far behind. He's the only one I'd trust right now."

"Okay."

"He drives a white pickup with Nevada plates."

"Did you happen to bring a gun?"

"I brought us both guns. I brought bolt cutters, too."

"This is a lousy business, Klick."

"Yup."

"I prefer girl-watching."

"You and me both."

●

Although I knew it would take longer, I parked at the abandoned mine and decided we would circle all the way around the far side of the ranch, remaining hidden by the ridge. I had been spotted from the other side, and this was too far away and too much country to patrol effectively. We had a good cloud cover overhead. We moved north-northeast for about fifteen minutes. I stayed in the lead and I stopped us two or three times a minute to listen. I read once that lions hunt with their ears—their night vision is horrible—and ever since I have done so as well. It requires this frequent stop-and-go procedure, but more than once it has paid off. Lyel was accustomed to it from other outings with me. He followed my lead well. Thirty minutes later we began to round to the west as we curved along the rim of the bowl-like ridge that contained the Sweetland ranch. We crossed through several fences, though we didn't come upon any livestock. Twice we reconnoitered our position from the top of the ridge; we were drawing steadily closer to the compound and the backside of the two huge barns. Fifteen minutes later we were right above them.

Lyel handed me the bolt cutters and, tapping his wrist, told me that he would give me ten minutes. If I wasn't in sight after that amount of time he would either leave for help or come get me, depending on the situation. I nodded as his big hands flashed *ten* at me. I felt for the gun in the small of my back and slipped over the crest of the ridge, descending the broken-rock face slowly and quietly. It was too dark to spot a sentry, and that bothered me. It's much easier to move when you know the position of your opponent. I crossed silently through two corrals. In the second, a pair of mares slept on their feet in the corner, not bothered by my presence. I didn't need the bolt cutters; the big sliding door on the back of the barn was cracked open slightly, enough for a man to walk through. I stepped inside and pressed myself up against the wall, waiting for my eyes to adjust.

There were six stalls straight ahead on my left, three of which each contained a pretty, young thoroughbred. A post-and-rail fence separated this area from the open center of the barn. At the far end I spotted two doors. The inside arena was large enough to work horses. Large funnel-shaped overhead lights were suspended at regular intervals. My heart was pounding with adrenaline and the dispirited coolness of failure passed through me. I was ready to leave when I noticed that the lights were attached to a flat ceiling. It meant the barn had a hayloft. In the darkness I looked for evidence of a ladder leading up to the loft and saw none. I couldn't see any way to get the hay down into the stall area either. I walked slowly down the aisle, studying the ceiling overhead. Halfway down the aisle I noticed the outline of the trapdoor that would allow bales to be thrown down from above, but searching the floor I saw no evidence of fresh hay indicating the trapdoor had been used recently. I remembered from my previous visit a haystack near the paddocks. Its presence implied the barn's hayloft was not being used. At least not for hay.

Unable to locate an access to the loft, I decided to try the doors. I opened the door to the first room and I could smell the rich leather and saddle soap mixed with the heavy animal odor. The tack room. I had fond memories associated with these smells, and for a moment I stood charmed by them. No way up from this room either.

I closed the door carefully and moved on to the next room. It was locked. In my experience with barns and ranches, it was tack rooms that were locked, and only then rarely. Tack is expensive and easily stolen. More often than not, trophies are kept in with the tack. But the tack room was unlocked, so why was this one locked? I returned to the tack room and looked for and found the small refrigerator that kept various drugs and medicines cool. For a moment I had thought that perhaps the other room was locked to restrict access to the medicines, but this was obviously not the case. Then why lock it? I was frustrated to be denied entrance to the room. For a moment I debated putting a shoulder to it. But that would hardly do. It would make a racket and leave behind evidence of my visit.

On my way out I passed below the trapdoor and it gave me an idea. I scrambled up the side of a stall and I could easily reach the ceiling. I leaned out and pushed against the trapdoor and it moved. It wasn't locked. It was heavier than I had expected— something had to be resting on it. I heaved against it and managed to open it about an inch before its weight overpowered me. I didn't get a look at anything. I didn't see row after row of mature pot plants. I didn't see the clever lighting arrangement that provided grow lights for each of the plants. I didn't have to. I could smell the thick, pungent, skunklike odor of fresh pot. I felt triumphant. Evidence that supported one of our theories. The Sweetlands were not just horse ranchers.

I jumped down and hurried to the far end of the barn and finally out the door into the corral. I spotted the electric box at the far corner and headed directly over to it. Two additional pieces of Romex had been cut into the box. They were crudely tacked to the outside of the barn and ran overhead, disappearing at loft level. I popped open the fuse box. By the color of the plastic I could tell that three 40-amp breakers had been added recently. It was further proof.

I heard the footsteps to my right and immediately pushed up against the rough lumber of the barn. A heavyset man came out of the barn, looked directly at me, then the other way, and paused. I heard him fish out a pack of cigarettes and when he struck his lighter I saw the angry, garish face of Larry Sweetland. He was no longer wearing the fancy belt buckle or shiny boots. He was even bigger than I remembered him, and he seemed solid. It had been Larry who had been banging the young girl on my last visit, and I remembered that now and wanted to hurt him. He stood there smoking his cigarette, not twenty feet away. Then I noticed the bolt cutters. I had leaned them up against the wall. They were directly behind him, and as he backed up to rest against the barn to smoke his cigarette, they were between his calves and the wall, only inches away. I wanted to reach out and grab them. I wanted to move him away from them. How much longer could he stand there and not notice them? He lifted his foot and placed the sole of his boot against the building, barely missing the bolt cutters. Then I saw them move slightly. They shifted to the right and slipped silently along the wall. They stopped. The big man continued to smoke the cigarette. Again he looked directly at me and didn't see me. I must have looked like a shadow against the wall, partially hidden by the electrical junction box. His eyes had been affected by the flame from the lighter, and remained unadjusted to the darkness because of his attention on the cigarette's orange ember.

Then the bolt cutters fell over and thumped to the ground. He jumped and looked back at them. At first I think he mistook them for a neglected farm tool, for he kicked them and leaned back against the wall. But then he seemed to reconsider and he turned to have a look. He reached out and touched them, and I saw his recognition of what their function was in the sudden stiffness with which he carried himself. His head moved in little jerks, first toward me, then toward the other side of the barn. He stood up and hurried inside the barn.

I ran to the doorway and heard him run and stop at the far door that I had found locked. He unlocked it and hurried inside. I could hear him climbing a ladder, heard a board move, and then, a few seconds later when he turned on the lights, I could see two thin gaps in the ceiling where light now trickled through. I heard his footsteps at the far end of the hayloft.

I debated taking the bolt cutters with me—I wasn't worried about prints, I was wearing thin gloves—but decided to leave them. If I removed them, it might alert the man to my immediate proximity. If I left them, there was no telling what his reaction might be, but there was a chance that I would buy Lyel and myself an extra few minutes. If they pursued us on horseback, we would need every bit of a head start we could muster.

I cut through the two corrals quickly and in doing so I startled the two mares, which I had forgotten about. I stayed as low as I could and still run effectively. With my size that wasn't very low and I knew it. I paused twice to have a look. The first time I stopped, Larry Sweetland wasn't anywhere to be seen. The second time, I could just barely make him out at the doorway. That meant he could just barely make me out as well. The sage grew thicker and taller on the slope and helped to hide me better. As I crested the ridge, Lyel said in a whisper, "What happened?"

"The bolt cutters," I explained, moving past him and down the other side quickly.

Thirty minutes later we were back in the truck, headlights out, cruising very slowly through the darkness toward Pole Road. I turned left, electing to take the long way home in case they had driven to the end of their road and were waiting for us.

By the time I got home, Nicole was in her room, fast asleep

25

I woke up late. Nicole was out for a run, having left behind a note signed with a stick figure taking a long stride. Hot coffee was waiting. I poured a cup and fixed myself a bowl of Grape-Nuts. I don't take a morning paper. The regional papers are too poorly written for my tastes, and the national papers arrive by mail three days late. I read *Time,* turning to "People" first.

She was out there running somewhere, and she was all I could think of. My infatuation was quickly turning into a problem. I was too far gone, and we both knew it. She had cooled noticeably, preparing me, I feared. I experienced that sickening, hollow feeling of grief. I was about to lose her and I wasn't sure why. Had I been too honest too quickly? It is something I'm famous for.

Time provided no diversion. The photographs of the swells and the glamorous did nothing to distract me as they sometimes do. I found myself substituting Nicole's face for the women. Here she was a princess on the arm of a prince, here a motion-picture queen, here a best-selling author of romantic intrigue, and here a star athlete competing for a place on the U.S. Olympic team. I tried to isolate my insecurity, tried to think it through rationally. She had come to me the night before. Had I misunderstood everything? Had she been waiting for me to return the interest last night? Was I really vain enough to think she would come to me two nights in a row? Was this horrible feeling driven by sexual frustration or had I sensed in her a reluctance to allow our partnership a chance to evolve?

I ate only half the cereal. I rinsed the bowl and placed it in the dishwasher and poured myself another cup. I knew I should have been focusing on "Red" Clay, on Sheriff Dean Hudson, on the Sweetland brothers and on my findings of the night before. So I pushed the Nicole matter out of my mind temporarily, though I continued to anticipate her return, and tried to think what my next logical step was.

Lyel stopped by his guest house. He looked the part of the country gentleman, only he was far too big. He said, "It has just occurred to me that the discovery of the bolt cutters may prompt a speedy reorganization out at the Sweetland ranch. It is my recommendation that I conduct some reconnaissance in the back country on horseback in an effort to confirm or disprove our suspicions."

"Not such a good idea, friend—"

"They don't know me from Adam," he said, interrupting.

"That's not the point. The point is that if you happen to see something, and they happen to see you, there's a good chance they would kill you without asking any questions."

"Point well taken. Another idea then."

"Yes?"

"Tim could take me up in a glider. He can keep that thing aloft for hours, and it's completely silent from the ground. Even if they spot us, the last thing they would think is that I'm spying on them."

"Has anyone ever told you that you're brilliant?"

"You have."

"Always evaluate the source, my friend. It's a fine idea. Might I recommend a camera with a telephoto, just in case?"

"You might. And binoculars."

"Those too."

"I'll call you later."

"Yes."

"Don't push him too hard, Klick. We don't know anything about him. Better to tread lightly. He may not be the patient type."

"Point well taken," I said, mimicking him. He's never liked to be mimicked.

●

Twenty minutes later, still stalling around hoping she would return, I fired up the truck and drove off. I passed her on the bridge and we both waved. She wore that same Lycra top. I followed her with my eyes briefly in the rearview mirror. She was running away from me. I then focused on the road and when I looked back she was gone. Just like that, gone. And I feared this is how it would be. One morning I would wake up and she would be gone, off to lick her wounds. To distance herself from any involvement. Leaving me behind to whimper wistfully, wondering why.

I wanted to tromp on the brakes, turn the old truck around and catch back up to her. I wanted to keep her in my sight, to make certain she wouldn't disappear. I wanted to fix it, whatever it was. I wanted a year to have gone by, and for her to be eagerly awaiting my ardent advances.

But I did nothing. I knew what was right for her. We both did. Trying to change it wouldn't solve anything, would only distance us further. She needed herself now, not me, and this realization left me feeling unimportant and small. I gripped the wheel more tightly, inhaled deeply, releasing the breath in a long, steady flow, and drove on.

●

The sign read RED CLAY RANCH, just like the mailbox. Running Rain "Red" Clay owned about six hundred acres up Slaughterhouse Canyon. There wasn't any red clay for three thousand miles.

The dirt drive curved through overgrazed pasture but was well fenced. Recent work. As I rounded a bend I noticed three man-made ponds—stocked with trout, no doubt—and a spanking-new wind pump spinning rapidly atop a steel tower. No lack of cash here. The ponds were too perfectly shaped, void of any landscaping, and looked awful. The house was pushed back away from one of the barns, but nearly surrounded by paddocks housing what appeared to be Arabians. Arabians are an expensive breed. Rich man's breed. A white satellite dish stared patiently at the sky.

Clay had recently put on weight, or he hadn't bought clothes in years. The buttons on his silk Western-style shirt threatened to pop lose. He was too short for his jeans and too fat for his leather vest. His face was oily and his hand was cold and damp. He had lost some of his jet-black hair and limped noticeably. His mouth was infested with rogue teeth attempting to escape. He spoke with a slight lisp.

He led me into his very Western living room and I took a seat in a vinyl chair, leaning against a Navajo rug that someone had forgotten to remove the MADE IN TAIWAN label from. There was imitation money spread around everywhere, like margarine heaped on toast, including the tasteless original oil paintings and the fake Remington bronze on the coffee table.

He killed twenty minutes with insipid verbal drool, telling me some obviously made-up story about his Indian ancestors, sweating the whole time and sucking down the remainder of an iced tea he neglected to offer me any of. He was effeminate and soft, and quite sunburned considering his adopted heritage, reminding me of a tomato left too long on the windowsill. He had about as much Indian blood in him as I did. He pretended to know nothing about me, and I was delighted. But he was too nervous to know nothing about me. I knew he had spoken to Hudson. I would have liked to have heard that conversation.

"You defended Greg Sweetland at his trial."

He nodded.

I smiled at him and stared until he squirmed in his seat. Leaning against vinyl makes me sweat. I stripped my back off the plastic and it made a slurping sound as it released me.

"He offered to pay, I defended him," he said somewhat apologetically.

"The way I understand it, he was convicted of growing grass, yet received probation. How did that come about? I thought Idaho has a mandatory jail term for cultivation."

"The man is . . . is dead, Mr. Klick. How can you possibly be interested in such things? Let sleeping dogs lie. That's what my grandpappy, Running Brook, would have said."

His insistence on playing Sitting Bull aggravated me. The plight of the American Indian is complex and even sad. Association with men like this was obscene. He was an embarrassment, even to himself.

"I have my reasons for being interested in Sweetland," I told him. I wondered why he had agreed to see me. Perhaps Hudson had foreseen my eventual interest in the court case and had encouraged Clay to handle me. Perhaps Clay himself was curious as to how much I knew. "Specifically, I'm wondering about the direction of your legal defense."

"That's confidential," he tried.

"That's public," I reminded. "Court transcripts are public information."

"Then why not consult the transcripts, Mr. Klick?" he asked, a sudden attempt at an expression of all-knowing confidence. Confidence was a stranger to this man and it looked more like a cheap mask.

"Because, come to find out, they're missing from the court records."

"You don't say?"

I nodded.

He sucked air through his teeth. "Still, from my end, it's confidential information."

"But, as you pointed out, Sweetland is dead, so what possible harm can come from sharing the information with me?"

He was confused. His eyes darted about and settled back onto me as if he hoped to find me gone, or, better yet, an apparition that had never been here. He was frightened all of a sudden, and it wasn't of me. Just then I had the feeling we weren't alone. It excited me. There was nothing I would have rather done than to find Hudson listening in.

He said, "I have a reputation to protect. I don't discuss past cases for any reason, unless with a professional colleague, of course, and then only with good reason." He dragged that cold, soft hand across his oily brow and wiped his palm dry on his tight jeans.

From what Lyel had told me of the man's reputation, there was little to protect. And by the looks of him that rumor was confirmed. He was a transplant here. A misbegotten city sleaze hiding in the high desert of Idaho. I disliked his pretense and I disliked his wormy manner. I came here to get away from people like him.

He became cocky, with a high, raspy, obnoxious tone to his voice. The voice seemed to fit him well. "Mr. Klick, I can't see how any of this could possibly pertain to some grieving widow." His eyes continued to dance and I realized he was unaware of his slip. He had called Nicole a *widow*. And he somehow knew I was working for her. Two mistakes he would be held accountable for.

"Can you tell me about Dean Hudson?" I said, fighting off the desire to one-upman him and point out his mistake.

"Sheriff Hudson? Why, he's a fine man," he said, dragging his hands on his pants again. I was surprised the fabric wasn't threadbare from the unnerving habit. "Fine man. He works hard for this town. Has a lot of ground to cover, with little or no manpower. Does a damn good job of it, if you ask me. Why?"

"Being a lawyer in this town, you must cross paths with Dean Hudson quite often."

"Course we do, it's a small town. We aren't always sitting on the same side of the fence, mind you, but you can't let things like that get in your way. Not here."

"And what was his relationship with Sweetland?"

"What's that?" he said, trying to buy time for his small mind to think of something to say. If this man played poker, he had never won a hand in his life.

To rattle him, I repeated the question.

"No relationship; I don't know what you mean."

"With the brothers, then. He seems to know the other Sweetlands pretty well."

"Sheriff Hudson knows everyone in this county on a first-name basis. Nature of the beast. What the hell are you driving at, Klick?"

"What I wonder," I said, "is how Greg Sweetland could have been given probation after being caught cultivating marijuana. There are laws against such things. There's a mandatory sentence."

"This is a small town, Mr. Klick."

"Even so."

"An entirely different set of standards than a fellow like you would be used to. This here is country where people care about each other. Really care."

"Right," I said, thinking of Nicole and the cold shoulder Hudson had given us both. "But it still doesn't explain how a mandatory sentence can be ignored. That is," I said, thinking aloud, "unless the Sweetland case had something to do with the judge or the judge's daughter."

It struck a nerve. Clay turned scarlet and dragged both hands on his pants. "That's *wild* speculation," he said, infuriated. "With innuendo like that, I see no purpose in furthering this discussion. I think it is time for you to go, Mr. Klick."

"I just got here," I objected. "I drove ten miles out here to see you, to ask you some questions, and considering the circumstances—"

"The circumstances! What circumstances, Mr. Klick? You come in here full of nuance and speculation and accusation and I resent it, sir! I have nothing more to say to you. Now, if you please, get out of my house."

"Or we could talk about you referring to Nicole Russell as a *widow*. Perhaps we should start there. Is Paul Russell dead?"

For a moment I thought he had stopped breathing. He didn't move. His eyes grew large enough to pop. I remained seated, sticking to the vinyl, wondering what to do next.

He finally jerked around and looked out his dirty window. "Get out," he hissed, avoiding any further comment.

"You might be better off to deal with me," I proposed. "This thing's going to come down on all of you," I added, as if I knew what I was talking about.

"Out," even softer now, a defeated resignation in his voice.

I walked out the door and closed it behind me.

He was too numb to think straight. I was certain of this. That's why I paused briefly and then circled around the house. Peering in through the same dirty living room window, I expected to see him on the telephone, in panic, or perhaps in conference with Hudson.

But he was not on the phone. He was sitting on the edge of the ugly brown couch, head in hands, shoulders shaking.

As frightened as a child.

26

I carry a small transistor radio in my glove box because of the truck's broken radio. I tuned in to the only local station in time to hear Brother Al sign off, which meant it was ten o'clock sharp. Brother Al Pine is a close personal friend and fellow musician, and just hearing his voice makes me feel good.

The local news followed and led off with a story that forced me to the side of the road. The horribly nasal newsman said, "Top story this hour: Local physician, Dr. James Kupps, died last night in a single-car automobile accident. Kupps, valley resident and respected family physician for over thirty years, was found near the three-mile marker off Broadmore Road, where his car had apparently run out of control and struck a cottonwood tree. Sheriff Dean Hudson said he estimates the accident took place between one-twenty and two A.M. Kupps was last seen at a local establishment at around one A.M. last night. He was pronounced dead on arrival at County Hospital. No further information is available to us at this time; however, we sure will keep you posted on that one, folks.

"In other news, fish and game management—"

I switched off the radio and my heart began to pick up speed and force. Kupps, a chancy player at best, had been eliminated from the game. It meant the rules had changed. Someone—Hudson, no doubt—had decided to start setting boundaries and close ranks.

It suddenly occurred to me that with Lyel off with Tim, Nicole had been left alone, and my pounding heart tried to tear through my chest.

I had the twenty-year-old truck out on Pole Road, and though I must have been pushing seventy-five miles an hour, I found myself willing the crate to go faster. I continually glanced at the speedometer. It had to be wrong.

I could picture her relaxing at home. Maybe she had neglected to lock the front door. Perhaps the security system was not enabled. As I was bombing down Pole Road, someone could be abducting her as a way to get to me.

I turned onto Highway 39, which serves as Ridland's Main Street, forced to downshift and obey the speed limit. All I needed now was another run-in with Sheriff Hudson.

The next five minutes seemed more like twenty. I finally pulled onto the gravel lane that led to the house. When I came through the unlocked front door, she was nowhere to be seen. "Nicole?" I shouted. "Nicole!" And I began swinging open doors and looking inside rooms. Panicked. When I broke open the folding doors to the laundry room I saw her sitting quietly on the floor, stroking Harper's head and looking into my eyes with a good deal of alarm. We caught eyes and she saw the terror in mine. I bent down and swallowed her up in my arms. She hesitated a moment and then squeezed me back. "What is it?" she wondered.

"I . . . oh God, is it ever good to see you." I refused to release her. Harper reached out and pawed my thigh and I chuckled. He wanted her back. He wanted her as badly as I did. This had to be the luckiest dog in the world, bar none. I hadn't noticed until now, but the dryer was thumping rhythmically, a zipper clanging against the metal tub periodically.

I can't be sure who instigated it. She was giggling and we were coming out of our clothing and before I knew it she had forced the door shut with her heel and had rolled me onto my back. Naked, she lay atop me, warm and soft-skinned.

Quite some time passed—it could have been years, for all I

knew—before I felt the wet nose of the dog attempt to pry its way between us. We both laughed, and our rib cages thumped together. She drew herself off me, took my hand and led me naked through the house (she ran on tiptoe) and into a hot, steaming shower, where she proceeded to lather me up and inspire me once again.

Later, over coffee, I looked into her eyes and saw a great deal of happiness, and I felt perhaps as good as I've ever felt, and I knew now that I loved her. Though I still couldn't explain it to myself. Certainly not to her. And I think I knew that if I didn't explain it soon, it wouldn't exist. Unmanifested, it would find no perch and would fly onward.

The wheels of a car grinding gravel in my drive brought me out of it. I detected sadness, even a finality, in her reluctant release of my hand. I rose and went to the door to have a look. I considered scolding her for not having the security system turned on, but decided to let it pass. People like Nicole rarely saw the need for security. Lucky them.

It was Sheriff Dean Hudson. Again. I was tempted to ask him how he knew I was home, but I guessed how. He came out of his car, took hold of his wide hard-leather belt and yanked his pants up on his belly. As he came around the hood he saw me by the door. "You're in a shitload of trouble, Klick."

"Sheriff."

"We pulled Doc Kupps out of the woods this morning—"

"So to speak," I said.

"Clowning around won't help things. I'd keep my mouth shut if I were you."

"You're not."

"What's that?" he asked like an old man hard of hearing.

"Never mind," I told him.

"I think you're getting a little big for yourself."

"Whatever that means."

"And wise to boot."

"Good golly."

"Doc is dead."

"A little birdie told me."

"And the only suspect I have is you."

"Try your brother-in-law. Or how about your friend, Mr. Clay? How about yourself?"

He looked at me strangely and then we both noticed the glider passing low overhead, silently, like a gigantic white hawk. The glider rocked from side to side in hello. I waved.

"Friend of yours?" the sheriff asked.

"If you check with the passenger, he'll tell you I was hiking with him last night, nowhere near Kupps."

"Hiking?"

"I'm on a health kick."

"That mouth of yours is going to get you in trouble."

"It already has. I've learned to live with it. It's the only one I've got."

"There ain't nothing to stop me from bringing you into town again. This time I might hold you."

"Oh yes, there is."

He looked at me curiously.

"Me," I answered. "I already told you: I can account for my every minute last night, Sheriff, from the time I was with you on. Can you?" His face turned bright red. "What were you doing late yesterday afternoon? Take a drive out to the Sweetlands, did you? Take the polish off a pair of boots? Pay a visit to Mr. Clay? And Bates? Did you tell Bates to kill Kupps, or did he think of it himself?"

His face went scarlet, his eyebrows white. Then he began to smile. That's when he scared me. People who smile when they're angry either make me laugh or scare me. Hudson didn't make me laugh. There were two men inside him, and I had just let one of them out to vie for control. His tongue lapped at the corner of his mouth. His eyes were glassy. He shook his head and coughed a laugh. "Stupid fuckhead," he said. He turned and walked back toward his patrol car. "Good luck," he added with a grin as he climbed in.

I gave him one of my press-release smiles and waited to make sure he'd left. Then I let out a deep breath and tried to get the wobble out of my knees. I felt seasick. I switched on my gate alarm quickly and waited to hear the bell that indicated he had driven completely out, and had not decided to sneak back up on me and blow my brains out. That, I decided, he was saving for later.

"What was that all about?" Nicole asked from the table.

"I think I made someone mad."

"Is it smart to make a cop mad?"

"No, I don't suppose it is."

"Then why do it?"

I shrugged.

"He's involved, isn't he?"

"Up to his neck."

●

The bell sounded. Both Nicole and I looked over at the wall. A minute later I saw Lyel's car rolling down the lane. He came in through the front door, ducking his head out of instinct. "You never know what you're going to find out," he said.

"I hope you'll tell us."

We all sat down at the kitchen table. Lyel said, "A lot of activity around the barns. If they did any loading, it was done inside. What I did see, however, whetted my curiosity."

"Which was?"

"One of the house trailers, not the one to the side of the barn, but the one out in back of the house"—I nodded because I knew which one he meant—"is not a home for humans, unless humans eat alfalfa, which I somehow doubt."

"Come again."

"I saw one of the kids carrying a flake of alfalfa into that trailer. A little while later a wheelbarrow came out, filled to the rim, if you know what I mean."

I reminded him of the three young horses I had seen inside the Sweetlands' barn. "The Sweetlands are involved in more than illegal crops," I said.

"Illegal breeding?" he asked.

"A cigar for the big man," I said. "He's a known horse thief, right?"

Lyel said, "I suggest we research Sweetland's past travels. If he is alive—and we still can't be sure of that—then he may be hiding somewhere he feels comfortable with, somewhere he's been before."

"Agreed. I'll check with the travel agency," I told him.

"What about me?" Nicole asked.

"I think it's time you paid Debbie Benton a visit. Find out exactly what Paul's plans were on the day he disappeared. I have a feeling you may get more out of her than me."

"I doubt that," she said. "I seriously doubt that."

"Give it a try," I encouraged. I didn't want her here alone, and Lyel had that look that said he had something planned.

I had used Fare Weather Travel in Butte Peak on a number of occasions. Everyone who lived south of Snow Lake used them. Kim Cross was a tall and healthy-looking woman who wore her hair short, kept her desk neat, and taped *New Yorker* cartoons on the side of her terminal. She wore jeans and an Oxford shirt and little or no makeup. In front of me was one of those cylindrical tubs that hold paper clips with a magnet. She smiled enthusiastically, and authentically, I thought, and asked how she could help.

There was one other desk, manned by the boss, a red-eyed, tired-looking young man. I said to Kim, "I'd like a fare rate from Butte Peak to Las Vegas, coach, leaving within the next two days."

She punched some keys, and before the screen responded she told me, "If you make that three days, it adds a discount."

"I doubt I can, but give both rates, if you would, please."

She read off the fares and I asked her again, this time substituting Bangor as my destination; and then once again if I stopped in Vegas and then flew to Bangor. I scribbled away as she spouted fares.

The red-eyed boss greeted an arriving customer who joined

him at his desk, wrote a check and handed it over. The boss typed something into his terminal and excused himself to a small enclosure that held a whining dot-matrix printer that had just started to generate the customer's ticket. He stayed in there for a good long minute, collating the ticket with an itinerary. I timed him: sixty-three seconds. I looked over to the bank of file cabinets that took up the far alcove and decided I might have enough time if I hurried.

"Anything else?" Kim asked.

"Can I refund these if I change my mind?"

"No problem."

"I'll just run to the bank, be back in a few minutes."

I looked at my watch on the way out the door. It was eleven-thirty. I hoped young boss would go to lunch first.

●

He did. I waited in the post office across the street until I saw him. Then, knowing she had no customers, I rushed across the street and pushed through the door. "I'm back," I announced.

She smiled.

I handed her the exact cash for the trip to Las Vegas and got ready to trip my stopwatch so I could pace myself. She danced her fingers across the keys, nails clicking, and then rose to head to the small room with the printer. "Be right back," she said.

I grinned and nodded. The moment she entered the room and the printer began singing, I jumped up and moved quickly to the file cabinet marked "S." His was the only Sweetland file. I fingered through at least two dozen copies of dated itineraries: Baltimore, Maryland; Lexington, Kentucky; five or six for Monterrey, Mexico; San Francisco; Los Angeles; and three for Las Vegas very recently. I slid the drawer closed. I had used up my time. I stepped closer to a poster of a ravishing beauty lying on an air mattress in aquamarine water over white sand. I've seen dozens like it. I like them all.

I tried to hold the destinations in my head. I thought of them as lyrics to a song. I'm good at remembering lyrics. I was a bit rude as I accepted my ticket and left quickly, although I did manage to thank her.

I climbed into the truck and wrote down everything I could remember on the back of some junk mail.

Lyel's house was too large a home for a single man, and I once again reminded him of it.

"Was Mr. Sweetland a traveler?" he asked. I handed him the envelope. He said, "It's addressed to you, and besides, I have all the credit cards a man could need, and then some."

"Other side, wise guy."

"Oh, really?" he said sarcastically, flipping it over to read. "Quite a bit of traveling."

"How about you? Did you have any luck?"

"I called Addison Electric Supply in Boise. I told them I was Larry Sweetland and that I had lost the receipt and needed a figure for my tax accountant. You may be interested to know that the Sweetlands purchased twelve hundred thirteen dollars and fifty-seven cents' worth of fixtures from Addison. Must have spread out the buying of the grow lights. I only found one order for fifteen bulbs from an outfit in Pocatello. They might have bought the rest out of state and had them shipped up here. The fifteen were bought recently, probably as replacements." He scanned the list of destinations again. "Yes, he certainly got around."

"And then some."

"Several trips to Mexico. No, thanks."

"Several indeed."

"I noticed. Why do you suppose he'd go there so often? A supplier?"

"Not if he's growing his own up here."

"Could be his source for starts or something," Lyel said.

"Maybe."

"Perhaps a consultant. If you had problems with a thirty-thousand-dollar crop of grass, you might seek advice on how to save it."

"Could be," I said. I had reached my own conclusions. We had missed the obvious. Just this once I relished being one up on Sir Lyel.

"But you don't think so," he said.

"No, I don't. He could find the same advice, even starts, for that matter, in northern California or Hawaii. He wouldn't have to go to Mexico."

"Good point." Lyel didn't like being the underdog. I could nearly hear him thinking.

"Maryland, Kentucky, San Francisco. What's that tell you?" I hinted, loving every minute of it.

"Horse country," he thought aloud. "As we discussed earlier."

"Big money," I reminded in a tutorial tone.

"Okay, okay," he said in a panicked voice. The game was on and we both felt the stopwatch running. "These trips have nothing to do with the pot business," he guessed.

I nodded.

He bit down hard on his lower lip, eyes dancing. I knew that feeling. He had cornered *me* in this same way before. I gloated. "A man of many talents," he finally said.

I smiled.

He saw the smile and took it as acknowledgment. "We've been looking at the wrong expertise," he said.

"You're warm," I told him.

"We've known all along that his real strength is training horses," he thought aloud.

"Warmer . . ."

"He's traveled to a bunch of places where thoroughbred is a way of life."

"Toasty."

"Hunt country and furlongs."

"Monterrey, Mexico?" I asked.

"He had bigger things going down there."

"Now you're hot. Very hot."

"Something less than legal, perhaps. But not drugs."

"Shall I tell you?"

"No, no, please don't," he said. "Another hint, perhaps."

"When I spoke to Debbie Benton, she said that she and Paul Russell were supposed to *fly* down to Las Vegas that afternoon."

He stood. "Awfully hard to fly with twenty keys of pot."

"That should have occurred to me at the time," I apologized. "Where to?" I asked.

"I'm heading to the library, aren't I?"

"I suggest you try Angie's Consent. It's a stud, believe it or not."

"You haven't researched it completely, I take it. You don't know for sure."

"No, not for sure."

"We allowed ourselves to be misled," he complained.

"We ignored Paul Russell's love of gambling. We misunderstood the Vegas connection. Lots of horse lovers in Vegas, people who race horses. We were sucked in by the obvious. We got caught up in the pot deal. We overlooked Sweetland's prior arrests. We goofed."

"But it wasn't a pot deal at all. That wasn't the deal between Sweetland and Russell."

"No. That wasn't the deal that got Russell killed."

Midafternoon I received a call from Red Clay. He pleaded with me to come right over. It meant a twenty-minute drive and I was less than enthusiastic considering my earlier talk with him.

Driving into his place, I scratched my head, downshifted and parked over by an old mechanical hand pump mounted in a footing of concrete. It looked something like a dark-green neck of a disfigured flamingo.

I missed my birds. I missed sitting out on the porch with a St. Pauli Girl and waiting for the faint clucking of a feeding mallard. The true art of life is keeping it simple. The devoutly religious once understood this. There is little art to getting one's life so crammed with things to do, bills to pay, and relationships to maintain that one ceases to enjoy the fundamentals of existence. The givens. It's the accepted norm, and it isn't very hard to find your way into. But certainly enjoyment of life was one of the first intentions behind whatever power put a pulsing muscle in the center of our chests and started it working. The Man With Blue Hair understands enjoyment and simplicity. He holds court up on my wall, overseeing all that goes before him, watching over all who pass below, and he manages to maintain that wonderful smirk on his face. I should like to manifest his sublime attitude into my physical existence someday. For after all, in one sense he is nothing more than oil pencil on black paper. He doesn't understand the pleasure of a garden-fresh salad and a bottle of Chardonnay. On the other hand, I have no idea what it's like to hang on a wall all day, ever happy, and play God. It's hard to say which of us has it better.

The door knocker was a bronze-plated cowboy hat hanging by a hinge. I thumped gently, sending deep reverberations throughout the log structure. Clay's face was so oily and reflective I could have used it as a mirror. He was ashen-white and he kept both hands rammed into his front pockets to hide their shaking.

He said, "From what I can tell, you're out to help the woman find out what happened to her husband. Am I right about that?" He led me into the living room and offered me the vinyl seat again. I took a wooden rocker instead. He sat down on the couch. It hissed.

"Why did you call me?" I asked.

"I'm scared."

"Of whom?"

"People. Certain people. I wanted to warn you, but I didn't dare talk specifics over the phone. He may have my phone tapped. You never know."

"Hudson?"

"Listen. What you're doing is stupid. It's a stupid thing to do. Both of us, you and I, we should learn from Kupps. Okay? That was a message. We'd be stupid to ignore it."

I studied him a moment. I was surprised. I said, "You're not part of it, are you? Not like the others. I thought you were."

"Me?" he asked indignantly. "What, are you crazy? I'm an attorney."

"That isn't the best defense. You were Sweetland's attorney. You rigged that."

"And you want to know why?" he asked. "Because they knew I'd look the other way just to win a case. Business has been bad, I mean real bad, for me. I needed that win, and I suspect they knew it, too."

"What else do you know?"

He ignored me and spoke more to himself.

"Hudson came by yesterday," he added. "He must have known you would contact me and ask me about the trial. He told me you would. And you did. There, see? He has the whole thing figured. Don't ask me how."

"And he told you what to say."

"He *threatened* me." He trembled. I felt sorry for him. He was soft like over-ripened fruit. The slightest prodding and he would burst, with foul-smelling seeds. "He told me there would be plenty of need for public defenders in the coming year and there was no need to bite the hand that feeds you. Hudson knows everything about everyone in this valley. He knows I'm two months in arrears on my payments on this place. I've had it listed for six months. Without work, I've had it."

"Threatened?"

"This morning. A little while ago. He told me Kupps had spoken with you. Then he told me what happened to Kupps, and what a shame it was. Then he hung up. There was only one message in that call and that was that if I talked to you, he'd kill me."

"Then why the hell did you call me?"

"To *warn* you." He paused and wormed his fingers in a ball. "I couldn't call the cops. Who the hell was I supposed to call?" He looked at me hopefully.

"Sweetland's alive, isn't he? You know he's alive."

His face tightened up on itself and I couldn't recognize him. "I saw him. I saw him a full twenty-four hours after he supposedly died."

I nodded. "He wanted legal help," I theorized.

"What?" he asked frantically. "No. No. Not at all!" He paused. "Our ranches connect. My land runs quite a ways east. I was out on a ride. My herd's short a couple of calves.

"I never connected it," he continued. "I used to hear an occasional plane, you understand, some of 'em damn big, but what with the cloud-seeding Snow Lake does every winter and all the crop-dusting and air traffic in the summers, I never paid much attention."

"A plane?"

He nodded. "Saw him loading stuff into a plane. A *big* plane. Got back, called Hudson, and told him about it. I was thrilled. I like Greg. I told him there had been a mistake, that Greg was alive, that I had just seen him." He worried some more and added, "I had gone along with some dicking around on the Sweetland trial and Hudson reminded me of it. We pressured the judge right out of town. Rigged the thing. Got a rumor going that his daughter was dealing for Greg. In a town this size, that's all it took. His daughter was a wild thing and he bought the rumor. Hudson suggested to me strongly that I was mistaken, that I hadn't seen Greg at all. I got the hint. I agreed it must have been Larry, apologized for taking up his time and hung up. You wouldn't believe what he was doing," he said.

"Loading horses into the plane," I told him.

He looked at me with complete disbelief. Astonished. We sat in silence. So Sweetland had driven Paul Russell's Audi out of state, but had then flown back in to get a few of his more valuable possessions. I had met their brothers and sisters in the Sweetland barn. "Yearlings, right? Maybe younger."

"Younger. That's right. Now how the hell did you know that?"

"I suggest you leave town."

"Not a chance. I couldn't take a chance like that. If Hudson or one of his deputies caught me, that would be the end of it. I'm sitting tight. I suggest to you that you do the same. If I hadn't warned you, I would have hated myself. But now I have. What you do about it is up to you. Just calling you may get me in trouble."

He looked terrified. I told him, "There's another way, you know. You saw Sweetland. We can go to the proper authorities."

He shook his head. "There are no proper authorities. Don't you see that? Hudson knows everybody. He *is* the law. This is the West, Klick. Hudson still thinks this is the old days. He controls things. There's no telling how far his connections go. For all we know, they go all the way to Boise. Probably do. There are no proper authorities," he repeated. "I don't want to end up like Kupps. I wanted to warn you, that's all," he whined, looking at me with his sad, pathetic eyes.

I stood. When I reached his front door I said, "I'd keep this locked if I were you. Locked and the shades drawn at night."

"What are you going to do?" he whined. Then his face lit up.

"Say, what if I called Hudson, got him over here and got him talking? I could tape it. That would do it. That would give us what we need. How about something like that?"

"No, I don't think so, Mr. Clay." There was no way a man like this could pull off such a thing. He was far too nervous and out of control. "Let sleeping dogs lie," I told him, using his words. "I liked your original plan. Low profile. Remember, doors locked, shades drawn."

I left.

"How'd you know it was horses he was loading in that plane? Why the horses?" he called after me.

"You said a big plane," I reminded. "Greg's specialty is horses. Doors locked," I said again. My truck starting up drowned out whatever he shouted back.

●

She was sitting at my kitchen table, her delicate fingers wrapped around a cup of coffee. She had been crying. Her eyes were red and the bottom of her nose was blushed. "You made me see her for a reason," Nicole said. "Didn't you?"

"Yes."

She nodded. "I thought so. It was selfish of you, Klick."

I felt a knot in my throat. She was probably right. "I didn't look at it that way, honestly. I thought you needed to meet her."

She shook her head. "No. That's one thing I didn't need."

I wanted to hug her, but I knew it was wrong. Fading away from me, and the harder I reached, the farther away she moved, like someone standing on the other side of a trick mirror.

"Paul used me," she said.

"That's not your fault."

"Oh, really? That's not what my heart says." She began to cry again. And then she wept. Sobbed. I placed my hand on her back. She was hot. She reached up and took my hand. Relief surged through me. It felt right to touch her. "I suppose I never would have known if I hadn't talked to her."

I remained silent.

"And I never would have gone to her if you hadn't convinced me to. I suppose I should thank you. I've never thanked someone for making me feel like this." She forced a smile. I bent over and kissed her lightly on her lips. She threw her arms around me and held me tightly. I stood up and in doing so pulled her from the chair. She was warm all over, and soft, and even through our clothes I felt us unite in the same way we had while making love. She smelled earthy and bitter. She was frightened and clutched to me to prove it.

"Greg Sweetland killed Paul," I confirmed. I didn't want to delay it. I didn't want to get her back on her feet and then knock her off again. "Paul turned up in the wrong place at the wrong time, and he happened to have fifty thousand in cash on him. Sweetland needed a way out. Paul was supposed to be it."

"Good," she said, and she stopped crying at once. "I hope he saw it coming," she mumbled into my shirt. "I hope he saw the whole thing coming. I hope he felt the fear clear down inside of him. I hope he was sorry." Then she came unglued. I held her for five minutes. She dried up and collapsed back into her chair. I poured us both a bourbon and kept the bottle out. I chased mine with a green Girl. She took a couple of sips off my beer and poured us both another shot. A double. We toasted to Harper's recovery and she gave me the first glimpse of a genuine smile. The bourbon quieted her. We both watched out the window as a pair of mergansers fed in the slough. She reached over and took my hand. I rubbed my thumb across her knuckles. She liked the ducks as much as I did. She understood them now. A few minutes later she excused herself and went off to take a nap. I gave her five minutes and then went into her room and tucked her in. Her clothes were in a pile on the floor. All of them. Her shoulders were bare and I could picture what it would feel like to slide in next to her and swallow her up. She thanked me as I pulled the door shut, twisting the handle slowly to close it as quietly as I could. "You're welcome," I told the door, so softly that even I couldn't hear.

29

When Lyel arrived back from the library, I signaled him and he closed the front door quietly and tiptoed inside. Lyel trying to tiptoe is like an elephant trying to tap-dance. We moved into a section of the house where we could talk in normal voices without worrying about awakening Nicole, and I opened the blinds so I could see the mergansers on the slough. We both watched the ducks feed as we talked, our pale, translucent reflections shimmering in the clear blue glass of the double-pane window.

He set a pile of photocopies down in my lap and said, "We were right."

"An ounce of research is worth a pound of investigation. We couldn't be sure until we had these," I reminded.

"You look worried," he said.

"I think I know where Greg Sweetland is. I think I know why. I think I know what Paul Russell intended to do with that fifty thousand, and I can guess why he died."

"Angie's Consent," he said, nodded toward my lap, "and the others."

"Stolen from a stable in Kentucky, a little over a year and a half ago, wasn't it?"

"One year, ten months, to be exact." Typical Lyel. "But how did you—"

"It made national news at the time," I interrupted. "Some dates you don't forget. I was lying in a Detroit hospital at the time with a stab wound in my back and a pharmaceutical running through my veins. Not a date I'll soon forget." I looked over at him now. He continued to watch the ducks. I had poured him some bourbon in Nicole's glass. I took a healthy amount down my throat and felt it burn. "The same date was on his travel itinerary."

"Kentucky," Lyel said. "You don't like coincidences."

"No."

"According to that, syndicated value at time of theft was a little over nine million. Stud fee, seven hundred and fifty thousand dollars," he recited, having read the clippings he had Xeroxed. "Greg Sweetland stole thoroughbreds for a living?"

"I believe so," I said dramatically. "At least he stole Angie's Consent, drove him down to Monterrey, Mexico, and set up shop. Collect the stud's sperm, freeze it, ship it to artificial inseminators in the states willing to pay the price. Get breeding papers on another matrimonial arrangement so there are no questions asked, and get the genes of one of the highest-pursed horses this decade has seen. Run the horse and pray the genes come through and pay off. What would you guess would be a good price for black-market thoroughbred sperm?"

"Fifty thousand dollars?" he asked.

I grinned. "The price Paul Russell paid to Sweetland. The thing of it is, Russell had some high-rolling connections in Las Vegas. Try this out. Russell uses Vegas as his source for grass all the years he was dealing. He makes a lot of friends down there, some of whom have an interest in racing. An *active* interest. Then he starts to deal pot through Sweetland up here. The two become hunting buddies. Sweetland maybe lets it slip that he can get hold of some incredible thoroughbred sperm or even breeding stock for the right price. We have other horses missing, right? Mares?" I asked, lifting the Xeroxes.

He nodded.

"So Russell checks out his Nevada friends and finds a buyer for the sperm. He's going to buy for fifty thousand, sell for seventy-five or a hundred. He can carry the sperm onto the plane with him. He and Debbie Benton are planning on retiring. Only he makes a single miscalculation: Greg Sweetland is in the hot seat from some local romance. He's also been alerted by Hudson that some federal agents are snooping around. He needs to disappear. It's the perfect time to die. But to die effectively you need a corpse. Along comes Paul Russell with a briefcase full of fifty thousand in cash. There's a simple solution here: two barrels into Russell's face and Sweetland comes out smelling like roses just as long as the locals are willing to cover for him—"

"—which they are because Hudson already has several of them on his payroll," Lyel finished.

"He spends what—ten of the fifty?—to ensure silence on the part of his friends, takes Russell's identity and car and heads south. A while later he takes one last risk: he flies back here to pick up a couple of valuable fillies he was working up here." This caught Lyel by surprise. "I had a chat with our friend Mr. Clay. He's a liability to them, I think. He spotted Sweetland after Sweetland was already dead."

"A liability indeed."

"At any rate, it's back to Mexico to spend time in the sun with a joint and a bottle of mescal, selling sperm and breaking colts."

Lyel said, "Required reading: Angie alone has a five-hundred-thousand-dollar reward on his hooves. Even after taxes that's a small fortune."

My heart began to beat fast. Anything over a hundred thousand has that effect on me. "He's bound to be well guarded," I pointed out.

"Well guarded for potential adversaries. Potential business would be another story entirely."

"Buyers?"

"A certain member of a certain notorious family in Atlantic City owes you a certain favor for a certain daughter you recently found."

"Carmine Catiglio? You want me to call Carmine?"

"Your scar is barely healed. He's perfect. He's rich, a known criminal, and he loves racehorses. Who better to send two lads down to buy a little seed? You earned the favor, use it while you still can. In another three years he could be in jail, or dead, or both."

"You're right."

"Yes, I know. Even Greg Sweetland wouldn't be dumb enough to screw around with a couple of boys sent by Carmine Catiglio."

"You're coming along? I thought you hated Mexico."

"Wouldn't miss it for the world. It's getting late in Atlantic City. I suggest you make a phone call."

My gate bell sounded. It was muted by the closed door. I assumed it had awakened Nicole. "Visitors," I hissed, already moving toward my bookcase. When the garage had been re-modeled into a television room, the finish carpenter had been asked to leave the bottom shelf of the recessed bookshelf un-nailed. He had cut the vertical grain fir to a snug fit and left it at that. With a row of paperbacks on it, it looked like any other bookshelf. Hidden in the architectural void beneath the bottom shelf, I kept two Detonics Combat Masters, a sheathed hunting knife, four loaded magazines, and four hundred hollow-point rounds. Early in my music career I had recognized the need for a working knowledge of self-defense techniques. However it wasn't until my somewhat late-in-life career switch that I was able to polish what little I had picked up on the streets of towns like Providence and New Haven. With a loan from Lyel—he considered it an "investment in our friendship"—I was able to enroll in a survivalist's training camp that came as close to a ter-rorist boot camp as I ever hope to come. Hand-to-hand, small arms, and creative explosives 101 were the daily diet. In six weeks I came away with a better-than-average working knowl-edge of the Dark Side, and I hone these skills whenever possible, whether at a shooting range or a gym, because even one scar is one too many, and I have several. The shelf lifted easily, and the snug fit allowed it to remain propped up. Hidden in the front closet of the house I had a Colt Government Issue and another two hundred rounds, but I preferred the Detonics. It's the finest—and the smallest—.45 in the world. The size of a snub-nosed .38. The Mercedes of handguns. The Colt had required me to have my gunsmith pin the grip safety. The Detonics is one of the only .45s sold that comes off the assembly line with a deactivated grip safety. It is a defensive weapon, designed and engineered to be shot. It means business. Twice a month I spend several hours shooting, whether in Los Angeles or Idaho. It's not like riding a bicycle—you get rusty quickly. I wasn't feeling rusty.

I handed Lyel one of the Detonics, along with two of the magazines. He aimed it at the floor, popped the safety off, did a blind check for one in the tube and, finding it empty, slapped in the magazine. He cocked it with his thumb and held it out at an angle pointed away from himself. He thumb-clicked the safety.

"Where can we put her?" he asked.

We were thinking alike. When facing an adversary, the most common response is to freeze. To panic. It is built into the genetic pattern for some stupid reason. One must train the response away. In a tactical gunfight, you have less than two seconds to respond to the challenge. If you fail to respond, it is often your last failure. My training helped me there: I have wandered into darkened houses with dummies jumping out from nowhere and firing blank rounds at me—something like a haunted house on bad acid. Once, about two years earlier, Lyel had come along as an observer on a refresher course in Gunsight, Arizona. He found it so interesting, he started with basic training and worked his way through. As a result I could feel comfortable around him with a loaded .45 in his hand. There were not many people I could say that about. "In the crawl space," I said. "Bottom of my closet. You get it open. I'll bring her."

He was out of the room in a flash.

30

We waited for headlights. I had switched on the outside floods, fully aware of the effect of their intensity. This was the set of floods that I used to light the croquet court for night games. They were mounted high on the roof and angled out to illuminate a full third of the front lawn. If our visitors were coming in on foot, the lights would tend to blind them, and I figured that would force them around in back of the house.

We put a frightened Nicole into the three-foot crawl space below the back bedroom. She was armed with the hunting knife. Giving her a handgun was unthinkable—something else I'd learned in tactical training.

There was little question of who was coming—it had to be Hudson. The only true unknown was how many men he had along with him.

"Inside out?" Lyel asked.

"I think it would be the best, don't you?"

We hurried out of the house. I ran toward the slough. Lyel went around the house and hid behind the satellite dish.

What Lyel and I called an "inside out" was a simple-enough concept. When someone plans to take you by surprise from the outside, you turn it inside out and do unto others as they see fit to do unto you. I moved toward the slough slowly, keeping low and quiet. I knew it would take a lot of noise to invoke flight at this time of night, but then again, if the mergansers did fly, they would give me—and our strategy—away. I sat down between the field grass and willow facing the house.

Lyel was perfectly still. He had a good view of the other side of the house as well as my position. I could see the south corner, and through the large windows into the living room.

Several minutes passed before I heard the first distinct foot-falls in the stand of aspen on the other side of the fence—one man coming toward the house very close to Lyel.

Without any floodlights on this side of the house, it was held in a shadowy darkness. To my left I could see a piece of the illuminated croquet court; some of the light spilled around the corner onto the ditch, casting elongated shadows. Again, the floor of leaves well beyond Lyel alerted me of the same approaching man. He was moving more confidently now, tree to tree, closing the distance to the house quickly. I saw the faint outline of Lyel as his spine became more rigid. I knew for a fact that he would not fire the weapon unless his life depended on it, but he would use it. In weapons handling, the proper defensive tactic is to prove to your opponent in the first few fractions of a second that a firefight will result in at least one death—his. The correct procedure is then to conduct a mutual retreat, turn and hightail it. In the case of a "spontaneous urban assault"—a mugging—this procedure works well. It is something altogether different when a man comes hunting you. But we were both trained for that as well.

I couldn't be certain of Hudson's intentions. If it was to kill me, or us, then I would be better prepared for the impending firefight if I could anticipate his strategy—second guess him and use his efforts against him. If your opponent is aggressive, then return the aggression. If he is conniving, then retreat. I considered Hudson *both* aggressive and conniving which left me in something of a pickle.

This raid was Hudson's last-ditch effort to maintain control of a situation that had quickly gotten away from him, which made me question the well-being of "Red" Clay. I had the sickening feeling he had gone ahead with his plan to try and trick

Hudson. Or, worse yet, Hudson had gone out there and tortured the man, and knew what Clay and I had discussed.

I had trouble believing Hudson had come to kill Nicole and me, but try as I did to look for other solutions to his problem, eliminating the two of us seemed his only recourse. He could have told his men that I killed Kupps, and that I'm believed dangerous. If Nicole then "happened" to get killed in the cross fire by Hudson, who would challenge the sheriff?

I thought about Nicole, hidden in the dark crawl space, frightened and alone. Her presence gave me determination to win whatever battle was to come.

The headlights to Hudson's patrol car appeared a few short seconds later and I began to see the bigger plan. If we tried to sneak out, Hudson had a backup to catch us in the act. A deputy, no doubt. Keep it nice and legal.

We were in a squeeze. Hudson was still an official of the law. *The* official of the law. Any confrontation with him would only mandate arrest—on a statewide level if necessary. On the other hand, he still had the power to detain us and do with us whatever he saw fit—probably kill us—while he reorganized and tightened the loose ends he had allowed to come undone. As far as I could see, this assessment of our situation allowed us only two choices: Kill Hudson and his accomplice and suffer through an agonizing trial where our only defense would be circumstantial evidence, or run.

If we could expose Sweetland and effectively pressure him, we might handle Hudson without killing anyone. Shooting another human being is a sickening experience, no matter how much training one has. Killing a person is a living nightmare. I had no desire to suffer through it again. Once is enough, and I had been forced to kill more than once.

Lyel saw my hand signal. He understood that to neutralize the man between himself and the house he would have to move while the noise of Hudson's car provided him cover. I watched as he moved stealthily toward the other.

At the last possible moment, the man felt Lyel's presence. In the eerie slow motion that accompanies these experiences, the man lifted his weapon and began to turn toward Lyel, who was himself momentarily screened by the satellite dish and unable to see his opponent. My effective range in a prone position was somewhere around fifty yards—a long shot for a handgun. But the tall, overgrown hay and field grass would not allow a prone position, which cut me back to an accurate range of somewhere between thirty-five and forty yards. I would have to take the shot kneeling, but it was not a tough shot. In this case I was trying to hit "the broadside of a barn." As the deputy continued to turn toward Lyel, gun drawn, I fired a single shot into the Thermopane window to the deputy's right. The stout pop of my Detonics was followed by a loud crash as the vacuum seal between the twin panes of window glass exploded, spraying fragments both into the room and out into the face and left arm of the deputy, who was now fully turned around.

I left him to Lyel, my attention immediately on Hudson, whose car came to a rolling stop in the driveway, lights on. Inside the vehicle and on a gravel driveway, Hudson hadn't heard the single report of my gunshot, and the house had effectively blocked the sound of the window shattering. I lost sight of the car then behind the house, and quickly looked back at the deputy and Lyel.

The two were entangled in a flurry of limbs, fighting on the lawn beneath my fragmented bedroom window.

Hudson's headlights switched off and he shut off the car. There is no silence quite like the tranquil silence of the evening countryside. On any other night, the steady rumble of the slough flowing behind me, the whisper of field grass in a light breeze would have stimulated some comment of gratitude for my blessings. On this night, however, the silence was more like the silence in a theater, where a single cough demands everyone's attention.

Lyel lowered his arm toward the deputy's head. He must have found one of the fist-sized river rocks that are used as a border for the planting that rims the perimeter of the house, for I could hear the *thud* of the contact clear across the field. His opponent fell still. I was up and running at a crouch. As my angle changed, through the house I could see Hudson coming up the brick path approaching the front door, seemingly cool as a cucumber.

In situations like these, Lyel and I tended to think alike; it was what made us work so well together. He possessed a mechanical form of thought, based on a studied, principled rationale of logic and reason. Of the two of us, he is the academic, encyclopedic in his judgment. I tended to work from my heart, my emotions. I moved on instinct. He moved according to what that complex data base of his told him to. Nonetheless, despite the differences, in these must-do situations, we would often speak the same words at the same instant.

"We can't win, right?" he asked. "He's the law."

"We're out of here," I replied and hurried through the broken window into my bedroom as I heard Hudson ring the front bell. How considerate, I thought, wondering if I had misinterpreted Hudson's plan. No, I decided. That was just the kind of overconfident man Hudson was. Certain I would open the door for him. Certain he would have the jump on me.

I knocked twice softly on the crawl-space hatch in my closet floor, opened it and lowered myself in. I motioned to her. She came stumbling across the rocky earth and threw herself into my arms, her face streaked with tears, her shoulders trembling. I whispered, "We've got to make a run for it, okay?"

She nodded bravely.

I helped her up through the hatch, the smell of her nightgown and her skin dizzying. In these life-threatening moments, all my senses were stimulated, all my dials turned up to ten, my instincts base and directed toward survival and continuation of the species. I could have taken her right there on my bedroom floor. I wanted her. God knows how I wanted her. Such a strange and desperate feeling, my body on autopilot, begging, pleading with me.

Lyel was there and he pulled her out. Her flannel nightgown brushed my face again. She smelled of scented soap and body lotion. Her skin was soft and warm beneath the covering. I stuffed her feet into a pair of my sock-slippers.

The door chimes sounded again.

We left the house through the back door and moved away, angling toward the densely willowed banks of the slough that promised to help hide our moving forms as we stole through the darkness, escaping to the north, away from Hudson and the finality he promised.

•

Fred Peck's pickup truck was parked in the garage, keys in the ignition. I didn't know Fred well enough to use an explanation at this hour, so I stole his truck. In the rearview mirror I saw Fred come out the front door waving his arms and shouting at us. Waking Fred presented us with an additional problem: he would certainly report the theft to the sheriff's office, which meant Hudson. This time of night, the call would be automatically call-forwarded to Hudson's home and would awaken the man's wife. She, in turn, would call him on the radio. It meant we only had the narrowest of leads. I pushed the pedal down farther.

"Where?" Lyel asked.

"I need clothes," said Nicole, pulling on the flannel.

I turned right, sped down Main Street at seventy and turned left onto Pole Road. They both looked at me curiously. "We have to take Clay with us," I told them. "He won't make it without us."

"I'll call Tim," Lyel said. "He can help."

"Help?" a frightened Nicole asked.

"Lyel and I are going to Mexico," I told her.

"And what about me?" she wondered.

"You and our friend Mr. Red Clay are going on a short vacation," Lyel explained, throwing his thick arm around her and holding her tightly. "Don't you worry about a thing."

She reached over and took my right hand off the wheel and pulled it into her soft, warm lap. It was a moment of heaven for me, despite our circumstance. Friend Lyel with his big arm around her shoulder, my hand finger-laced with hers. I could have just kept on driving.

I probably should have.

31

It didn't feel good to run from a man like Hudson. His abuse of the power entrusted to him and his overindulged self-confidence made me want to stand up to him. But not yet.

I turned Fred Peck's truck into Clay's long driveway, gravel spitting out behind the rear tires sounding like faint applause.

"Do you feel it?" Lyel asked.

"What?" I said.

"Him," he replied in a raspy voice. I applied the brakes and we came to a stop.

"Stay here," I instructed Nicole, "and lock the doors behind us."

"Who?" she wondered.

I looked into her eyes. My look must have frightened her, for her brow knitted and she bit down on her lower lip before saying, "God, no."

We shut the truck's doors and she locked them. Lyel, weapon drawn, waited by the front door. He looked over at me and I nodded. He turned the handle and held the brass cowboy hat against the knocker, preventing it from bouncing against the door and announcing us. The heavy door opened smoothly and silently.

We stepped inside and quietly closed the door behind us. Lyel was right, and we both knew it before taking another step. *Him:* the black-hooded one who eventually sinks his long talons into your soul and extricates you for points unknown. Clay had been caught in those talons.

He was slumped on the couch, a bloody bullet hole in his left shoulder, another just below his right eye. He had been beaten badly, and the room had been tossed to support the look of a robbery. Some of the art was gone from the walls. The stereo had been ripped from the bookshelf, leaving behind stretched, broken wires. This had nothing to do with a robbery. His cocktail was spilled across his lap, its ice melted. The vinyl chair across from him still held the impression of where his murderer had sat.

I felt somehow responsible. He had been a weak imitation of a man, and in death he was tragic. In his own way he had challenged Hudson, and Hudson had prevailed.

"We shouldn't touch anything," I said.

"You really think Hudson would have been that careless?" Lyel asked.

"You never know." I moved slowly out of the room. "I'll use the phone in the kitchen."

"Who are you going to call?"

"I'm going to leave an extensive message for Agent Blokowski."

"But what do we have? The federal boys can't handle a guy like Hudson. Not without Sweetland's testimony."

"We should have killed him. Now I'm sorry we didn't."

"No, you're not."

"No. Maybe I'm not." I placed the call. I had to call Salt Lake City to reach anyone this late at night. The man I spoke to denied an agent Blokowski was working the Snow Lake area at first. As my story unfolded, he acknowledged that certain aspects of it interested him and then he had the gall to suggest I phone the FBI. I told him in no uncertain terms that he was appointed that task, and I slammed the receiver down. Lyel was right. They wouldn't do anything.

Lyel called Tim and made the necessary arrangements. We wouldn't risk meeting at the hangar in case Hudson had the airport covered. Tim would taxi the private jet to the end of the runway before takeoff. The runway bordered a sixty-acre hay field owned by the Flying Heart Ranch. We would meet Tim at the end of the runway, approaching on foot from the ranch.

When he hung up he asked, "What about Nicole?"

"I have a cousin in Santa Fe, Wayne Penny and his wife Susan. We'll drop her on the way."

●

An hour and ten minutes later we left the valley below us, and for an instant, while I tried to ignore the resonant thunder of propulsion, I could imagine I was a merganser in the initial throes of flight. I could feel my wings outstretched and extended, my muscles frenzied and frantic. As the wheels clunked into their holds I felt my webbed feet slap back against my white downy underside, and I banked sharply to the left, the world growing tiny beneath me, the dark sky swallowing me up like the comforting warmth of a blanket being tossed over my head.

Nicole reached out and took my hand. Her fingers were ice cold and a pervasive sadness emanated from her. I turned her head toward mine and kissed her once gently on the lips and stroked her cheek fondly. I reassured her with all those things you say to reassure a person, and I'm quite certain they had little or no effect. She forced a smile. She was beautiful even in sadness, which so few of us are. She couldn't turn her beauty on and off like some people can. She had no choice about it; like a swan, she was stuck with her splendor.

I felt her slipping away from me and I wanted desperately to do something about it, but I feared I would only drive her farther away if I tried. What a strange feeling this desperation was. Sitting side by side, I felt the bonding force between us diminishing, like the dissipating strength of a harmony as two strings slip out of tune. What had once been sonorous and filled with wonder was for some reason escaping me, and I felt choked with the knowledge I would lose her. Tears welled in my eyes, and I turned to gaze out the window into the velvet blackness that enveloped us. Blackness all around me. And the haunting image of Clay's final stare burned into my memory, seared deeply in my memory, branded there forever, reminding me how fickle this thing called life really is. Paul Russell knew. Kupps knew. Clay knew.

32

We arrived at Sweetland's ranch after six hours of hunting around the outskirts of Monterrey, Mexico. Lyel had paid out over a hundred U.S. dollars in bribes. Sweetland's place was a confused mix of lush and dusty. We passed a number of Mexican workers, shirtless and sweating as they worked to erect a long fence that edged a large corral. There were a number of tin-roofed outbuildings that appeared as if they might go over in a weak breeze. The house was modest. It had a red tile roof and cracked exterior in need of paint. It had once been beautiful, no doubt. A small bunkhouse for ranch hands sat off to one side, partially hiding several laundry lines and a play area where a number of small Mexican children were busy with a big red kickball.

We parked the four-wheel-drive behind a dilapidated pickup truck and climbed out. A huge Mexican came through the front door looking anything but hospitable. He had deep-set chocolate eyes and arms that threatened to tear the T-shirt he wore. The Incredible Bulk. A bodyguard, no doubt. Lyel eyed him and approached him without the slightest degree of fear. Lyel had already taken on his new identity and was quite comfortable with his superiority. Lyel was born with superiority. "My name's

Ward," he told the bodyguard. "This is Mr. Bailey. We're here on behalf of Carmine Catiglio. Here to see a Mr. Sweetland. Would you announce us, please."

"No one named Sweetland live here," said the man in chopped English.

Lyel took another step closer. "Don't fuck with me, friend. I've traveled long and hard. I don't particularly like this country and I have business to attend to. Sweetland lives here, and he'll see us. And if you try to bullshit me again, the two of us will tangle. Your choice."

He didn't bully the Mexican. For a moment I wasn't sure the man had even heard him. He looked over at me and I said, "Bailey. This is Ward. Here to see Sweetland." He glared into Lyel's eyes and then backed off and went inside, slamming the door. He was gone a long time. I stepped under the portico to get out of the deathly sun. Lyel had two huge orbs of sweat below his pits. He looked uncomfortable.

When the man returned, Sweetland was standing behind him. I knew it was Sweetland without any introduction. We were the same height, damn near the same weight. He had conspiracy in his eyes, masked by an unnerving confidence. Lyel said, "Carmine Catiglio was supposed to contact you through mutual friends, Mr. Sweetland."

"Yes. He did." He eyed us suspiciously. I was well aware that there was no way he could possibly know who we were, or why we were there, but I felt he did. I could see him lift the shotgun and fire it point-blank into Paul Russell's unsuspecting face. "Dead aim," Dr. Kupps had called it. A man like this would have no trouble doing such a thing. He made me suddenly cold, which was something of a miracle considering the climate. "Come on in," he added. "How 'bout a beer?" He turned and walked inside. He had made no attempt to shake our hands. He knew nothing of manners.

The inside of the house was a combination of a variety of tiles. Some ugly art adorned the walls. He led us into a room that had once had a fountain running in the corner—a small Mexican boy made of ceramics, peeing into a now stagnant pool that had been allowed to grow mossy algae. The room smelled moldy, as if mildew was hiding in every crack. Sweetland handed us both beers. I couldn't read the label. His was half empty. There was a pool in a courtyard. A dark-skinned young woman wearing only a G-string was soaking up the sun from a reclined position in a chaise. She had sensuous brown breasts with dark, almost black, nipples. Her hair looked like a horse's mane. It shone in the sun. Sweetland caught me staring and pulled a cord that closed a pair of yellowed white draperies. "A friend of mine," he said, indicating private property. And in that instant I saw his vulnerability. I had come down here hoping to find a way to provoke him. I had tried to talk myself out of it several times, but had failed. I wanted to rile him. I wanted him to try for me. My opportunity was drinking in the sun, covered in a shimmering oil that gave her a look of seductive invitation. She was young and ripe and brimming with possibilities.

Lyel said, "You have some seed Mr. Catiglio may be interested in."

Sweetland kept his bloodshot eyes on me. Stoned, I thought. He was waiting for an acknowledgment from me that I understood the gist of his warning. I gave him no such pleasure. He had controlled people for months now, possibly years. He was directly or indirectly responsible for the death of at least three people. I would not be controlled, and he obviously sensed it.

Lyel tried again. "Carmine is more interested in bringing a mare down here and breeding. You have any problems with that?"

"We guarantee fertilization. There's no need for that." He drank. He still hadn't looked at Lyel.

"Still, that's the way Carmine would like it. He wants to know exactly where the sperm comes from, if we understand each other. He's buying bloodlines, not sperm. He's prepared to pay a premium for this service."

"It's possible," Sweetland said. "It's been done before."

"Can you give me a figure?"

"There are problems with that, okay? These horses are still being looked for. A good mare can attract the wrong kind of attention. Things need to be worked out," he repeated.

Both Lyel and I noted the plural. As expected, Sweetland had stolen more than one prized quadruped. It meant he was more than lucky. He was shrewd and cunning and had both brains and guts. And he was sitting across from me.

"I'm listening," Lyel said.

"I don't like you," he said to me.

"Too bad," I told him.

"Now, now, boys," Lyel tried. "Let's keep this professional, shall we?"

"I've seen you somewhere before," Sweetland announced, squinting his stoned eyes and searching for where he had seen me.

It hadn't occurred to me. There was, in all likelihood, the possibility that we could have crossed paths a number of times in Ridland. There are only two gas stations and one grocery store. However, I didn't recall ever having seen him and I told him so. I couldn't tell if he accepted my response. He drank the beer down to only a few fingers remaining and clapped it onto the coffee table in front of him.

"Problems," Lyel reminded.

"Later," Sweetland said.

"I'll tell you what I told your overfed friend. I'm not fond of Mexico. I don't like the shits and I don't like the smell of trash and excrement."

"The dollar's strong down here," Sweetland quipped.

"So I would just as soon get business over with and get back to where we came from."

"Just exactly where did you come from?" he asked me.

I paused. It was a mistake. "Atlantic City," I said.

"Awfully tan for Atlantic City, aren't you? I hear they've had several weeks of rain there."

"I get around," I told him.

"I'm sure you do." He leaned forward. "So where the fuck did you come from?"

"Atlantic City," Lyel insisted. "We both met in Atlantic City last night. Flew out this morning. That's all you need to know."

"Vegas," he said to me. "I've seen you in Vegas, haven't I." It was a statement, not a question. "At Catiglio's place in Vegas."

"My assignments are my business, not yours," I told him.

He seemed satisfied with his deduction. "That's where it was. I thought so."

I had no desire to correct his mistake.

"You guys go back to your hotel. Dinner's at seven-thirty, drinks an hour before. We'll talk after dinner."

"I was told you could accommodate us," Lyel said. "What's this about a hotel?"

He grinned and nodded. "Just checking." He eyed me again. "Pedro will show you to your room. I hope you don't mind sharing a room."

"I'd like to take a look at the studs," Lyel told him.

"That can be arranged."

"I'd like a swim," I said.

He studied me, that dark look returning to his eyes.

●

We both assumed Sweetland might have wired our room, so Lyel and I playacted. I told him how I thought Sweetland was a jerk with all his suspicions. I told him I wished Carmine had sent somebody else, and that the only thing good about the trip so far were the tits on the babe out by the pool. He claimed to have missed her and complained that I always got all the women. I told him I couldn't help it. In the meantime Lyel had changed into khaki shorts and a white shirt. He had pale, muscular legs and knobby knees. I put on a pair of tiny swim briefs that emphasized my bulge and tied them loose. I'm proud of my flat stomach. I slapped it once.

"Doesn't leave much to the imagination," Lyel said.

"That's the idea," I replied, acting my role. "I'd like to find myself between those oiled legs, in a little bit of natural oil—if you know what I mean."

"I don't think our host would appreciate that."

"Fuck him. Anyone would tire of a no-brain like that in no time. A fresh salami's always appreciated by these brown bitches." I hoped he was listening. I wished I could see his face. "You ride the horses. I'll ride the woman."

"Don't mess up this deal. Carmine'll cut your dick off."

"Carmine loves to fuck other guys' women. Gives him a sense of superiority."

"That's true. But he's Carmine."

●

When I reached the pool she was gone. No surprise there. I swam about twenty laps and then lay out to dry, which took all of about a minute. When I was up to two thousand degrees I hopped in the pool and waded around to keep cool. She called down from a balcony. She introduced herself as Cristina. A rather bold move, I thought. She wore a shift that seemed to be made of translucent gauze. I wondered if she knew what kind of a view she was giving me. She wasn't wearing anything underneath, so I assumed by her wet hair that she was just out of the shower. "Greg told me we had guests," she said in conversation.

"What a lovely hostess," I complimented. Her wet hair continued to drip down onto her chest where the gauze seemed to disappear.

"If you need anything, just call," she said.

"Anything?" I asked.

She grinned. Her teeth were exceptionally white and perfect. She turned around and went back into the room where I couldn't see her. I was glad I was standing in cool water. I swam a few more laps. Round one was complete. I had made my point with her. Now if I could charm her in front of Sweetland . . . if I could elicit a response, an unmistakable response, I might have what I needed. Then the thought crossed my mind: What if Sweetland had instructed her to charm *me*? What if he was the type of guy who liked hurting people he didn't like? It fit him well. What if he was setting me up? What did I care? I decided. Either way I would get my chance at him. I would just have to be careful that I didn't let her timing control me. If they were in this together I could find myself vulnerable.

I moved into the shade and let myself dry. When I looked up I saw her brushing her hair in the window. She was watching me. And she was smiling.

I smiled back.

33

"He's got Angie's Consent and No Holds Barred," said Lyel in a slightly affected voice for the sake of any listening device. "I can hardly believe it. What a pair. Carmine will be happy. He's wanted to breed to Angie's Consent for a long time. He has the perfect mare for him. I'm going to call him, as arranged, and see what he says. I'm sure he'll give us the go-ahead to make the arrangements."

"I met his companion," I told him. "What a knockout. She has mahogany skin and Hawaiian hair. Jesus, I'd like to take her out for a test drive."

"Don't screw this up, Bailey. We're here on business. This isn't the Strip."

"I don't like Sweetland. He strikes me as a dumb hick. I don't trust him for a minute. I think Carmine is right in demanding the horses get it on."

"We make the arrangements and we're out of here. Another day at the most. Don't get so hot under the collar. Speaking of which, can you make this air conditioner cooler?"

I walked over to the quiet machine and switched it on high.

Lyel leaned into my ear and whispered, "One full-time guard on the stables, but I think he's a juicer. There's a trailer with a gooseneck hitch out back but I couldn't see a truck that could pull it. There's a two-horse hitch with a standard hitch but it's parked near one of the small outbuildings that may be a bunkhouse." I nodded, turned the machine down and adjusted the thermostat. "That ought to do it," I said, patting the machine. The light was different here from the light this time of year in Idaho. Looking from the window, I knew I was in another land. No mergansers down here. No mallards. I wondered how Nicole was. I hoped everything was fine, but I couldn't bring myself to believe it. I still felt her slipping away, even this far from me, and my heart hurt as if someone had slugged me in the chest. I am one of those people who hesitate to admit they have fallen in love—really in love. I fight it off like I would a bad cold. I've had too many sure things disintegrate before my eyes to have much faith in forever. I tend to put my faith in today and let forever take care of itself. But with Nicole I wanted to know forever, and perhaps that's why I never would.

●

Dinner was fair. Mexican chicken, spicy hot. We capped it off with a cup of thick Mexican coffee that promised to keep me awake half the night. Sweetland and I were into a drinking contest. We did a couple of shots of mescal out on the porch while Cristina sang us all a traditional song. She was good with a nylon-string guitar and had an above-average voice. I added some harmony the third time the chorus came along and it made her smile.

Sweetland came undone when I started singing and he interrupted the music to take us on our tour of the stables. Cristina exploded at him in Spanish. He stood and struck her, and that brought me out of my chair. Lyel laid his hand on my sleeve and I sat back down. We'd all had too much to drink. All but Lyel. Cristina rattled off more Spanish. Sweetland's neck turned scarlet and he spat at her. Quite unexpectedly, she reached behind her neck and her dress fell away. She walked fluidly over to the pool wearing nothing but low black heels and black lace panties, faced us, peeled off the panties, kicked off the shoes and dived in.

"Fucking whore," Sweetland mumbled. "Come on," he said to us. Something about the whole charade made it feel contrived. In my inebriated condition I thought I saw through it. Was he setting me up for something? Getting me drunk and having his woman disrobe in front of me. What was the point?

On his way through the living room he poured himself another shot of mescal. I declined his challenge to match him shot for shot. She was splashing around gracefully in the pool. I was worried.

•

The stables were worn down and contained the sweet, pungent odor of fresh manure and straw. Cobwebs clung to the overhead lights, which glowed slightly yellow. The guard sat in a chair directly in the middle of the walkway in front of the stalls. It would be an impossible location to jump him. We would have to come up with another way to incapacitate him. He had a shotgun lying on the floor next to him and a large-caliber revolver in a holster at his side. He looked like something out of "Gunsmoke," except that his bloodshot eyes gave away his weakness for the bottle. The horses were indeed exceptional specimens. I'm no expert, but who has to be an expert to know a woman is beautiful, or a sunset spectacular. These horses were exceptional, although one had a runny nose and the other an infected hock. Lyel hadn't noticed the infirmities. I pointed them out, thinking that we'd better appear as if we knew what we were doing. One of my neighbors, Joyce Wunderlich, is a horsewoman. She knows about everything there is to know about the beasts. I've helped her doctor her herd a few times and I've acquired a limited working knowledge of quarter horses. Sweetland tried to brush over the runny nose, but I knew it might be more serious than he was letting on and I told him so. He was getting more drunk by the minute and he was starting to scare me. People our size are dangerous when we overindulge.

"Where's Pedro tonight?" I asked.

"Around," Sweetland answered. "Why?"

"Haven't seen him."

"Pedro isn't real social," he said. "But he's there when you need him."

"I bet he is," I replied.

"I wired Mr. Catiglio," Lyel told Sweetland. "I don't expect his call to come through until much later this evening, after he's through at the casino." We were leaving the barn now, the three of us walking side by side. We must have looked like the front line of the Washington Redskins. "Would you mind if I waited for his call in the living room?"

"Hell, no," Sweetland replied. "I'll turn off my bedroom phone so it doesn't wake me up. I'm glad you told me. But don't expect it on time. The phones down here suck." As we approached the house he said suddenly, "She acts like a whore. That's what she is." He laughed, but it was a dark laugh. This man had an evil in him, an insensitive evil that made him thoroughly unpredictable. At this moment he was drunk, was being too friendly to both of us, and it made me feel exceptionally uneasy. I preferred him angry and mean—it rang more true.

"I think I'll take a swim, if you don't mine."

"Suit yourself." He paused and looked at us both. "Breakfast is at nine. If you're up earlier than that, Anita can make you something. Good night."

We both said good night. He was almost stumbling. He stopped in the living room and poured himself another shot. He crossed the courtyard by the pool where Cristina's clothes were still piled in a hump and disappeared into the darkness of the other wing.

"You sense it?" Lyel asked.

"I sure do."

"What do you suppose he has in mind?"

"He wants us relaxed and comfortable. I'm feeling just the opposite."

"Do you suppose he knows? Do you suppose he remembered where he saw you?"

"It's a possibility. That could be it."

"He's not as drunk as he's letting on, so why the playacting?"

"He's baiting us, I think."

"It's tonight or not at all," Lyel said.

"That's what I keep thinking."

"And Pedro. Where the hell is Pedro? He's one hell of an obstacle if we have to deal with him."

"Did you spot the truck?"

"Yes, I did."

"It looks easy enough."

"That's part of what bothers me. What if he made the mistaken assumption that Carmine sent us down here to steal the horse?"

"You have a strange mind, my friend," I said. "Do you suppose he wants us to try for it?"

"Could be."

"I had a thought tonight."

"What's that?"

"It occurred to me we could bring Sweetland back with the horses."

Lyel looked at me. "You're certainly feeling adventurous," he said.

"It's either that or kill him," I said. "I've made my mind up about that."

"Yes, me too. He's the kind of dangerous that must be dealt with. For one thing, if we steal his horses and leave him here alive, he'll come after us someday. Sometime when we least expect it. And he'll probably blow our faces off with a double barrel. Somehow that doesn't appeal to me."

"Nor me."

"So he's part of the bargain."

"It would look that way."

"And if we're smart, we'll handle him first. It increases our bargaining position with the hired hands."

"Agreed. Tonight?" I asked.

"I'd rather wait until daylight."

"I hadn't thought of that."

"Neither will he, I don't think." Lyel grinned.

"Good point."

"He'll expect something tonight, and we won't give it to him. Carmine's call won't come in, because he isn't going to call."

"And our host will stay up all night waiting for it," I pointed out.

"And drinking."

"That will make him weakened tomorrow."

"Don't count on it. I'm not sure a man like him weakens easily."

"We'll see," I said.

"That we will," he said.

I had shed my clothes. I dived in the water. It was cool and it sobered me immediately. The stars were out. I swam several laps of backstroke watching the sky. I sat naked in a chair and waited to dry off.

When I reached the bathroom down the hall from our room I grabbed a towel to dry my hair. As I turned around to replace the towel she was standing there in that same white transparent dressing gown. The door was closed behind her. She took a step toward me. I could smell the wine on her breath. Her body was warm and fluid. "Take me," she whispered, helping her gown to fall to the floor. She was flawless. But she did nothing for me. I understood Sweetland's plan now. If he could catch me in the act with his woman, then he'd have the excuse to beat me, or even kill me. With a man like Catiglio behind me, he wanted a damn good excuse. Had he recognized me? Did he know?

"No," I told her, reaching past her and opening the bathroom door quickly. I raised my voice. "No, thank you." I picked up the gown, handed it to her, patted her tender bare bottom and ushered her out the door.

Was Sweetland standing down the hall in shadow, watching? I thought he probably was. Waiting with that shotgun of his.

I glanced nervously over my shoulder several times as I headed back to our room. I half-expected Sweetland to step out of the shadows and pull the trigger.

34

Around three o'clock I thought I heard something down the hall. I rose to my elbow and strained to hear more clearly. I have a keen sense of hearing, but even so, after the initial sounds no others followed until I saw the handle to our room turn and the door slowly open. I lowered myself back down and kept my eyes open long enough to see Sweetland peer inside into the dark. Checking up. He pulled the door closed and soundlessly returned to wherever he had come from.

So he was suspicious, I thought. He was expecting us to do something in the night. Had he doubled the guard on the horses as a result? Had he had extra men hidden and waiting to kill us if we tried something? I fell asleep after that and slept soundly until the horizon began to glow with the first hint of morning. Then I gave up trying to go back to sleep; I showered and went downstairs, beating even Anita into the kitchen. I put some bottled water on to boil and went for a walk. This was the coolest part of the day. Even so, it was still in the mid-seventies. When the kettle was going at a full roar, I made two cups of drip and headed out to the barn. I kept alert to see if extra manpower had been added. I only saw one man other than the guard in the barn, to whom I offered the extra cup. That was Pedro. He was furiously working on some sort of mower, trying, I assumed, to beat the heat of the day, when such repairs would be torturous. I waved to him, but he ignored me.

The guard was thankful for the coffee. He appeared exhausted, not at all alert. We tried to communicate, but you can only say so much with your hands when you're holding a cup of coffee. We ended up sipping together, blowing steam off the surface of hot, bitter coffee. I checked that hock again. It didn't look any better. Sweetland was in a pickle. He needed a veterinarian, but couldn't trust any of the vets in nearby La Rosa, who might double-cross him and try for the reward money, which would far surpass any fee for medical services. On the other hand, both his horses needed immediate attention. The witch doctor, be-your-own-vet method was failing miserably. All this served to heighten my determination to liberate the animals from this man's care.

I looked around the stall to see if any preexisting circumstances or conditions might interfere with our plan. Although the stall doors leading to the outside were padlocked, the door of the next stall over—an empty stall—did not appear to be. The guard would have to be silenced and the entire operation would have to be done very quickly even if we managed to get Sweetland. Combined, even black-market, these horses were worth hundreds of thousands of dollars. A man like Pedro would be well aware of that fact and would be prepared to lose Sweetland. Threats to harm Sweetland then would be useless. We needed to take swift, effective action and, simultaneously, eliminate or reduce the possibility of others' following us or interfering—and all in broad daylight.

I was growing anxious to have this over with, to be gone from here. There existed an underlying violence in Sweetland, a disguised danger, like the somewhat passive threat of a resting volcano. I inspected the overhead rafters, alert to possibility of a backup, but saw no evidence of one. I stood, drinking my coffee while my friend smoked a cigarette and smiled at me and occasionally rattled something off in Spanish that I didn't understand. I would wait until he finished, nod and smile back, hoping it was an appropriate response. I wondered if this was how two-year-olds felt before they finally began deciphering the language. What a frustrating existence.

On my way out of the barn I plotted how to put the various elements of our plan together so that no more than five minutes would be consumed from beginning to end. The truck and trailer were at opposite ends of the compound, the main house in between. A small toolshed or machine shop was closest to the truck. The trailer, on the other hand, had been stored near one of the bunkhouses. As I came into the kitchen, Anita, a wide-bodied cook with miserable teeth and a nice smile, said, *"Hola."*

"Buenos días," I tried, failing miserably.

She liked it. She giggled and nodded at me. *"Buenos días,"* she replied.

I poured myself another cup of Java. Cristina came through the door looking ravishing in an aquamarine cotton blouse and white shorts. Her flip-flops clapped her feet as she walked over to me and said, "Good morning, Mr. Bailey. Did you sleep well?"

"A little bit restless," I told her.

She grinned. I watched her finely tuned body pump over to the coffee.

Sweetland came through the kitchen door with a sawed-off shotgun in hand. He looked me in the eye, motioned for Cristina to leave and take Anita with her. He said, "You two had me fooled," he said.

"I—"

"Shut up. I don't mean you and her, asshole. I mean you and your buddy. Jesus, I let you walk right in here. I don't know how you managed to involve Catiglio. That must have taken some doing—"

"What are you—"

"Shut up!" He waved the gun at me. His bloodshot eyes darted back and forth like the eyes of a hung-over man on amphetamines. "You fucked up, cowboy. I knew I'd seen you someplace. And I knew it wasn't Vegas. I thought maybe it was up in Ridland—"

"No way—"

"Shut up. I had Pedro do a little looking around for me, Mexican-style. *Gringos* stick out down here, you know? Your jet landed at Saltillo after landing in Monterrey. It was a mistake to keep that jet around. That's where you fucked up. Come to find out, it's registered as a charter out of Butte Peak. Imagine that. So that means you aren't who you said you are, and that means you're trouble of some sort. I called Catiglio and he swears by you, so that means I gotta think you guys is federal." He added, "Who else but feds could apply pressure on a guy like Catiglio?"

He waved the gun again, and I had the feeling he was going to kill me before he let me answer. Where was Lyel? Why wasn't Sweetland worried about Lyel? I looked over at Cristina. She led Anita from the room. Out of the corner of my eye I saw him glance over as they left. In that instant, I launched my hot coffee into his face and I fell backward, kicking up at the barrel. The second chamber went off and blew several pots off an overhead rack that hung over a chopping block. I lunged feet first, hooked his ankle with mine and tugged hard, pulling him over.

He had to drop the gun to catch himself, and the coffee had blinded him. I sat up and moved for him, but he had grabbed hold of a huge meat cleaver and he cut a swath through the air blindly, missing my face by only inches. He continued swinging as he pulled himself together. I took hold of an iron skillet and fended off his next attempt to sever me. Then I threw it at him, caught his shoulder, and he grimaced in pain. His arm came up and I took hold of his forearm and stopped the movement of that cleaver. He was as strong as they come. He used his left effectively, surprising me with a rib shot that stole my wind and my strength.

We were both on our feet. I defended his next left well, still keeping that cleaver out of my face by driving his forearm as high as I could. He flicked his wrist and threw the cleaver at me. I dodged to my left, but it was too heavy and fell quickly, slicing a hot, painful line through the neck muscles at the very top of my shoulder. It spurted blood and I lost my strength in my right arm. His next two lefts were directed at the wound. He pounded me there unmercifully. I cried out and landed a left of my own, an ineffective punch that failed to do anything but surprise him. Then I shifted my head right, left, right, and kicked him in the knee. I didn't catch it well enough to break it—he was too fast and agile—but I hurt him and I could see him favor it immediately.

He threw me against the refrigerator and before he could punish me, I thrust forward with a head butt and caught him in the chin. I felt a few of his teeth go and heard him wince as he staggered backward. I had dazed him. My head felt as if someone had dropped a brick onto it from four stories up.

He tried to swing with his right but I blocked it and connected heads with him again, this time flattening his nose. I lifted my knee into his gut and crushed the wind out of him. He went limp, though he remained conscious. I took his head in both my hands. And there I was. One tough jerk to either side and I could break his neck. End his life. The power to do so was in my hands and the determination was in my mind. The fight was no longer with him, it was within myself. It was me looking at the stranger in the mirror again. It was me coming to grips with who I am, attempting to communicate with a side of me I keep locked well away from sight. The dark side. I *wanted* to kill him. I wanted to dominate. To win. To hear his neck break, to feel the cartilage give way and the vertebrae separate. From somewhere well outside of myself came the idea that I had already won. There was no *need* to take this any further. This would not be an act of survival. This would be a predatory act. It would be what a Greg Sweetland would have done.

I dropped him and kneed him once more in the face to make sure he was spent. He collapsed into unconsciousness and I sank down alongside of him, breathless, my shoulder screaming in pain.

I found a clean dishtowel and held it firmly on my wound. I cut the electric cord off the toaster with the cleaver and tied Sweetland's hands. I used the cord from the refrigerator to bind his feet and then gagged him with a towel, careful to allow him a chance to breathe. That nose wasn't going to be of any use to him for some time.

As I reached the stairs, Lyel was just coming down. "That bastard locked me in," he said, immediately forcing a look at my wound. "I heard the women screaming—saw them running from the house. I broke the door down." He paused. "Did you kill him?" he asked as he lifted the soaked towel from my shoulder and made a sound of disgust. "That's an ugly slice."

"It's not too bad," I said, still breathing heavily. "I'm a fast healer. I had my chance to kill him," I explained. "But I couldn't do it."

He nodded and gave me one of his Lyel looks. "I'll get the shotgun," he said after a second had passed. "You sit down," he ordered. I wandered over to the bar and took two large swigs of mescal from the bottle. Lyel reappeared a moment later with a grim look on his face. He was carrying the shotgun. He said, "He only had two more shells on him."

"We've got the Detonics," I reminded.

He pulled his out from behind his back and handed it to me. "With that shoulder you would be useless with this thing," he said, referring to the shotgun. "Wait here."

When he appeared again he had Sweetland in tow. The man was still unconscious. Lyel dragged him across the tile floor and deposited him by the front door. Then he returned for the shotgun. I watched as he placed the shotgun under Sweetland's chin and then pulled open the front door. He screamed incoherently until one of the hired hands appeared in the distance. He was well armed and kept his distance. Lyel motioned that he was prepared to remove Sweetland's head from the man's body if need be. The hired hand backed up and let his weapon hang at his side. He seemed to understand the situation. If they had known Lyel, they would have challenged. But his size and his big bones were deceptive. To them he appeared capable of killing a man in cold blood. "Your turn," he told me.

I moved painfully to the front porch and aimed my handgun at Sweetland's right eye. Lyel stepped out into the driveway. He said over his shoulder, "There's one to my right, and this guy. That's all I see."

"We better tell them what we're up to," I said.

"What the fuck, mister?" It was Pedro and his chopped-liver English. He had come through the house and was standing in the living room aiming an ugly pistol at me.

"I'll kill him," I said.

"Look like you already have."

"He's alive," I insisted. "You don't bleed once you're dead."

"What you want?"

"We want one of the horses and Sweetland. We leave you the other horse."

"I keep all the fillies," he said.

"I want Angie. He's the sickest. You keep No Holds," I said.

He nodded. It didn't feel right. I wasn't sure what was keeping him from killing me, unless he knew that Tim was waiting for us at the airport and that if we didn't show up at a given time there would be an investigation. Which there would be.

"What do you make of it?" Lyel said softly.

"No idea," I admitted. I said to Pedro, "Tell your boys to load Angie for us. We want the pickup and the two-horse trailer. That leaves you the gooseneck."

He nodded and began shouting loudly in Spanish. The man across from Lyel hurried off. Pedro put away his weapon in an act of conciliation, but I couldn't be sure it was sincere. I kept mine on Sweetland, who began to stir, with one eye trained on Pedro. It took them fifteen minutes to load Angie for us. But, as promised, the pickup and trailer arrived at the front door. They had even given us a full tank of gas.

Pedro had sat down. He now stood and said, "In an hour the horses and all of us will be gone from here. We keep one of you until that is handled. We leave you on the edge of town."

"No deal," I said.

"Then say your prayers, mudderfucker." He raised the gun.

"Wait," Lyel interrupted. "I'll remain behind."

"No way," I said.

"You need some minor medical attention," Lyel reminded. "I'll take him at his word. He has nothing to gain from killing me. All he wants is some insurance."

"Insurance," the big Mexican repeated.

"Get in the truck and go," Lyel demanded, moving toward me and helping put Sweetland in the horse trailer's front compartment, which is meant for saddles and tack. "Get to Tim and have him arrange a doctor. I'll be along."

"No way," I said again.

"I have two shells in here, Klick. If they try anything, their numbers are going to be greatly reduced. I'll be fine."

"Really," said the Mexican.

"Go," said Lyel.

I climbed in behind the wheel and started her up. When I looked in the rearview mirror I saw Lyel with his back pressed up against a pillar, the shotgun held firmly in hand.

35

I took twelve stitches in my shoulder and the arm was supposed to be confined to a sling—something I shed immediately. Lyel arrived on schedule with one of those looks on his face that indicated he was lucky. Extremely lucky. We decided our best bet was to send Tim back alone to alert the authorities of our arrival by truck at the Brownsville crossing. Any private jet would be searched thoroughly on the United States side by Immigration and the DEA. We didn't have Sweetland's passport, and without advanced warning of our arrival we would face too much potential trouble.

Lyel and I would pour enough mescal down Sweetland to keep him unconscious, and would turn him over to United States authorities upon our arrival.

It came off without a hitch.

Tim had made all the necessary phone calls. We were met by a United States marshal at Brownsville as well as an FBI agent and a DEA agent. We were debriefed most of one night and the better part of the next day. We explained, to the best of our ability, the way Sweetland had arranged Paul Russell's murder. We also detailed Dean Hudson's role and implicated him in the murder of Red Clay.

On Wednesday morning we were summoned to a conference room, welcomed by three tired and glum faces. Randoff, the FBI man, who was group spokesman, sat us down and said in a disappointed voice, "Sweetland won't cop, won't bring Hudson into it at all. We've got him on the horse theft. He left prints behind that have been on record ever since. No problem there, but the drug charge probably won't hold. DEA boys raided the Sweetland farm last night and came up dry. The Russell murder is sketchy. Nothing but allegation there. We'll keep working on him, but for the time being, we're stuck without someone else's testimony."

Lyel was undone. He came up out of his seat, which was something like the space shuttle at lift-off and said hoarsely, "You have to be kidding me!"

Stepping back, Randoff said, "We don't like it any more than you do. You'll get the rewar—"

"The *reward*?" Lyel bellowed. "Have you any idea what Mr. Klick's life expectancy is at this moment? Or mine? Or Mrs. Russell's? My God, man, you've placed us on the butcher block. Laws are laws? That's a hell of a comfort."

"Sweetland will remain in custody. There's still a good chance we can break him or one of his brothers, or Paul Bates. Hudson might even cop, though we'd hate to lose him in a plea. He's the one we'd like to nail. We have a good feeling about Mr. Bates. He won't want an accomplice-to-murder charge. He breaks and this thing could play exactly as we're hoping. Based on Mr. Klick's testimony of Dr. Kupp's statement, Bates will be in federal custody by this afternoon, in Salt Lake by this evening. By tomorrow we could have an entirely new case. All I'm saying is that for the time being I'd lay low if I were you. Leave Hudson in Ridland, and Mrs. Russell in Santa Fe, as planned."

"And if Bates is not living by the time you reach him?" I asked.

Randoff looked at me angrily.

"What then?" Lyel asked, leaning across the table.

"I don't have an answer for that," Randoff said.

36

News of Paul Bates' death did not make the Boise papers. Lyel and I didn't find out about it until we landed at Butte Peak and overheard a noon-hour radio news broadcast. Bates had reportedly been attempting single-handedly to load a refrigerator into the back of his pickup truck when something went wrong. They found him crushed beneath a frostless Kenmore with ice maker and water cooler. Butte Peak Sheriff Dan Norton called the "accident" a "terrible waste of human life," praising Bates for his community service as coroner and past president of the Rotary.

We took the only local taxi to Lyel's compound. I reassembled the two Detonics, which I had broken down into a variety of pieces and had checked inside our "luggage," two cheapo bags we'd filled with secondhand clothing just to give us somewhere to hide the pieces of the Combat Masters. Lyel filled the Wagoneer with gas from his private pump. We drove into Ridland and parked at the sheriff's office, the Detonics hidden in the smalls of our backs beneath windbreakers.

Kay Collins, the wiry cowgirl with the scratchy voice and fast talk who fronted Hudson's office, had been crying. She saw me and lowered her eyes. "Kay?" I said, in my most friendly voice.

She shook her head slowly from side to side. Her hair needed washing. "I never had no idea," she promised us.

"Kay?" I repeated.

"But I got me a feeling it's all over. I seen him headed up-valley, and I got me a hunch it's all over."

"Up-valley?" Lyel asked.

"I know it was him who killed Paul Bates. I asked him about it point-blank. I asked him how a thing like that could happen, and I seen something in his eyes—never seen anything like that in a man's eyes. Lord Almighty. I just knew. That's all. I knew. He just stood there looking at me—he knew I knew. His eyes went all blank at me. For a second there—for a split second—I think he actually thought about killing me. *Me!*" she said in a frightened and disbelieving voice. Then she lost it. She came completely unglued, tears pouring down her face, hiding herself from us. She managed to find a cigarette and lit it up. It calmed her down. She took a deep drag. "And then I seen him heading up-valley a while ago with the trailer on his rig and I knew he wasn't coming back. It's all over."

"How's that?" I asked.

"He's gone into the backcountry for good," she said, crying again. "He knows all about the Sweetland investigation. Knows them FBI people were coming to get Paul. Dan knew. Dean and Dan had a long talk on the phone last evening. Been crazy around here the last few days. His rig was all full of stuff, just like when he goes hunting, but hell, the season ain't even open. He ain't going hunting. So where the hell's he going? I'll tell you where. A man like Dean Hudson? He's gone. He's running."

"His horse?" Lyel asked.

"Where, Kay?" I cut in. "Where would he be heading?"

"Where do you think?" she asked. "'Cross the border. Wouldn't you? I'd get on one of them old trails and get myself up to Canada."

"But that's a long way from here," I said incredulously.

She nodded. "Yup. But hey, what's three or four weeks? Hell, that's nothing. When my Phil goes on his fall hunt, it's two weeks on horseback. It ain't nothing. Ain't no roads for a hundred miles either side. Near solid wilderness area here to Canada. Dean Hudson been hunting different parts of this state his whole life. A man like him can just disappear into that country. Same as Claude Dallas did. Just vanish. Why, they've lost whole airplanes out there for more than forty years. Forty *years*! Dean knows better than to stay on the roads. He knows how fast the law can shut off those highways. Done it himself a few times.

"Hell," she continued, "there's only three roads running north to the panhandle. He's too smart for that. I'm telling you, he's gone. I just can't believe he'd do something like that! I just can't believe it." She started to cry again. I gave Lyel a head signal toward the door. He raised a finger.

"Miss Collins," he said formally. "Is there anyone you might recommend who could assist us? Anyone who knows that country? Preferably not a close friend of Sheriff Hudson."

"You going after him?" she said, lifting her head in disbelief, her eyes red, her cheeks smeared with tears.

"Yes, ma'am," Lyel said, as only Lyel can, "that we are."

37

Newt Wright was an ageless man with a square chin and narrow-set blue eyes. He talked with a Western twang and knew everything there was to know about the backcountry. He had thin hair that looked as if it might blow off his head in a strong breeze and leave him bald. So he wore a dirty-white cowboy hat inside and out, with a ragged rattlesnake skin, rattler and all, wrapped around the crown.

"We'd be kinda like a posse," he suggested from the other side of the small table in his cluttered mobile home, a grin stealing his face. "A three-man posse."

"That's it exactly," Lyel confirmed.

We had resigned ourselves to doing this alone. If people with Blokowski's talents went after Hudson in the back country, the sheriff would never be caught. If the Feds even bothered to go after the man, it would be with helicopters and search lights, and Hudson was far too savvy for that.

"I known Dean since he was a youngster, you know. Never did like him much. And once he became sheriff I knew this town had trouble. He lost his parents when he was just a boy, you know. Lost 'em both to one of those blood diseases. Leukemia, or something or other. Growed up with his uncle and aunt, Sam and Cheryl Williams. Kept his name, though. And boy, if he didn't have some kind of attitude. I'm tellin' ya! Was the school bully from about ten years old. Always pushing kids around. Sam and Cheryl were too soft on him. He ended up in Korea, then the rodeo circuit. Did pretty good, I guess. Then he lost that finger and came back here and bullied his way into the sheriff's office. Bullied the votes out of people. We had a feller as sheriff then that went pretty soft on the kids, the people of this town were ready for a change, which is what Dean Hudson promised them. They got their change all right. Hudson is tough as nails. But if you're his pal, you could do sixty down Main Street. Can't stand that kind of attitude. Not in a sheriff. Nope, doesn't surprise me he done boxed himself in. Hudson has a short temper, and isn't real long on brains. That's a bad combination in a man, regardless. You put a sheriff's badge on him and you got trouble. Never did like him."

"Miss Collins said you knew Paul Bates," Lyel reminded.

"Knew him and liked him," Wright replied, nodding. "I'm your man, gentlemen, if that's what you're asking. And as far as I'm concerned, with a man like Dean Hudson, if he's done everything you say he's done—and I believe it—then we leave him out there. We find him, we leave him out there. That's what a posse's job was, you know. Don't believe the movies. A posse caught a man and they hanged him. That's Western justice. That's just the way it works out here."

"If we catch him—"

"We'll catch him all right," Newt Wright assured us. "That boy don't have one-half the time in that country that I do. We'll catch him all right."

"We intend to bring him back," I said as firmly as I could. "We're not hanging anyone."

"He *killed* a man," Wright complained.

"Even so," Lyel said. "Our job is to find him and bring him back. We kill him only in self-defense, and even then, only if there's absolutely no other way out. That has to be understood up front. We don't condone what he's done, Mr. Wright. We have no intention of repeating his mistakes."

Wright nodded. "I'll go along with that."

"You sure?" I questioned.

"Promise you. But let me tell you boys something." He looked each of us in the eyes, and then looked down at his folded hands and said softly, "As long as that man has a breath left in him, or a bullet available, he'll be playing for keeps. And from what I understand, he's one hell of a shot. You boys any good with a rifle?"

"Klick is," Lyel said. "I can handle a handgun all right."

"It's been a while," I admitted. I had the feeling Newt Wright held some fairly high standards.

"How are you equipped?" he wondered.

I told him about my handguns. He'd never heard of Detonics. It figured. He showed us a pair of long-ranged rifles with sights. "We'll bring these along," he said. "And there won't be any fires, so bring your long johns. We'll bring a single pack-horse, pack the rest of what we need in saddle bags. I can round up all the gear. It's gonna cost you a hundred bucks a day for the horses, the gear, and me. Five hundred minimum. That sit all right with you?"

Lyel nodded and stuck out his hand. "I can live with that," he said. They shook hands.

"Funny way to put it," Wright said, "considering what we're talking about." He smiled. He had perfect teeth except for an eyetooth that was capped in shiny gold. "He's got a jump on us," he reminded. "Why don't you fellas go pack some things and round up some bedrolls. Keep it light, remember." He reviewed quickly what we would need. Rain poncho, flashlights, jackknife, long johns, hat, warm gloves, toilet paper. "But keep it light, boys. The lighter we are, the faster and the farther we can travel."

I hesitated, reluctant to ask at first, but finally said, "Mr. Wright, if we can catch him, about how long do you think it will take us?"

"We can and we will," he said, intentionally not answering my question.

He wanted me to understand something, and I did.

This was his show now. Lyel and I were along for the ride.

●

The ride that afternoon took us about ten miles into the forest along a drainage creek. We had located Hudson's truck and trailer on our third try. It was parked hidden, several miles east of the two-lane highway leaving Snow Lake. Wright proved his value immediately. He had second-guessed Hudson incredibly well, and he had spotted the hidden truck where Lyel and I might have missed it. We broke trail within a mile of the trailhead. Lyel questioned this, but Wright had explained that Hudson would expect the truck to be found. He would also head north as quickly as possible. "When you're on the run," Newt Wright said, "you don't waste time." There was a hint of experience behind his words. We didn't find out until dinner—cold Dinty Moore stew out of the can—that Wright had been part of the manhunt for Claude Dallas, the woodsman murderer turned prison escapee, who had successfully eluded authorities in the forested mountains of Idaho for over six months. Wright knew all about chasing dangerous men on the run. It explained why Kay Collins had put us on to him. It explained the high powered rifles.

Minutes before sunset, he signaled me off my horse. My shoulder wound didn't bother me a bit, it had healed quickly, but I was already saddle-sore. Two distinct sets of hoof marks were in the soft earth. "That's him," he said. "Packhorse is loaded full. That's in our favor." I was reminded of old Westerns where the scout leads the way for the cavalry. Newt Wright had that same camp-cookie feeling about him. I would never have spotted the horses' hooves. I couldn't remember what the captain said to the scout—Good work? Lead on! How far ahead of us is he?—so I simply nodded and asked, "What now?"

He was proud of the find. "I knew he'd come this drainage. You follow that trail down there, he'd be fifteen miles away from you by tomorrow morning. You'd never catch back up. Never."

"It's good work," I complimented.

"We'll have to go on foot pretty soon," he said, looking at the sky.

"What?" Lyel questioned, overhearing from his horse.

"You want to catch him, don't you?" he asked rhetorically. "You think he's going to stop because the sun goes down?" He looked up the drainage. "Not no-way, no-how. Not the first few days. If he knows his stuff, he'll be eating coffee raw and walking the horses until sunrise. He probably don't expect us, but even so, when he gets into that high country," he said, pointing, "he'll stop and give us a good long look. There's a clearing about a mile up where they did some logging about ten years back. We'll stay this side of the clearing until it's good and dark. We lose about a mile on him. Maybe two. But it's not worth the risk to cross that clearing until the sky is black."

"You're the boss," Lyel said.

"That's right" came the quick reply of Newt Wright.

•

We waited, hidden in the darkening forest, as Wright had suggested, until the final, faint glow lifted from the sky and was gone. Wright would not allow the use of flashlights. Our eyes adjusted, and we walked along. We had removed the bits and reins from the horses and were leading them by long ropes attached to halters. He strung us out, himself in the lead with both his horse and the packhorse, then me, with Lyel taking up the rear. A quarter moon rose after a while and made the going much easier except at those times when the canopy of pines thickened, returning us to absolute darkness. At a few minutes past midnight we crested the ridge our guide had warned us Hudson would use as a lookout. Sure enough, Wright pointed out a mess of hoofprints and some road apples that confirmed Hudson had stopped here. He asked us how we were holding up, and we both acknowledged that it was good to be out of the saddle. My shoulder hurt, but there was no need mentioning it. I was hungry—I imagined Lyel was famished—but we had to pace ourselves with the food in order to make it last as long as possible.

At half past two Wright stopped to consult a topo map. He unstrapped his greatcoat from the back of his saddle and had Lyel and me hold it over him to shield his brief use of a match as a light. His degree of precaution seemed ridiculous to me. I didn't say anything of the sort, but Wright proved once again to be a mind reader. Still studying the map, he said, "The thing about not taking no chances is you might live to tell someone about what you done. There's only one thing that will get us kilt, and that's letting Hudson know we're here. Once he knows we're back here, we're sittin' ducks. He'll find the right spot and we won't stand a chance. He'll end up with four horses and all our supplies, and even if we weren't after him, he'd kill us for that. He's a desperate man, boys. There ain't no figuring a desperate man. They'll make a fool of you every goddamned time."

He was right, of course. In my effort to locate Sonny Milligan, the famous tenor player from the bebop era, I had pursued an ex-flame of his, who to my surprise was at that time hitched up with a man wanted for armed robbery and murder. This man, whose name was Coleman, set my car on fire, with me in it. It was shortly after that near miss that I located Milligan, only to find out his ex-flame was not with Coleman by choice. She was a battered woman who feared for her life if she tried to get away from the man. Having a streak of white knight in me that goes back to fourteenth-century England, and the Norman Conquest before that, I found myself unable to return to L.A. and collect my due. Instead, I pursued Coleman across four states. Somewhere, somehow, he caught on to the fact that I was after him. I used up two of my nine lives on that adventure—one in a motel room and one in a truck-stop men's room. Ironically, Coleman was pulled over for speeding in Oregon, initiated a gunfight while resisting arrest, and was shot to death in the breakdown lane of I-84 overlooking the Columbia River. But he had indeed been full of surprises, as Wright would have said, and the only way I was around to tell the story was by being overcautious.

My problem here was that the magnificence, the sheer beauty of our moonlit surroundings lulled me into a false sense of awe. It seemed incredible that in such a spectacular setting there could be a killer lurking around the next bend in the trail. This was no black-and-white Western, this was full-color Panavision with the sharp smell of pinesap, the crisp cold of the northern Rockies, and the occasional distant hoot of a lonely owl. I was in heaven.

"And it's just for that reason we'll split up," Wright continued, as he retied the greatcoat onto the back of his saddle. "Since you're the better shot of the two of you, Klick," he said, "then you'll go alone. I'll take Mr. Chandler here," he said, still misunderstanding Lyel's name, "up this draw to the west. You'll continue on, following this streambed. It runs another three or four miles due north. When it peters out, you'll find an animal path or two over on the right side. It won't be easy going, you'll want to walk it, but that will bring you over the cirque by the spring there, and you'll pick up another creek a few hundred yards due west once you break that ridge. Maybe five miles down that creek you'll hit a fork. Wait there if you don't see us. We should beat you, but you can't tell if there have been slides or something that might slow us down. Wait there for us."

Lyel protested both to our splitting up and to my going it alone.

Wright explained, "He could have gone either way here. The ground's too hard to pick up his trail, and if he's on to us, we're sitting ducks, like I just said. Safest thing to do is split up. You got glasses with ya," he said to me, referring to my binoculars. "Use 'em. Before you come out into that cirque, you hunker down and spend a good thirty minutes checking every nook and cranny. Check the trails and see if you pick up his horses' tracks. By the time you enter that cirque it'll be daylight, and you can bet he'll be looking back. You fuck it up, Klick, and he'll shoot you dead. One shot. You'll never know what hit you.

"We got a similar problem over the other side of this ridge," he said, looking at Lyel and pointing up the draw. "We'll hit that about the same time of day. If I were him, I'd wait on a ridge for sunrise and check my backside. But he won't spend long at it, just long enough to glass the area and move on. That's why I say you kill a good half hour glassing yourself. You'll be okay."

I assured Lyel everything was fine. We would be meeting back up sometime after noon. He protested one final time and then gave me one of his tender Lyel looks that are few and far between. It was nice to have someone who cared, even if it was a two-hundred-and-forty-pound millionaire ape like Lyel.

Wright found me a can of peaches and another of tuna fish. I was carrying my own water, so I was set. We shook hands all around and soon—quite soon—I could no longer hear the reassuring slow pattern of their horses' hooves striking the hard pack. I was completely alone; alone in God's country, my breath a blue mist in front of me, my heart beating quickly, a killer with nothing to lose, making tracks for the Canadian border, somewhere in the darkness ahead. I knew I was following Hudson, and I thought Wright knew it too when he assigned me this trail. The little narrow-eyed fox was up to something, and I had the strange, exciting feeling that I was the bait.

38

I continued to think of myself as bait as I followed the creek north. What did Newt Wright have in mind? Or was I imagining things? Did he, in fact, believe Hudson might have skirted left up that small drainage to throw off any pursuers? This was big country back here, wide-open country, and I knew Wright was right in one aspect at least: if we didn't catch up to Hudson's trail early on, we would never find him. Therein lay the beauty of his escape—a few clever tricks along the way, and he would never be found. He would follow his instincts and his topo maps into Canada, unpack from his saddle bags many, many thousands of dollars, and attempt to live happily ever after.

But I feared Hudson now suffered the same psychological trap that befalls so many killers. He had accepted his abhorrence, and in the process had adopted a willingness to kill for even the slightest suspicion or reason—as proved with Kupps, Clay, Bates, and his visit to the slough house. Killing came easy now. Society offered the ultimate penalty for murder regardless of number; there was no reason to stop now.

I had read a great deal about the psychopathic and psychotic killers of our time—the famous, or infamous, ones like Ted Bundy. I knew that many of them actually enjoyed their own pursuit, reveled in the thrill of pursuit. A few had wanted to be caught, to be stopped. A few had gladly killed their pursuers. Hudson was no Ted Bundy, of course. Hudson was a pathetic small-town dreamer who had never managed to live up to his own image of himself. But certainly he knew he would be hunted. Certainly he knew that if he were on the other end, he would be coming after a man like himself. Certainly he was prepared for his pursuers.

For the next two hours I continued through the dark forest, following an unimproved trail that ran parallel to the trickling creek. My nerves jumpy, I stopped every fifty yards or so and tried to hear past the soft snorting of my beast of burden and the quixotic, hypnotizing drone of the creek. Several times I imagined I could hear the clip-clop of shod hooves in the distance. I stood there frozen then, one hand touching the cold stock of Wright's powerful hunting rifle, ready to defend myself. But each and every time it proved to be nothing more than an audio hallucination, a deceptive product of a fertile imagination.

I reached the edge of the forest, where the towering fir and lodgepole pine suddenly stopped, giving way to a variety of high-altitude shrubs and grasses, and, just beyond, to the bare slate-gray slopes of the box-canyon cirque, which, in the spring, fed this creek its melting snow. Even at night, in the dead of night, I could see the change in color ahead, I could sense losing my cover. I retreated several hundred yards, taking fifteen minutes to do so, in order to bury my mare deep within the forest and not risk her being seen where the woods thinned. Wright knew his stuff—this cirque would make a perfect ambush site. Hudson could be high atop the ridge, which at this hour looked like the silhouetted perimeter of a shark's mouth, as seen from somewhere inside the shark's throat—the jagged broken teeth would hide a man easily.

Overhead, charcoal-gray clouds and a chalk-white moon were playing a game of hide and seek in a checkerboard sky. I didn't like my location. There were far too many spots above me where I would never spot Hudson. The interior of the cirque I faced formed a semicircular bowl of football-sized rock. No vegetation, no rock outcropping. It looked like one imagines the inside of a crater on the moon. Its crest, the very top edge of the cirque, was composed of jagged rock face, which, over thousands, perhaps millions, of years had been chipped away by the elements and had spilled billions of rocks into the bowl. There are thousands of such formations in the northern Rockies, which collect snow all winter, hold it all spring, and give it back to the earth in the form of chilly runoff throughout the short summers. Far below, in places like Ridland and Hill City and the Magic Valley, there were farmers and families whose lives depended on these snow-collecting bowls. I sensed my life depended on it now as well.

Unhappy with my location, I scurried from tree to tree on the edge of the timberline, waiting each time for the cover of cloud. I could picture how I might appear through the eyes of Hudson high atop the ridge line—a faint gray shadow, jagging left and right, tree to tree. The way the edges of the backlit clouds swept over the barren rock reminded me of using my hand before a lamp to make shadow tricks on the wall. A duck. Scissors. A flying bird. I knew them all. The wind a thousand feet overhead drove the irregular sky of diamond-shaped clouds relentlessly. On the ground their shadows raced at surprising speeds, bending and sliding over all the contours in the same eerie way as a seemingly motionless snake whisks over obstacles of every shape and size. I followed the edges of these cloud shadows, darting my way through an ever-thinning forest, and finally began to stop and go up the western slope of the cirque, my binoculars pounding silently against my chest, the rifle slapping my back. The timing reminded me of bodysurfing, for I spotted an approaching shadow as it rapidly climbed the rock toward me, and then joined it for as long as I could, pausing as I was returned to the harsh glare of direct moonlight.

I wondered if he could see me. I wondered if he sat high above me in confusion, drawn to my moving form. I knew it would be nearly impossible to make me out in this light, for I found it nearly impossible to make anything out using my own glasses. The effect of the cloud pattern whisking across the bare, monochromic rock surface was near dizzying. Everything seemed to be moving. The rocks themselves seemed to be alive, jellylike, as if made of fabric and foam rubber. I climbed higher still, hoping, in effect, to gain an angle of sight he would not expect. If

Hudson was waiting for first light to watch the mouth of the old trail for someone following, then he would most likely hide in the darkened western shadows of the outcroppings as the sun came up. By working my way well up the western side of the cirque I would have a good view of his potential hiding places.

I became aware of my mistake much too late. I was too high up to attempt a retreat, too low to be able to take any cover. As the sky became a projector screen for the ever-approaching sun, the cover of the moon and cloud combination was diminished, the illusion of cover gone. Confident I would be nearly impossible to spot—unless I moved and drew attention to myself—I was, nonetheless, stuck, trapped, confined to sit absolutely motionless. To run back down toward the trees, toward the creek, even in this dim, bounced light, would give me away in an instant. I had left myself vulnerable, visible and unprotected. The mistake marked me as a backwoods novice. Hudson, a veteran big-game hunter, was anything but. My only saving grace was that if by chance I made it through this error, I had learned a valuable lesson. I would not repeat this same mistake again.

My sudden realization of the effect of the rising sun forced me to hunker down and remain perfectly still. I spent the next forty minutes glassing the entire ridge, concentrating on the backside of any outcroppings large enough to hide a seated man. Twice I thought I spotted Hudson, but there simply wasn't enough light yet to make sure. I knew Wright's supposition would prove to be true: Hudson would only remain long enough to glass the area several times in early light and then would move on. This for two reasons—to avoid wasting time, and to ensure not to be seen. The longer he remained on the ridge line, the more likely someone like me might spot him. He would not wait for the sun actually to rise. His eyes long adjusted to the moonlight, he would wait for this faint glow that was now occurring, conduct a quick reconnaissance, and then move on. A man with Hudson's self-confidence would not allow himself to believe anyone could be this close to him this soon anyway. He had jumped trail early, leaving his pursuers to continue out a trail he was not using. Had it not been for Newt Wright, I realized, Lyel and I would have continued on our merry way for days on the first trail, never realizing our mistake. This is why I now thought

Wright even more brilliant—for now, with our team divided up, we were covering more ground, putting more pressure to bear on Hudson, perhaps even closing in on him from two sides. Our small stone-faced guide had made an excellent decision.

Hudson had his hands full.

I spotted him ten minutes later when he had the misfortune to cough. It was a quiet, muted cough, but it was a sound that didn't belong here and it drew me to it in an instant. He was smooth. Professional. The moment he coughed he must have retreated, for all I caught was a disappointing glimpse of the back of his coat. I jerked my binoculars toward the sound immediately, and yet my only glimpse of him was fleeting. He was taking no chances. He was gone.

Worried he might be simply relocating, I remained hunkered down, fully aware that if he was heading on, I was losing valuable time. I felt the back of my neck prickle with sweat. I thought I knew how Hemingway's Francis Macomber must have felt as he watched the lion charge at top speed. I had that same sense of dread flood me. I had spotted the big game and my knees felt momentarily weak with expectation. Anticipation.

Frantically I surveyed the ridge line for another five minutes. They felt more like forty. Then I exploded into action, slithering back down the steep rocky face, reentering the woods and sprinting to my waiting mare, who, tied on a long line, had found some strong-willed grass to feed on. I rode her quickly to the tree line, forced there to dismount and seek out one of the foot-wide animal trails Wright had wisely known would lead from creek to ridge. I could see the disruption Hudson and his two big horses had caused the delicate trail, and my heart beat even stronger in the thin air. Win or lose, Hudson would not escape without a fight. I could only hope that Lyel and Wright were in position overlooking the fork in the creek. This was how I now interpreted Wright's strategy. Use me either as bait, or as a means to push Hudson forward into the trap. Either way the plan to divide made sense. I assumed Wright might be somewhere above me at this very moment, covering me in case I had coughed and Hudson had spotted me first, yet in a much better position to head off Hudson once he got moving again. I didn't know this particular backcountry at all, but it only made sense that if there was a fork in a creek a few miles from here, it could not be far from the ridge off to my left. Was I in sight of Wright and Lyel at this very moment? Or was I dreaming?

●

I crested the ridge, causing what amounted to an instant sunrise. The big yellow ball was several feet off the distant mountain-rimmed horizon and rising quickly. I left my horse briefly to its own devices so that we didn't cross the ridge as an inviting target, and it was a good thing I did. Below and to my left I could see Hudson and his two horses, amazingly tiny as he walked them down an opposing game trail on this far side. A crystalline, turquoise-blue, teardrop-shaped pond, rimmed with windblown trees and tall, verdant grasses, shone brightly in the morning light. Just past the pond, the trail dropped away as it followed the pond's exit creek. I waited for nearly ten minutes for Hudson, who had remounted his gelding, to pass the pond and disappear. He intelligently took several minutes to glass the ridge from where he had just come. I anticipated this, and slipped behind an immense boulder before he even brought his glasses up. I gave it a long time before I peered around the edge of the towering rock that hid me, knowing that, this hidden, I would be impossible to spot even from half the distance, and saw that he was no longer there. He had moved on. I began the long descent with my mare in tow, taking it slowly because the scree slope provided poor footing. The sun tried hard to warm the fall air, but a penetrating chill pervaded nonetheless, and my breath formed in front of me in a short cone of blue dissipating mist.

I kept my eyes intent on the trail beyond the small pond, so much so that twice I stumbled, and it was only the rope attached to the halter that helped me maintain my balance. I was thinking ahead now, thinking ahead to that moment of confrontation. I had the upper hand—I was aware of his presence, and I assumed the reverse was not true. I began plotting my attack. How could I gain enough ground to trap him? Could he be trapped, or would I have to follow him until he tired and finally slept? Even eating coffee grounds, he couldn't stay awake forever. And the longer he remained awake, the duller his senses would become, the easier a prey he would become. I imagined a dozen different ways of approaching him, of ambushing—yes, ambushing—him, but he represented a formidable opponent and I kept coming back to the fact that taking him between the sights might be the smartest tactic of all. Wright's rifle had a powerful hunting scope in place. If I gained the perfect opportunity, if I could place the cross hairs on his right shoulder, I might be able, in a single shot, to take him out of the game. A hollow .30-06 in the shoulder from a hundred yards would either immobilize or kill him. He would be reduced, in that single squeeze of a trigger, to a helpless, defenseless opponent, and despite the obvious lack of fair play involved, this was not a contest, I reminded myself, this was an effort to return a multiple murderer to custody. Hopefully, to justice.

Eventually I crested the lower ridge by the pond and followed his trail out. The earth was soft here and the route he and his horses had followed easy to identify. Although eager to apprehend him, I did not like the position of being in the rear. I would need to be in advance of him if I was to set the proper trap. Waiting for him to tire did not thrill me either. I was already tired myself, and if he did tire, if he did rest, it would most likely be at night, and in the woods costly mistakes can be made in the dark. No, my best bet was to leapfrog ahead of him and be waiting when he came riding by. He had a packhorse in tow, which made him much slower. In theory I could make much better time than he. But in order to get in front of him, I would have to risk an alternate trail, perhaps forge my own, at some point cresting a ridge and dropping down into the area he would be eventually riding into. He was choosing his route well, as Wright had first pointed out to Lyel and me—the trails he chose were in tight, narrow draws that allowed him a feeling of added security. It would be difficult, if not impossible, to come up from behind him without his knowing it. Wright had warned us that he might even set booby traps if he felt he was entering a vulnerable area where his backside could not be covered. Ropes with cowbells, flares attached to trip wires, the tricks varied, though their purpose remained the same. I kept my eyes open for any of these tricks, often riding off his exact trail by a few yards in case I missed such a ploy.

I reached the fork in the stream early, at a few minutes past ten. There was no sign of Lyel or Wright, and I was immediately faced with a dilemma. Did I endure what might be a two-hour wait, allowing Hudson the comfort of an additional lead? Or did I continue on? I convinced myself there was no choice but to continue on. I dismounted and collected a fallen branch, a few stones, and several small twigs, and placed an exclamation point and arrow in the middle of the trail by the intersection of two creeks.

If Wright didn't understand the symbol, I was counting on the fact that Lyel would. I made my decision then: that if I was going after Hudson alone, I had better make my move soon. With his trail following the tiny creek to the left, I took the dry creek to the right. A hundred yards downstream, a hill developed that became a range a quarter mile later. I could picture what we looked like from a bird's-eye view. Hudson with his horses on the left of a small course of steep hills, myself to the right, each of us following creeks that pulled farther and farther apart from one another. My job was to make better time than he, cross back over this range and drop down in on top of him. I brought my mare into a brisk walk, nearly doubling my earlier pace. I thought about Wright and Lyel back there somewhere. I thought about them coming across my crudely crafted comment. Wright's position might have been that two hours was nothing—we had him now, that was what mattered. But this wasn't between Wright and Hudson. It wasn't even between Lyel and Hudson. I knew who was involved here, and knowingly or unknowingly, I was allowing myself to be controlled by it.

39

Without a map, I realized I had big problems. I couldn't be sure what the geometry of our movements was. I had a good sense of direction and was feeling right about my plan, but if the streams grew too far apart, then no matter how much ground I gained on him, I might lose it all back in the time it took me to cross the ridge. For this reason I altered my plan immediately and rode up the near side of the hills that separated us. Once at the top, I dismounted, tied off the horse and went on foot for several minutes before coming to the edge of the ridge that overlooked his creek and trail. It was better than I had hoped, not worse. The range of hills between us, which I was now on top of, was narrow and long and appeared to twist and turn, leaving our streambeds and trails nearly parallel. An hour into it, I had already gained on him significantly. At twenty past eleven I saw him briefly, as the motion of him and his horses broke some light inside the woods where he traveled.

Excited, I ran back to the mare, mounted up and stayed on top of the ridge, but on the far northeast edge, away from where he might accidentally spot me. I took note of the time, and when we had good footing I brought the mare into a trot and gained considerable ground. At twelve-fifteen, I scouted the northwest rim once again. I had him. I had picked up enough ground to allow myself time to ride down into his side and set my snare.

But why risk it? I wondered. Why bring the horse down with me and allow her to spook the others, or make noises that might alert a sharp Dean Hudson to my whereabouts? My earlier mistake in the rock cirque paid off. I was thinking several steps ahead now, I was looking at this rugged country as an easy place to die rather than a beautiful place to be.

I removed the bit and bridle and was about to hook the lead rope onto her halter when something spooked her. She backstepped away from me and her eyes went white with fear. I took one step toward her and she turned and bolted. I chased after her briefly, but it was no use. She was off and running down the far slope, away, away, away, everything she was carrying still strapped securely to her side. Including the rifle.

I had another choice to make then, as the fox shot down the ridge to my left and I realized what had spooked her. She wouldn't go far. It wasn't like I had lost her for good. But recapturing her would take me at least twenty minutes, perhaps longer. I would lose my lead on Hudson. I would be forced to start over, forced to risk Lyel and Wright stumbling down the trail and alerting Hudson. I had the lead rope to the halter, a ten-foot nylon strap. And I had the Detonics and two clips with a pocketful of spare ammunition. I was not exactly unarmed.

I hurried to the ridge, looked back toward where Hudson would be coming from, and seeing no one, ran—yes, ran—down the steep face, dodging my way through three-foot-high sagebrush, slaloming my way down the slope like a skier through the gates. At the bottom I was greeted by the haunting sound of my own pulse at my ears and the deathly silence of the woods in the fall when the songbirds have headed south, and the only sound is of a determined trickle of water coursing through a smoothed stone creek.

I dodged my way, tree by tree, to the very edge of the small-game trail and pressed my back against the sticky bark of a lodgepole pine. My wait seemed interminable then. The minutes ticked off my watch, and I reviewed my plan a dozen times. Of most importance was getting Hudson off his horse. His rifle would be strapped to his horse, and God only knew what else might be available to him, and in the saddle he had the advantage of speed and mobility. On foot, matched against a man on horseback, I was at a definite disadvantage. But I had the decided advantage of surprise, and if used effectively I believed I could quickly gain the edge I needed. With my Detonics drawn and cocked, I had my backup in hand. If anything went sour, I would shoot to kill.

●

I heard the deceptively peaceful clip-clop of the horses' hooves a few long minutes later. My heart began to pound and I felt my body priming itself for combat. I put myself in a mental state where I would hopefully deflect surprise, react with training. I stepped myself through my plans and my various options one final time. I reminded myself I was the hunter, not the hunted, and that the fear associated with sudden surprise was to my benefit.

Twenty yards and closing. I could hear the steady hot breath of the two horses. I switched hands, placing the Detonics in my left, the lead rope with its metal clasp into my right. It dangled silently at my side. I reminded myself that this was the man clever enough to kill at least three men, a rodeo man, a big, strong man more than capable of putting up a good fight.

That was what I wanted, I realized: a good fight. I wanted to hurt Hudson, not kill him. I wanted to render him useless so we could bring him back to stand trial at the mercy of the very legal system he feigned to defend. I wanted to see him humiliated, dressed in the dull-orange jumpsuit of county offenders, handcuffed and ankle-cuffed as murderers were. Killing a man like Hudson was being too easy on him. It was the trial I wanted. The trial and the newspapers and the disgrace. Sweetland and Hudson side by side, their lawyers attempting to convince Mom and Pop Idaho that what they did was understandable. I wanted to see the faces of the jurors. I wanted that badly.

Ten yards.

I held my breath then. I took a deep breath and held it and counted the steps as his horse approached. Would the horse balk as I expected? I prepared myself for that. The horse would flinch and jump away from me. I could not allow that to frighten me. It might scream, might even kick, but I must not allow it to frighten me.

Two yards.

The horse's head passed by me.

It stopped.

It did not rear, did not flinch, did not buck. It simply stopped in curiosity—the one reaction I had not anticipated. But I would not have my plans dictated by a horse. I remained absolutely still. The second or two it took Hudson to nudge the horse along seemed more like a minute or two. His horse took two steps forward, and there was his leg to my left. I lifted my arm high, and as I brought the metal clasp down hard on the hindquarters of his mount, Dean Hudson and I caught eyes. The look on his face delighted me: absolute terror.

The horse came off his front legs in a Lone Ranger lift, just as I had hoped. The Detonics was now held in both hands, legs spread, the Weaver stance—arms out—supporting it for firing. I was prepared for Hudson to come off the horse in a back somersault, which he did. I was prepared for the noise and the confusion as both horses briefly hesitated and then thundered forward, leaving Hudson behind.

I was unprepared for the circuslike performance as the former rodeo cowboy was able to snag the stock of his rifle and actually begin shooting at me before he even hit the ground. Bark flew off the tree, pine needles exploded at my feet. I dived to my right, rolled once into a prone position and squeezed off two quick shots, continued my roll and came up behind a tree. I thought I might have hit him, but in the confusion of fleeing horses and the rounds dancing all around me, I couldn't be sure. I dived then—dived into a somersault, came up on one knee, sighted for the closest tree and squeezed off two more shots, pinning Hudson behind the tree and preventing him from even getting a shot off.

At least that was what I thought.

I saw the stock end of the rifle coming at me from my left. He was swinging it like a baseball bat. My head was supposed to be the ball. I raised my hand to block it. It smacked my hand and sent the Detonics flying. He tried next to lunge it into me, and in the split second of my deflecting the effort I came to the realization that the rifle had most likely jammed when he struck the ground, and its only use was as a ram. My hand was numb, perhaps broken. I let his next effort land in my back as I tackled him and brought him down. As he thudded into the root-wormed, needle-covered earth, I speared him in the abdomen with the top of my head, hoping to take the wind out of him. Hudson was tough, and in better shape than I suspected. Spearing him felt like hitting my head on a carpeted floor. That big fat hand of his came into a little iron ball and smacked me in the ear. It sounded like someone had knocked a rack of handbells over onto cement. Something purple and shapeless loomed briefly in front of my right eye. I lifted my elbow as he struggled to get out from under me and caught him on the chin. I heard his teeth crunch and his sickening scream as he spit out the tip of his severed tongue at me. His tongue was bleeding badly, but he recovered quickly enough to introduce me to another of his steel-fisted hits and send me reeling backward. The man had a delivery like Sugar Ray. I was punch-drunk. It took everything I had to keep my senses.

I dodged his next effort. He was clumsy with his body work and I put this to use. I got to my feet and began to dance around to bring my feeling back and to keep him guessing. He stepped solidly toward me like the old white boxers used to fight, the ones who knew a single hit would put you out. But I wouldn't allow him to connect. I danced to the left and smacked him in the upper arm. I could see it go heavy on him and I sneaked in again and let him have it. I knew that feeling: the arm is attached to you but it weighs twice as much as it usually does. He stepped toward me again and fooled me. I was thinking too much of his right. That left maul of his came out of nowhere and gave me back some of my own medicine. For a moment I thought he might have dislocated my shoulder. I stumbled back and struck a tree and he got in on me and with his heavy right arm worked on my belly, tiring me out, bending me over slowly, waiting for my hands to fall, for a chance to cut up and take my head right off my shoulders.

As I bent with his first few punches, I saw my own chance for an uppercut. I was fairly stout in the gut, and although he was wearing me down, he wasn't hurting me too much. No permanent damage. I had hit that right arm of his well, and he was too overeager to punish me and it was costing him strength. The right arm fell lower and lower. My right shoulder was a mess. He'd hit me well and only then, as I bent even further to avoid too much punishment, did I realize he was both dropping that right arm and ignoring the possibilities my left offered. I came straight up with that left, fist clenched, like an amateur at an auction—right out of my chair. I caught him directly below that ugly-looking mouth of his and stood him straight up. He swung wildly then, and struck the tree because I overestimated my strength and stumbled to my left, leaving nothing but bark in front of him. I hammered repeatedly on his right shoulder then—one, two; one, two; one, two—ducked low and came in strongly on his gut, with both arms moving like pistons. I backed him up. He was dizzy, bad on his feet. I backed him up some more. He flailed again, but his vision must have been fuzzy and his right arm was useless and the left easy to defend against. We sparred briefly—he still had something to him. Determination. Anger. Desperation. I landed some beauties and I knew I had him. I had the momentum. I had the confidence.

He had the knife.

It was a big sucker and it came out of nowhere. Flashy and silver. Sharp. That tongue of his made it look as if he were dying. Blood everywhere. Ugly. He had no right hand to work the knife. That slow right arm saved my life. Tip of the blade nicked my neck but didn't slice me open. I bled from the wound, but I knew all the parts were intact. I didn't feel the wound. I had taken a bullet through me once and I hadn't felt it either. Combat does that to you, I think. The body shuts off some systems to reserve power and sensitivity for others. He lunged at me with his weapon and I managed to jump back and away. I kicked hard into the side of his knee and tried to get behind him, which forced him to spin quickly. I caught him in the same knee again and this time I heard it. He went down hard. It looked like a hinged door when you pull the last pin and the door falls off the jamb. All the little parts that hold that peculiar joint together were snapped, torn, or stretched. The sports doctors call it hyperextended. It looks something like a doll with her leg twisted off. I was all too familiar with that knee pain, and I knew he wasn't coming up. Not for six or seven weeks and a lot of physical therapy.

I was too tired and too beat to move quickly and I relaxed too far, thinking my opponent helpless. He reared back his arm and launched the knife like a professional knife thrower. Despite my training, despite my precautions, despite my understanding of what he had done, I failed to move quickly enough. Fatigue and astonishment won out. As I made a desperate half-turn to avoid the projectile, it lodged deeply in the meat of my upper left shoulder. I knew better than to yank it out. I reached over for it, my head swimming, the intense pain beginning to creep slowly into my system, and I stopped myself from pulling the plug. Hudson was dragging himself awkwardly toward my Detonics, which I had lost track of until that moment.

40

With his one leg stiff, Hudson clawed his way over the exposed tree roots, fingers groping for purchase, and dragged his heavy weight toward the .45. I had dropped to my knees with the knife wound, and Hudson was closer to the handgun than I. My strength sapped, like something from a recurring nightmare, I found myself too heavy to lift. I could not get to my feet. I could not stand. Hudson continued his snail crawl along the forest floor, ever closer to the gun. Ever closer to killing me.

I had no weapon other than the knife, which was buried several inches in my upper chest, and I knew I lacked the strength to fight him much longer. It would have to be quick and purposeful, or it would be over for me.

This realization drew some chemical out of some fleshy sac deep within my gut and I felt suddenly as if I were a robot and someone had just plugged me back in. Like losing your brakes on ice, sliding helplessly into an accident, there were so few choices. Cut the wheel and duck.

I crawled forward on my knees. Hudson saw me coming and this must have squeezed the same sac in him, for he was no longer a snail; he was a water snake on the glassy surface of a lake. He flew toward that gun.

We were an interesting match. In this final act of survival, I found myself appraising both my opponent's and my own strengths and weaknesses. His leg was completely useless, his upper body weakened, but no doubt coming back. My upper body was holding an eight-inch hunting knife, but my legs, weakened by the stabbing, were on the mend. We were opposite bookends.

There would be no second try. No second heat. This was a single-elimination tournament. I fell forward, reached out and took hold of his right foot. I pulled hard and felt that bad knee come completely undone. Hudson exploded with the pain. But to my surprise his intention remained on the weapon, and as he came up off the forest floor like a killer whale sounding offshore, he threw himself forward toward the Detonics, now but inches away. There was no thought to my next move, no conscious planning. My training failed me completely. The circuit blown. Something called instinct took over, and there was no fighting it. I found myself with the knife in my hand, not in my chest, and as Hudson made one final lunge for the handgun, I drove the blade of the knife completely through his hand and pinned it to a root below.

He looked over at me then, not with pain, not even anger, but with complete and utter astonishment. He looked at me, back at his bleeding hand, and back at me. It was strange that I didn't go for the gun then—another failure of my training. I came to my feet and dropped all my weight onto that knee of his, like the groom in a Jewish wedding smashing the glass. Stomping the glass. I powdered his knee into soft tissue. He managed only a short cry of agony before he blanked into unconsciousness.

I reached for my shoulder and attempted to close the wound. I looked up then: Approaching me cautiously on foot, rifle outstretched, finger on the trigger, was the slight frame of Newt Wright; behind him, my dear friend Lyel, looking full of worry and concern. Perhaps it was the relief of seeing him, perhaps it was the wound, but a thick blue-black jelly settled in my head, all sound slipped peacefully away. I saw their lips move, but I couldn't hear. I was falling away. Falling, falling away into that thick blackness that welcomed me. And nothing I tried could stop it.

Newt Wright built a small fire and spent several minutes carefully bending the large needle he carried to repair his leather work. He used lengths of fishing line as sutures, stuffed a towel into my mouth, and put two crude stitches into my shoulder. He put one on either side of Hudson's hand and then bandaged both wounds. Lyel, pragmatic and typically silent, watched the whole event without comment, acting as nurse, attempting to keep our wounds as sterile as possible. They splinted Hudson's knee and tied his wrists together around the saddle horn to allow him to keep his balance on the steeper trails.

We spent the night there, all of us too exhausted to continue, and the three of us rotated watch on Hudson despite his immobility. We suffered through a cold drizzle for much of the next two days, and aside from Hudson's saddle slipping twice, the trip out was uneventful. Midafternoon, two days later, we pulled into the sheriff's office in Snow Lake and turned Hudson over to him. As we had expected, two FBI agents were in the area, still organizing what was to be a search for Hudson, and they took custody of the man by evening. The news was mixed: Sweetland had wised up and had plea-bargained the expected murder charge to manslaughter in turn for information connecting Hudson to the cover-up of the Russell murder. Both men were going away for a long time.

As we parted, I looked crusty old Newt Wright in the eye and asked him, "Did you send me into that cirque as bait, or just exactly why did you split us up when you did?"

He grinned at me in a way I will not soon forget, for it is a grin I would like to own: devilish, cunning, thoughtful and yet ambiguous. "Son," he said to me in a twang reminiscent of *Gunsmoke*'s Chester, "We jes' got lucky." I never would know the answer.

Lyel arranged a surprise for me the next day, secretly hiring Tim to fly down to Santa Fe and pick up Nicole. I was out on the porch, despite the cold, watching the mergansers feed when I heard his car drive up and saw her climb out. I felt silly with my arm in a sling.

She walked up onto the deck, a radiant vision of beauty, and kissed me warmly. She headed to the fridge and fetched us two St. Pauli Girls, kicked a deck chair over next to me and sat down. "I'm glad you're okay," she said.

"I'm glad," I told her.

She took my hand in hers, and we sat in absolute silence for another two hours and three more beers. I grew sadder and sadder. Something was different here—or perhaps it wasn't; perhaps nothing had changed as I had hoped it might. Like the ducks and geese, Nicole was heading south. I could feel it deep down in my aching bones. It made me want to cry. Nothing I could do to stop it. Absolutely nothing.

●

I spent two awkward days with Nicole. We smiled a lot and she doted over me, working more as a nurse than a companion. I wanted to feel good about it, but I did not. We slept together, but we didn't make love. I was too exhausted the first night—at least that's what I told myself—and she didn't come to bed until I was asleep the second night. I knew what was coming next, and I had neither the desire nor the strength to face it.

I sank into a depression, despite word from Lyel that Angie's recovery had netted us a hefty reward that would more than cover Nicole's missing money. I felt sad, desperately sad. I didn't like losing a lover. It made me feel like a failure.

Finally, that Tuesday, I got up my nerve. A bourbon in hand, sitting out on the deck, bundled up against the crisp chill, I said to her, "What's changed?"

She shook her head, staring out at the slough.

"I love you, Nicole."

She nodded. "Yes. I believe you do."

"But you don't love me?"

"I won't allow myself."

"Why?"

"I need time."

"Can't I do something? Can't we talk?"

She looked at me. "You're easy to talk to, fun to be around. You don't take yourself too seriously—you know when to laugh and when to be silent. I can't tell you how much that means to me. I can't tell you how much you mean to me. I'm frightened of you. It's too soon. Too soon after Paul. I made such a big mistake with Paul."

A friend of mine, Amos Galpin, had written a song called "Big Mistake." I heard it ring through my head. "Okay," I said.

"I haven't known how to tell you. I owe you so much. I'm so grateful, so thankful—"

"Please don't."

She stopped and sniffled.

I said, "This isn't a commodity. There's no owing. There's no owning. I can't even explain it to you." I'd had my chance to explain a few short days earlier. Now I regretted letting that opportunity pass. I wasn't sure how to say it. I said what came to mind, watching a red-shafted flicker swoop through the air. "What it is . . . You're the wind under my wings, Nicole. You are what lifts me up. You are what carries me aloft, what gives the perspective, what drives me on. You are all those intangibles in life that make it worth living. You are beauty and knowledge. You are the greatest gift that has ever been given to me. And I selfishly don't want that gift taken away."

She reached out and took my hand.

"What can I do?" I asked.

She shook her head and cried. "Nothing," I thought I heard her say.

A pair of mallards came in low and swift. A pair. A couple. A team. They must have seen us, for they jerked in unison away from us and frantically climbed back into the sky, wings singing. How badly I had wanted them to land. How much I was counting on that. How symbolic it was to me. My eyes stung as they flew away, for at that moment I was certain.

●

Lyel joined us for supper that evening. He prepared grilled salmon, rice, and baked Brussels sprouts as only Lyel can. We drank two bottles of Dom. He entertained us in typical Lyel fashion. Not a care in the world. We laughed a good deal, and by the time he left I felt cleansed. Lyel is one of the good ones, one of the ones you can count on.

Nicole looked ravishing, as always. She moved me over to the fire and started to giggle. "I'm going to give you a night you will never forget," she said, her eyes a little red and her voice unintentionally husky.

"Whatever you say," I told her. I was nervous. Even afraid. The ending was drawing near and I couldn't bear the thought. I couldn't win, and I hated to lose.

We spent hours on the sheepskin rug in front of a dwindling fire. Some of the best hours of my life. Near dawn, watching her sleep soundly beside me, cherishing the moment, I finally was stolen away by sleep, the fire long since spent. Gray ashes.

And in the morning she was gone.